What the hell was this woman doing to him? Nathan asked himself bitterly, looking down at Valeri's unconscious form.

How could he have let her get under his skin like this? The chances were that she was married.

Yet he couldn't seem to get her out of his mind. There was no way to ignore it any longer. He wanted her in the worst way. He had ever since he first set eyes on her.

How had a woman like this gotten mixed up with someone like the man who claimed to be her husband? How the hell had *he* managed to get himself mixed up in this?

Now, more than ever, he wanted to get to the bottom of this crooked deal. But first he had to try to forget how Valeri Richmond was driving him wild....

Dear Reader,

It's month two of our special fifteenth anniversary celebration, and that means more great reading for you. Just look what's in store.

Amnesia! It's one of the most popular plot twists around, and well it should be. All of us have probably wished, just for a minute, that we could start over again, be somebody else...fall in love all over again as if it were the first time. For three of our heroines this month, whether they want it or not, the chance is theirs. Start with Sharon Sala's *Roman's Heart,* the latest in her fabulous trilogy, THE JUSTICE WAY. Then check out *The Mercenary and the Marriage Vow* by Doreen Roberts. This book carries our new TRY TO REMEMBER flash—just so you won't forget about it! And then, sporting our MEN IN BLUE flash (because the hero's the kind of cop we could all fall in love with), there's *While She Was Sleeping* by Diane Pershing.

Of course, we have three other great books this month, too. Be sure to pick up Beverly Barton's *Emily and the Stranger,* and don't worry. Though this book isn't one of them, Beverly's extremely popular heroes, THE PROTECTORS, will be coming your way again soon. Kylie Brant is back with *Friday's Child,* a FAMILIES ARE FOREVER title. Not only will the hero and heroine win your heart, wait 'til you meet little Chloe. Finally, welcome new author Sharon Mignerey, who makes her debut with *Cassidy's Courtship.*

And, of course, don't forget to come back next month for more of the best and most excitingly romantic reading around, right here in Silhouette Intimate Moments.

Leslie Wainger
Senior Editor and Editorial Coordinator

THE MERCENARY AND THE MARRIAGE VOW

DOREEN ROBERTS

Published by Silhouette Books
America's Publisher of Contemporary Romance

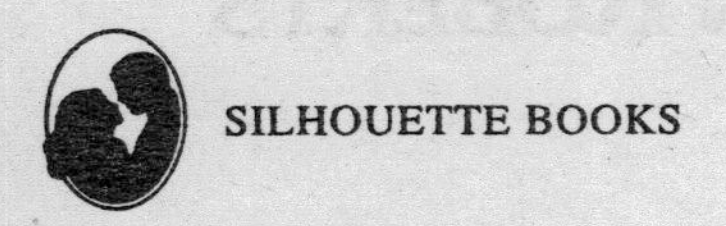

ISBN 0-373-07861-7

THE MERCENARY AND THE MARRIAGE VOW

This edition published by arrangement with Harlequin Books S.A.

Printed in U.S.A.

Books by Doreen Roberts

Silhouette Intimate Moments

Gambler's Gold #215
Willing Accomplice #239
Forbidden Jade #266
Threat of Exposure #295
Desert Heat #319
In the Line of Duty #379
Broken Wings #422
Road to Freedom #442
In a Stranger's Eyes #475
Only a Dream Away #513
Where There's Smoke #567
So Little Time #653
A Cowboy's Heart #705
Every Waking Moment #783
The Mercenary and the Marriage Vow #861

Silhouette Romance

Home for the Holidays #765
A Mom for Christmas #1195
In Love with the Boss #1271

DOREEN ROBERTS

lives with her husband, who is also her manager and her biggest fan, in the heart of the Oregon wine valley. She believes that everyone should have a little adventure now and again to add interest to their lives. She believes in taking risks and has been known to embark on an adventure or two of her own. She is happiest, however, when she is creating stories about the biggest adventure of all—falling in love and learning to live happily ever after.

To Bill, who knows me better than I know myself.
You're wonderful, and I love you.

Chapter 1

Nathan Thorne smiled as the blue Honda ahead of him turned onto the crowded Interstate 5 out of Sacramento. Luck seemed to be with him for a change. His assignments didn't usually turn out to be this easy.

He settled in a couple of cars back behind his quarry and relaxed his shoulders. She wasn't going to notice his ancient, beat-up Volvo in the dark. All he had to do was follow her to wherever she was going, wait for the right opportunity and strike up a conversation. Judging from what he'd been told, she'd bite, all right.

He wondered where she was going. Probably some hot spot outside of town. He'd met plenty of women like Valeri Richmond. Women who knew how to use their bodies to get what they wanted. Women who would stab their best friend in the back if they felt threatened. Women who lived for excitement, and didn't care how they got it.

When he'd first seen the pictures of her, he'd found it hard to believe she was that kind of woman. She was attractive—early thirties, with the kind of dark mysterious looks that could turn a man's head, yet with an air of class that would make him think twice about following up on his urges.

Especially a man like Nathan Thorne. Nat didn't usually waste time with niceties. He knew what he wanted and he let a woman know what he wanted. If she was interested, he'd go for it. If not, he'd walk away. No promises, no regrets. No one got hurt that way.

As for Valeri Richmond, she was an enigma. According to the one man who claimed to know her best, she was a selfish, hard-hearted opportunist looking for adventure. If Nat hadn't known what he did, the woman in the photograph could have easily fooled him. And very few people fooled Nathan Thorne.

Now that he knew who he was dealing with, he was prepared. Normally he would have balked at this kind of assignment. Forcing a woman to do something she didn't want to do was not the way he operated. But this case was an exception.

He'd take her back where she belonged—the easy way or the rough way. It all depended on how cooperative Valeri Richmond would be. And he knew just how to make women like her cooperate. He didn't foresee any problem at all.

To his surprise, she turned east onto Highway 50. He frowned, wondering what game she was up to. She was on the road to Nevada, the last place he expected her to be heading. Just in case, he narrowed the gap between them. It would be much easier for her to lose him on the highway.

He followed the blue Honda for an hour or two, growing more uneasy all the time. It was now almost midnight and the traffic was thinning out, making him more visible. He wove in and out of the two-lane highway, sometimes pulling slightly ahead, always ready to react if she made any sudden moves. She was speeding enough to keep him on his toes, yet he was pretty sure she was unaware of him on her tail.

When it happened, it happened fast. She'd pulled about four car lengths ahead of him when he saw her brake lights flash. Automatically he stomped on his own brakes, swearing as she fishtailed off the road and plunged into darkness.

Fighting the wheel, he followed her onto the uneven, desert-dry ground, bouncing over ridges and potholes until his teeth rattled. She'd fingered him after all. Damn her. She was doing her best to lose him, and she was tough to see in the faint glow of moonlight.

His headlights picked her out now and again as she plunged without lights through the dry brush. She had guts, he'd give her that. She was heading back to where the road curved around to the right.

He'd just sit tight on her tail and wait until she hit the road, Nat thought grimly. Sooner or later she would have to stop. He'd make up his mind then whether he wanted to tip his hand or wait for another opportunity.

In any case, considering the road she'd taken, she could well be going back on her own. If so, his services would no longer be needed.

And that was just fine with Nat. He hadn't liked the smell of this assignment from the beginning. He was starting to like it a lot less now.

He had just about convinced himself that he was off the hook when all hell broke loose. She was just a few yards off the road when her car must have hit a gully. The car flipped like a tossed pancake, landing on its passenger side.

He was out of his car and racing like the devil before the sounds of the crash had died away. In the darkness he'd seen sparks, and he knew what that meant.

The first explosion almost hit him in the face. He ducked, then scrambled up onto the car and yanked on the door. Miraculously, it opened. If she had locked it, she wouldn't have stood a chance.

He leaned down to undo her seat belt. Her head rested on the wheel, her arms hung limp at her sides. Flames were already licking along the underbelly of the Honda. He had seconds, at most. He gripped her under her arms and pulled. Sweat trickled down his face as he dragged her out. Acrid smoke stung his eyes. She was unconscious, which was just as well. He had no time to be gentle. She felt light in his arms when he picked her up and ran with her, half stumbling, to a small outcrop of rocks.

He felt the heat of the blast as it passed overhead. He was flat on his face, her body crushed under him. He waited for the flames to die a little and then eased himself off her still figure.

She was alive, her pulse strong. Thank God. He couldn't have lived with his conscience if she hadn't made it. He ran expert hands over her, but couldn't find anything broken. In the glow from the flames she looked defenseless lying there, her eyelashes a dark smudge above her high cheekbones.

He studied her features. She was beautiful all right. But then it had been too damn long since he'd been interested in a woman. The last thing he needed was to get excited about this one.

Apart from the fact that she probably needed medical attention, she was so far off-limits that it was ridiculous. Right from the start he'd had the feeling that he should have turned this job down. Now he was sure of it.

He looked up at the stars and swore long and loud, recalling the phone call that had caused a defenseless woman pain and had brought him to his knees beside her on this dark, empty desert road.

She came awake suddenly, the way she always did after a bad nightmare; heart pounding, mouth dry and a sickening sense of confusion. The first thing she noticed was that the wooden paddles of the fan in her bedroom ceiling were no longer there. They'd been replaced by a cold light beaming down at her from two fluorescent strips.

A steady, monotonous beeping came from somewhere on her right. She shifted her head, wincing as pain sliced viciously across the back of her eyes. She waited a moment or two for her vision to clear.

A plastic tube ran from a bottle of clear liquid suspended above her head into a needle, which stuck into her arm just above her wrist. She stared at her other wrist. She was wearing a plastic name tag...and someone else's watch.

Sunlight filtered through the blinds of a small rectangular window set high in the pale green wall. A small TV set looked down at her from a high shelf at the foot of the bed.

She was in a hospital room.

Panic hit her, swift and debilitating. *What was wrong with her? How did she get here? Why couldn't she remember?*

She looked back at the gold watch that she'd never seen before. It was ten after three. She'd slept through most of the day.

A phone sat on the bedside table, and she stretched out her arm, striving to reach it—though she had no idea what number she wanted to dial.

The door opened and a serious-looking man in a white coat entered the room, followed closely by a matronly nurse. His face lit up when he looked at her.

"Well, Valeri, it's nice to see you awake, at last. How are you feeling?" He paused at the foot of the bed and unhooked a clipboard. "I'm Dr. Harrison. I attended to you when you were brought in here last night."

She ran her tongue over her dry lips. Valeri. Her name was Valeri Richmond. "What happened to me? Where am I?" The fear clogged her throat, and her voice came out a husky whisper.

Dr. Harrison studied the chart for a moment or two, then looked up with a professional smile. "You were involved in an auto accident last night. You've been unconscious until now.''

She waited while her muddled mind absorbed this shocking news. ''Am I badly hurt?''

The doctor shook his head. ''Fortunately, your friend managed to get you out before any serious damage was done. Apart from a few bruises and a slight concussion, you were relatively unharmed. You're a lucky young woman. If it hadn't been for Nathan Thorne, you might have ended up in the morgue instead of a hospital bed.''

She seemed to be having trouble following the words. Apparently she'd wrecked her car. The shock of it must have wiped the memory from her mind. But there was something else—something that wasn't right at all. ''Who's Nathan Thorne?'' she asked warily.

The doctor narrowed his eyes and peered at her intently. ''Exactly what do you remember?''

She tried to think, but the effort intensified the pain in her head. ''Nothing about the accident,'' she admitted.

''Well, try not to worry. That happens sometimes in cases like this. It will most likely come back to you eventually. Headache?''

She nodded, then wished she hadn't when the agonizing pain exploded inside her head again.

''We'll give you something for that,'' the doctor said, scribbling something down on the chart. ''Every four hours, Nurse.''

''Yes, Doctor.'' The nurse gave Valeri a wide, encouraging smile.

''Just try to lie still and relax.'' Dr. Harrison handed the chart to the nurse. ''The pain should pass completely in a few hours. In the meantime, I need to ask you a few questions. Is that all right?''

''All right.'' If she had answers. Right now she didn't seem to even have answers to her own questions.

''Do you feel like sitting up?''

"I think so."

He nodded to the nurse, who pushed something at the side of the bed.

She heard a low hum as the top portion of her bed slowly raised, allowing her to view more of the room. She could see out of the window, but the view looked totally unfamiliar. Unless she was seeing things, those were mountains in the distance, shimmering in summer heat. That didn't make sense.

"Where am I?" she asked sharply.

"You're in the recovery room of St. Sebastian's General Hospital." Dr. Harrison glanced at the nurse. "Ms. Richmond is well enough to see Mr. Thorne now. By the time he gets up here we should be through."

"Yes, Doctor."

Valeri could feel the panic rising again, threatening to suffocate her. "Wait! I don't want to see anybody."

"He's very anxious to see you, Valeri." The doctor's voice was soothing, but it had just the opposite effect on her.

Something was wrong. Something was very wrong, and she had to make him understand. "I don't know anyone by the name of Nathan Thorne." She struggled to sit up, but the pain made her groan and she sank back on the pillow.

"Get that medication. Stat."

"Yes, Doctor." The nurse hurried out the door.

"I've never heard of St. Sebastian's Hospital, either." She glanced at the view from the window. "What part of town is it in?"

The doctor sounded cautious when he answered. "It's on the west side of Carson City."

Her shocked gasp seemed loud in the quiet room. "Carson City? Nevada?"

He nodded.

"That's impossible. I can't be in Carson City." A wave

of panic engulfed her body. "I live in Sacramento. What am I doing here? How did I get here?"

"You came by ambulance." The doctor moved up the side of the bed toward her and tucked his finger under her chin. "Look at me, please."

She opened her eyes, mortified to feel the moisture of tears on her lashes.

"Now, tell me the very last thing you remember."

She fought the fog clouding her brain, struggling to make sense of everything. "I…I'm not sure. I remember leaving the office last night…" She frowned. "I thought it was last night. But it was cold and wet."

"Can you tell me what day it is?"

After a moment's hesitation, she gave him the day, month and year. She didn't like the look on his face. Alarmed again, she added quickly, "What is it? What's wrong?"

For an answer, he reached over to her table, picked up the newspaper that was lying there and held it open in front of her eyes.

Heart thumping, she stared at the headlines, half expecting to see her name emblazoned across the front page. Instead, she saw a story about the tobacco industry's fight over a recent court case.

Puzzled, she stared up at the doctor. "I don't understand."

"Look at the date," Dr. Harrison said gently.

She did so, and caught her breath. No, it wasn't possible. She stared so hard the numbers blurred together. "No," she said sharply. "This is wrong. This can't be today's paper."

"I'm afraid it is, Valeri."

"I don't believe you."

"You apparently have a gap in your memory. Probably caused by the blow to your head. From what Mr. Thorne tells me, you hit the steering wheel pretty hard."

She stared at him, her lips numb with shock. "But I couldn't possibly forget six years of my life."

"I'm sure it's only temporary." He folded the newspaper and then patted her shoulder. "Try to relax. Tell me what you do remember about yourself."

She had to remember. She had to prove him wrong. Her head throbbed as she struggled to grasp the elusive memories, painfully and slowly forcing the pieces into place. "My name is Valeri Richmond. I'm twenty-nine years old—"

"When were you born?"

She felt sick, knowing that she would have to accept what seemed to be fact, no matter how bizarre. "I guess I'm thirty-five," she mumbled.

"Anything else? You're not wearing a wedding ring, so I assume you're not married."

"Divorced. No children." Which, considering her present circumstances, was fortunate, she added inwardly. At least she didn't have to worry about someone waiting for her at home.

"Where do you work?"

"I'm a freelance public relations consultant and I live in an apartment in the suburbs of Sacramento, California. I just can't understand what I'm doing in Nevada."

"Let's not worry about that for now. Parents?"

"My mother's name was Sylvia Forrester. She passed away a little over a year ago…no, *seven* years ago." She shook her head, still unable to believe so much of her life was a blank.

"I'm sorry. Your father?"

Her father was still very much alive. At least, he was the last she remembered. She was about to say his name when an odd thing happened. It was like seeing a momentary flash of a movie on a screen, there and gone in an instant. Yet in that moment she was quite certain that Alex did not want her to talk about him.

Shaken by the strange notion, she looked into the doctor's eyes. "I don't see much of my father," she said quietly.

"I see." Dr. Harrison glanced at his watch. "Well, I'm sure Mr. Thorne will be able to help you contact someone. I really don't think there's too much to worry about."

Valeri swallowed. "Will it come back?"

"Your memory? Probably. Partial amnesia is tough to predict. Sometimes it comes back gradually, a piece at a time. Or sometimes another trauma, such as another blow to the head, might bring it all back at once. Though that's not something I'd recommend."

She tried to smile at the weak joke. "What if the memory doesn't come back? Will it affect anything else?"

"Physically you have nothing at all to worry about. Very often people injured in an accident remember nothing about it, or the events leading up to it. In rare cases, such as yours, the time lapse can be even longer. You might have to get help filling in the missing details from the people you know."

"What about the people I don't know?"

Dr. Harrison smiled. "I can assure you, Valeri, if you're talking about Nathan Thorne, he tells me he is a good friend of yours. He's very concerned about you. He spent the night in the waiting room, and I'm quite sure he'll be very happy to know you're all right. Once you see him, everything could very well fall into place. I'll have a word with him, and then I'll send him in, all right? "

She didn't want to see anyone, much less a man she'd never heard of. On the other hand, if he knew her well enough to fill in the missing pieces, it would certainly help calm her fears.

She watched the doctor leave, then settled back to wait, wondering if she looked as messy as she felt. She put her hand up to her head, and received another shock. She'd lost about six inches of hair. It barely reached her jaw now. She must have had it cut. How could she not remember such a drastic move?

She concentrated, trying desperately to remember what she was doing in Carson City, but her head ached with the effort. She closed her eyes and was already dozing when the door opened again.

"Valeri!" a man's deep voice exclaimed. "Thank God, you're all right. I was worried sick about you."

She opened her eyes. He was tall, with big shoulders and an impressive build. His legs had been crammed into a pair of jeans, and he'd tucked a denim shirt into the waistband.

He was not a handsome man, but he certainly commanded attention. His face was what her charitable mother would have described as full of character. His mouth tilted up at one end, one jet black eyebrow sat higher than the other, and his hooked nose was just a little off center.

His eyes were his most striking feature. Trimmed with thick dark lashes, they were the color of burnished gold—and just as inflexible. She was quite certain she would never have forgotten eyes like those. As far as she was concerned, this man was a complete stranger.

Considering the only thing that stood between her and total exposure was a thin hospital gown, she found it difficult to muster any dignity. Nevertheless, she gave it her best shot. Fixing the stranger with her coolest stare, she said distinctly, "I don't think we've met."

The man moved around the bed and sat down on the side of it, a little too close for comfort. "You look a little pale. The doctor says you might have a headache for a few days, but he's giving you some medication and—"

She drew back, annoyed by his familiarity. "Who are you?"

"I'm Nat, of course." His eyes crinkled at the corners, intent on her face. "Nathan Thorne, your closest neighbor and, I hope, your very good friend. Don't you remember?

The doctor said you had trouble remembering things, but I'd hoped you wouldn't forget me."

"As far as I know, I've never seen you before in my life." She was utterly convinced of that. Nathan Thorne was the kind of man a woman didn't forget easily. The kind of man she'd always avoided. The earthy, primitive, sensual kind of man who screamed danger.

She hoped fervently that her tone had conveyed her opinion that she wouldn't be caught dead in his company. Admittedly, according to the doctor, the stranger had missed a night's sleep. That hardly excused the thick growth of dark stubble on his jaw, or the shaggy haircut. No man like this would ever be considered her friend. Not in a million years.

Nathan Thorne sighed. "The doctor warned me this could happen."

He reached for her hand, but she snatched it away. The nurse should be back any minute with her medication, she assured herself. She had nothing to worry about.

"I'm sorry. I know all this must be a bad shock for you."

He actually did look concerned. She tried to make herself relax. "You were with me when I wrecked the car?"

"Thank God I was. I dragged you out of there before the whole thing went up in a ball of flame."

She shuddered. In all her confusion, she'd lost sight of the fact that this man had saved her life. "Thank you," she said awkwardly, still not wholly convinced. "I guess I owe you a lot."

His smile looked almost cynical. For a second she felt an involuntary stirring of response, and immediately stifled it. She couldn't have feelings for this man. She just couldn't. No matter what had happened to her in the past six years, she was reasonably sure of that.

"Forget it," Nat said easily. "I'm just glad I came along for the ride. If you'd been alone..." He paused, letting his silence fill in the rest.

"Where did this happen?"

"About thirty miles outside of town. We were on our way home when you missed a turn and overturned the car. Must have hit a patch of oil, or something."

"Home?" Surely not with him. She couldn't possibly live with this man.

"To Windridge. Your house in the mountains."

"What mountains?" Aware of sounding stupid, her voice was brittle.

"Valeri, try to remember. You live on a fairly large acreage in the Sierra mountains, not too far from a small town called Sylvan Springs."

She started. The name did mean something to her. She'd heard it somewhere before. She repeated it over and over in her mind, but couldn't put a picture to the words.

"I live a couple of miles to the north of you," Nat went on. "You were coming into the city to do some shopping. I had some business to do here and you offered me a ride."

Relief washed over her. So he really was just a neighbor, and she was not personally involved with him. She should have known. He certainly wasn't her type, and in any case, men like him didn't look at women like her. She could just imagine the kind of women Nathan Thorne would go for.

But how in the world did she have the money to buy a house and acreage? Her business must be doing phenomenally well. She felt a spasm of uneasiness. Whatever she'd achieved in the last six years could be lost if she didn't get back her memory. Unless she had taken on some competent staff.

She was about to ask Nat what he knew about her business when he startled her by saying, "Sabhad will be so relieved to know you're all right. He's been really worried about you. If it hadn't been for the twins, he'd have come down here to the hospital, but he didn't want to leave them while they were so upset."

Valeri shook her head, trying to deal with this new

bombshell. "I'm sorry, I don't know who you're talking about."

Nat looked worried. "Oh, that's right. The doctor said you can't remember the last six years. Well, this might be another shock for you, but Ahmed Sabhad is your husband, and the father of your four-year-old twins."

She was having a nightmare. That had to be it. There was no way this was really happening to her. Only if this was all a dream, why did her head hurt so much? And where was that damn nurse with the medication?

"I'm sorry," Nat said quietly. "There just wasn't any other way to say it."

"It isn't true. You're mistaking me for someone else." She wriggled further up the bed, clutching the blanket to her chest. "I just got divorced. There's no way I'd ever marry again. And I'd know if I had children. Darn it, I'd *know*."

"You got divorced more than six years ago. You've been married to Sabhad for five."

"Then how come everyone is calling me Ms. Richmond?"

"You kept your former name when you remarried. Lots of women do."

"That's ridiculous." She waved her left hand in his face. "If I'm married, where's my ring?"

His expression didn't alter. "That I don't know. Maybe you took it off for some reason when you left. But I can promise you, you are married to Ahmed Sabhad."

"You're lying."

"I'm telling you the truth."

A cold, clammy feeling crept over her as she watched him reach into his jacket pocket and pull out a wallet. "Look, I have pictures of you and your family."

Her hand shook as she took the photos from him, almost afraid to look. She stared at the picture of the woman holding the hands of two identical little girls, both of whom had the same dark hair and eyes as her own. Her hair was shorter, and she looked thinner, but she couldn't deny that was her face smiling into the camera.

She studied the other photo. The swarthy, heavyset man standing next to her had his arm about her, and there was no mistaking his proprietary attitude. Good grief, was she actually married to this man? How could she not recognize him?

"That's Ahmed Sabhad," Nat said, pointing at the photo. "He's from Saudi Arabia. He still has business ties there, I believe. He's a very wealthy industrialist from what I understand."

That settled it. She just couldn't picture herself falling in love with a wealthy *sheik* and bearing his children. That sort of thing happened to other women. Bold, adventurous women. Not conservative, sensible women like Valeri Richmond. Period.

"Anyway, the doctor says you should be able to leave by tomorrow," Nat said, tucking the pictures back in his wallet. "I've rented a car, and I'll pick you up in the morning and take you home."

"You're not taking me anywhere." She heard the panic in her voice and made herself breathe deeply. "I'm not going anywhere until I have my memory back and I know exactly what I'm doing."

"That could take days...months...maybe never. What about your babies? They're waiting for their mother to come home to them. Surely you're not going to let them go on suffering?"

Guilt hit her like an iron fist. What if he were telling the truth? What if those two adorable little girls were really pining for her?

She looked wildly around the room. "I need my purse. It's probably in that cupboard over there. If I've got children, I'll have pictures of them in there...my ID... something that will tell me who I am."

His face was expressionless as he studied her, and she would have given a great deal to know what he was thinking. Finally, he said in a low voice, "Everything you had with you in the car burned up with it. I didn't have time to grab anything. I was too busy trying to get you out. I'm sorry."

She wasn't going to cry, she told herself fiercely. She was not going to cry.

"Your daughters need you," Nat said softly.

She wavered, trying to decide what to do. The door opened just then, and the nurse hurried in, holding a tiny paper cup. "Here's your medication, Ms. Richmond. This should make you feel better."

There wasn't a pill on earth that was going to make her feel better, Valeri thought. She took the tablets gratefully and swallowed them down with the help of a large gulp of water.

"You look a little pale," the nurse commented, after a sly glance at Nat. "Perhaps you should get some rest."

Valeri heartily agreed. She was relieved when Nat took the hint and stood up.

He waited until the nurse had left the room, then looked down at Valeri. "I'll leave so you can get some rest. I'll be back for you tomorrow."

She watched him go, wondering if it was her imagination, or if she really heard a veiled threat behind his words.

The room seemed strangely quiet after he'd left. She felt dazed, as if she were groping through a thick maze with nothing but dead ends. Nothing she had heard made sense.

The last thing she remembered before waking up in the hospital was leaving her office on a dark, dreary winter's afternoon. In Sacramento. Six years ago.

Her divorce had been barely six months old. She'd been heading for her apartment, which she shared with a rather bad-tempered cat named Claws and the occasional spider. She felt bad, wondering what had happened to the cat.

If Nathan Thorne was telling the truth, she had woken up to a completely different life. As a wife to a rich *sheik* and the mother of twins.

She gave her head a mental shake. Impossible. Nothing would convince her that she had children. That was something she would know. The physical and psychological changes to a woman who had given birth could never be buried by a blow on the head. Of that she was certain.

But if that were so, who was Ahmed—or whatever his name was? And, even more to the point, who was Nathan Thorne and why would he lie about all this? In spite of her convictions, she couldn't quite discount the odd feeling of having heard of Sylvan Springs somewhere before—though she couldn't remember why.

The pills were making her drowsy. She couldn't go to sleep, she decided, until she knew some answers. There was one person whom she could trust—who would tell her the truth. Her father.

Alex Forrester had walked out on his wife and five-year-old daughter one warm summer evening, and for the next twenty-four years his name was never spoken again between Valeri and her mother. It wasn't until Sylvia Forrester passed away that Valeri met her father again.

He came to the memorial service, and after Valeri had recovered from the shock, she'd agreed to have dinner with him—more out of curiosity than out of any real desire to renew their relationship. After all, she'd never forgiven him for abandoning her when she was a child.

Until he told her why he'd left.

Sylvia Forrester had been frigid. She'd made it plain from the start of their marriage that she found the physical side of marriage distasteful, and after Valeri was born she'd moved into the spare bedroom and refused to sleep with Alex again.

Alex had hung in there for five long years, hoping to change his wife's mind. When it became apparent that wasn't going to happen, the fighting became intolerable. He decided they would all be better off living apart. Sylvia had let him go without a word of protest. She'd simply told Valeri that her father had gone away and wasn't coming back.

Although he'd given up custody, figuring that it would make things easier for Valeri if her parents weren't fighting over her, Alex had sent letters and gifts for several years, until he finally gave up hearing from her. He was outraged later to learn that Valeri never received his offerings.

From the day she'd learned the true circumstances, Valeri had tried to make up for the lost years. Alex had turned out to be quite different from the man she had imagined, and had been a tremendous support while she was going through her own divorce.

She never told her father the reason for the breakup of her own marriage. Things had not gone well between her and Dan from the start. She just couldn't relax with him in bed, and began making excuses to stay away from him. Finally he'd found comfort elsewhere, and understanding why, Valeri had divorced him.

Now she needed Alex again. As she reached for the phone, she prayed that she'd hung on to the developing relationship throughout the six years that had passed. If not, she didn't know what she was going to do.

Chapter 2

With a shaky hand, Valeri punched out Alex's number on the phone, relieved that the number came back to her easily. It seemed odd to be dialing long distance for a residence that, in her memory, had always been just across town. She wondered if he'd married again. It didn't seem likely.

The phone rang once, twice, then the line clicked open. "Hello?"

Valeri frowned. The voice sounded too young to be her father's. "Is Alex there?"

There was a short pause. Then the pleasant voice said, "I think you must have the wrong number. There's no one by that name here."

She gave the address of her father's townhouse in Sacramento, knowing as she did so what the answer would be.

"Sorry. This isn't it."

Alex must have moved. Not surprising, given his restless nature. Six years was a long time for him to stay in one place. She thanked the young man, depressed the button and dialed again. This time her own phone number. A recorded message answered her in a voice she didn't recognize.

Her call to the office went unanswered. Two more calls to friends both proved fruitless. It seemed as if everyone and everything from her past life had simply vanished along with her memory.

Depression settled over her in a dense, black fog. The maze was getting thicker by the minute. The medication was working and she was almost asleep, but roused herself with an effort. This was ridiculous. Everyone she knew couldn't have died. All she had to do was track someone down. Starting with Alex.

She glanced at the clock. Of course. He would still be at work. She dialed the number, and was rewarded by a brisk voice announcing she'd reached the government offices in Sacramento. She was about to ask the woman for her father's lab, but the voice went on, advising her to dial the number for the department she wanted.

Irritated, Valeri stabbed out the number. Another disembodied voice told her to hold, and she waited, wondering what had happened to the cheerful receptionist who had always before answered her calls.

At last a human voice came on the line. "Can I help you?"

"I'd like to speak to Alex Forrester, please."

The pause on the end of the line seemed ominous. "I'm sorry, Mr. Forrester is not in the office today."

Valeri sighed. "This is Valeri Richmond, his daughter. I seem to have misplaced his home phone number. Could you give it to me, please?"

Again the pause. Valeri was beginning to get a nasty feeling that something was wrong.

"Could you hold for just a moment?" the voice said.

She waited, the phone feeling clammy in her hand. Finally a man's voice said pleasantly, "Ms. Richmond? This is Detective Chasen from the Sacramento Metropolitan Police Department. Would you mind telling me when you last spoke to your father?"

"I'm not sure...I—" She closed her eyes as pain burned across her forehead. As she did so, she experienced again that strange brief flash of recognition. She *had* talked to Alex recently. She remembered his voice, low and urgent, though she couldn't remember what he'd said. All she knew for certain was that she must not tell that to the police officer.

"Ms. Richmond?"

She started guiltily. "I'm...sorry. I'm calling from the hospital. I've been involved in an accident and I'm trying to get in touch with my father. He's all right, isn't he? I mean, he's not hurt or anything?"

Dear God, Alex was injured. He'd told her that.

"I see you haven't heard," the detective said gravely.

She gripped the phone, willing herself not to give anything away by her voice. "I haven't heard anything. What's wrong with my father?"

"Nothing, as far as we know. Not physically, anyway."

The detective paused, and she knew, with a dreadful certainty, that he was preparing to give her bad news.

When he spoke again, his voice had the careful note of someone watching his words. "Ms. Richmond, I'm sorry to have to tell you that your father is wanted for questioning in a murder case. He left the scene of the crime and is currently being hunted by the sheriff's department."

Her cry of dismay echoed down the line. "No, I don't believe it. Not Alex. He would never hurt anyone. He's the most gentle man I've ever known."

"I'm sure he is."

She winced at the irony in his voice. "Who is he supposed to have killed?"

"I'm afraid I can't disclose any details of the case." The detective sounded genuinely sorry. "I have to remind you that should you discover the whereabouts of your father, you must contact the sheriff's department immediately. I trust we can count on your cooperation?"

"Of course," Valeri mumbled, knowing full well she was not going to turn Alex in at any cost. There was just no way she was going to believe he was involved with murder. She had to find him and find out what really happened. She was fairly certain now that she did know where he was, but that she just couldn't remember.

"From which hospital are you calling?" Detective Chasen asked, his voice casual now.

"I'm sorry," Valeri said hastily. "I have to go now." She dropped the receiver into the cradle and sank back on her pillows. This latest news had shaken her more than anything she'd heard so far.

Up until that moment everything had seemed unreal, like a bad dream that would eventually go away. But now she knew that Alex was in deep trouble and needed her. What's more, she had a strong feeling that Nathan Thorne was somehow involved in all this.

She wasn't sure exactly what she knew, but somewhere in the shadowy crevices of her shattered memory lay the answers. She would have to dig them up. And soon.

Thanks to the medication she'd been given, she awoke the next morning after a long night's sleep. The fragile hope that her memory would return was quickly squashed, though she wasn't really surprised. The doctor had warned her that it could take some time.

During his final examination later that morning, he also warned her not to try to force herself to remember. That was a warning she intended to ignore. Alex was out there, somewhere—a fugitive, alone, injured and needing her. She had to find him.

One thing of which she was quite certain was that she was not going "home," or anywhere else with Nathan Thorne until she'd found her father and had answered all her questions. She'd worry about dealing with her so-called family if and when she was convinced she had one.

She wasn't looking forward to telling Nat of her decision. She didn't trust him. He was just a little too charming, and she sensed a hint of menace behind the smooth mask. He intimidated her. He had a way of making her feel self-conscious. She wasn't used to confronting that much potent masculinity.

He arrived after lunch, about five minutes after she'd signed the release papers. He must have called the hospital to find out when she was being discharged. It was almost as if he'd been waiting to pounce on her in case she tried to escape. The odd thought did nothing to alleviate her uneasiness.

She'd dressed in the chinos and soft blue rayon shirt she'd apparently worn when she'd wrecked the car. She didn't recognize the clothes, but she was grateful to discover they'd been sent to the hospital laundry by a thoughtful nurse.

The way Nat looked her up and down when he walked into the room, she might as well have still been wearing the hospital gown. Unsettled by his frank and thorough inspection, she took refuge in a cool, distant manner.

"Thanks for the offer," she said, when he asked if she was ready to leave, "but I've decided not to go back with you. I don't think it would be a good idea. I don't remember a husband and children, and it would only be confusing for everyone. Especially those little girls. I think it would be best if I remain close to the hospital until I get my memory back."

"I don't agree." His strange eyes mirrored his disapproval. "That could take months. What am I going to tell those little girls? That their mommy doesn't want to see them?"

"I don't feel that I am their mommy. It would be worse

for them to have a stranger come back and pretend to be their mommy, wouldn't it?''

She hadn't meant it to come out that way, but she saw something flicker in his steady gaze. More certain than ever that the man was lying, she felt a little more secure of her ground. ''In any case, that's my decision.''

''How will you manage without credit cards, or ID?''

''The staff here has been kind enough to arrange for me to go to a halfway house until my...background has been established.'' She had been going to say until she found her father, but had stopped herself just in time.

''I've already established your background. Once you get home, your husband can help you renew your ID.''

''I'm not ready to accept that yet. Dr. Harrison agrees that this will be better for me for the time being, until I'm ready to accept my new life. Until then, I'll retrace the years I've lost.''

She could tell by the way he tightened his mouth that he was annoyed. ''How are you going to do that if you don't have anything to go on?''

She shrugged, trying to appear unconcerned. ''I know my social security number. The hospital people are checking into it for me. It shouldn't take too long to reestablish my credit and my driving license. There are people out there who know me, who should be able to fill me in. All I have to do is find them.''

''Valeri, you don't have any friends. You live a pretty isolated life.''

''Then it's no wonder I left.''

He narrowed his eyes, and for an instant she saw a darkness there that frightened her. Something told her that Nathan Thorne could be dangerous when crossed. ''I suppose all this is on the level,'' he said, with just a hint of suspicion in his voice. ''After all, it wouldn't be all that tough to fake a loss of memory.''

A spark of anger sharpened her voice. ''That's a disgusting thing to say. You have no idea how terrifying it is to wake up and not know where you are...or who you are anymore. Surrounded by strangers in a strange environment, not knowing where you're going or where you've been. I can assure you, Mr. Thorne, this isn't something I do for laughs. And even if I were, just what business is it of yours, anyway?"

He studied her for another long moment from beneath his drawn brows. She stared back at him, daring him to contradict her.

Finally, he said smoothly, "I apologize. It was a dumb thing to say."

"Thank you. Now, if you don't mind, I have a cab waiting for me at the door."

He lifted his hands in a gesture of defeat. "Okay, I'm going. All I ask is that you contact your husband as soon as possible and let him know where you are. Here's the phone number. It's unlisted so you'll need this." He thrust a folded piece of paper at her, then, with a mock salute, turned on his heel and left.

Valeri let out a long breath. She was surprised to discover that her hands shook as she unfolded the paper. A phone number was scrawled across the page in a bold hand. If this was her own phone number, she didn't recognize it at all.

She shoved the paper into a pocket of her pants, then looked around the room. It seemed strange not to have a purse, or something to pick up. Her hands felt empty, and she walked out the door, feeling as if she were leaving behind the only real security she had.

She stopped at the desk, and the receptionist gave her a sympathetic smile as she handed her a small envelope. "Your cab's waiting outside, and there's your prescription. When we heard what happened to you, we collected a few dollars together to help tide you over until you can get back on your feet. It's in the envelope."

Valeri felt like crying.

"That's really kind of everyone. Please thank them for me."

The receptionist nodded. "Sure. Just take care, okay? We all hope you get your life back soon."

"Thanks. I'll let you know when I do." Valeri tucked the envelope into her pocket and headed for the door. Once she was settled, she assured herself, she could set about finding her father. There had to be someone who knew where he was. She just had to make some phone calls. Something would turn up. If the doctor was right, the more she found out, the faster her memory would return.

She couldn't escape the sense of urgency that had been with her from the moment she'd woken up in that hospital bed in this strange town. Whatever she'd buried in her mind, it was important. It was imperative that she remember. Alex was in trouble, and something told her that she didn't have a whole lot of time.

Nat sat in the front seat of his black compact, his eyes glued to the main doors of the hospital. He wasn't happy with this assignment. He wasn't crazy about Ahmed Sabhad, and might have turned down the job, if it hadn't been for one factor.

After Sabhad had given him the picture of those two little girls, he'd played a tape of them crying for their mommy. He'd begged Nat to find her and bring her back. He'd told Nat he hoped that once Valeri saw how her kids were suffering, she'd have a change of heart.

That had pushed a pretty sensitive button as far as Nat was concerned. Anyone who ill-treated kids was lower than low in his opinion. He knew, only too well, what it meant to children to be deserted by someone they loved. He'd been there.

Sabhad's story of Valeri abandoning her daughters—

simply because she'd grown bored—infuriated Nat. He'd acted on a gut instinct and agreed to accept the assignment.

When he'd heard that Valeri had lost her memory, he'd invented the story of being her neighbor. He had figured it would make his job that much easier than if he told her the truth: her husband had hired him to bring her back.

Now it looked as if he might have to play it tough, after all. She'd refused to go along with his plan, but he would have to insist. He had a big problem with that. It had been one thing to agree to bring back the hard, selfish thrill-seeker Sabhad had led him to believe his wife was. Valeri Richmond was something else.

She didn't seem at all the way Sabhad had described. That air of class he'd detected in the photos was even more pronounced in person. He had trouble acquainting the soft-spoken, fresh-faced woman in the hospital with the image Sabhad had conjured up in Nat's mind.

What was even more disturbing was that he found her attractive. She'd put on a little weight since the pictures were taken, all of it in the right places. He'd never cared for the bean-stick women who starved themselves to get into size-two jeans. He preferred a woman with curves, and when he'd examined her body for injuries last night, he couldn't help noticing that Valeri Richmond definitely had curves.

Staring out the window, his eyes squinted against the blinding sun, Nat silently cursed. If it weren't for the cries of those kids haunting him day and night, and the pictures he carried, he'd call the whole thing off.

Then again, Valeri Richmond wasn't quite what he'd expected. Maybe there was a spark of decency in her and she would change her mind as Sabhad hoped. If so, it would be worth Nat taking the risks involved. If only his own mother had had that chance, things might have been different for him, too.

Under any other circumstances, he could have sympathized with Sabhad's wife. Ahmed Sabhad was not the most pleasant man he'd ever met. It would be a shock for any woman to wake up and find herself married to a total stranger, especially a sleazeball like Sabhad.

Then again, if Sabhad was telling the truth about Valeri marrying him for his money, and then taking off to look for more excitement, she'd got exactly what she deserved.

Again he cursed. He had to stop questioning everything. The photos didn't lie; that was the clincher. That was Valeri Richmond all right, holding on to the hands of those two little girls. She belonged with her kids, and he was going to see to it that she got there, whether she liked it or not. What happened after that was between her and her husband.

And if he was going to do the job right, Nat warned himself, he'd better quit feeling sorry for her. He'd been down too many dark alleys to be taken in by the helpless female act. From now on, Valeri Richmond was a package he'd been hired to deliver, and nothing more. As he always did in his unpredictable profession, he'd worry about the consequences later.

The dry heat that greeted Valeri when she stepped outside was something of a shock. She'd gone from winter to summer overnight, practically. It was one more reminder of the hurdles ahead of her.

Preoccupied with her worry over Alex, she failed to notice the black car with the door standing open until a rough hand grabbed her arm and propelled her forward at such a speed that she had to struggle to stay on her feet. She opened her mouth to yell, but before she could draw breath a hand clamped over her mouth and she was forced into the car.

"Try to run," Nat said, almost pleasantly, "and I promise you, you'll be sorry. I'm faster than you think. And a lot more dangerous. Just in case you're wondering, I'm armed. Don't make me use it."

She shrank back in her seat, too terrified to protest. She wasn't about to argue with a gun. At least one question had been answered. Nathan Thorne was not her friendly neighbor who'd begged a ride into town on business. Therefore, she had to suspect he had some connection with the trouble Alex was in.

She went cold when the logical conclusion hit her. Nathan Thorne could be some kind of cop. He probably thought she knew where Alex was hiding. If so, he was wasting his time. Even if she did know, the last person on earth she'd tell was this big ox who seemed intent on kidnapping her.

When he slid in beside her, she shifted over as close to the door as she could get. It wasn't a big car, and his shoulders overlapped the edge of his seat. She didn't want him touching her again. The feel of his hands on her body had shaken her up enough.

"Where are you taking me?" she demanded as the car rocketed out of the parking lot at an alarming speed. "I think I'm entitled to know."

"I'm taking you home," Nat said grimly, his gaze concentrated on the road ahead.

Valeri squinted at the road sign coming up on her right. If he was taking her home, he was going in the wrong direction. "Really. Is that why you made up that ridiculous story about my husband and two little girls pining for me? Forget it, Mr. Thorne, or whatever your real name is. You're not fooling me for one second. I don't know what you want with me, but I do know you're not taking me back to any rich *sheik.*"

His glance managed to convey his disgust. "I might have lied about being your neighbor, but I didn't lie about the rest of it. Your husband and kids are waiting for you at home. Believe me, I'm doing this for your own good. Once you're back home with them you'll have a much better chance of getting your memory back. And those two little girls will have their mom back where she belongs."

Valeri stared at his harsh profile, struggling between suspicion and doubt. He sounded so convincing. Could he be telling the truth, after all? He had her pretty well trapped in his car. What did he have to gain by sticking to his story now?

On the other hand, if his intention was simply to take her back home as he claimed, why had he threatened her? It didn't make sense. Nothing made sense.

"I may not remember everything," she said, a little desperately, "and I can't explain the photos, but I am one-hundred-percent certain that I am not the mother of those two little girls. Or the wife of that man."

"Yeah, sure. And you didn't run away to have a hot time with your boyfriends on your husband's money, either."

Shock brought her upright in the seat. "I beg your pardon?"

"Oh, come off it, lady. You might be able to fool those doctors in the hospital, but you can't fool an old pro like me. I wouldn't be in the least surprised to find out this whole memory thing is just another ruse to get out of going back to your kids. Right?"

Outraged, she felt like hitting him. "How dare you talk to me like that. Just who the devil do you think you are?"

He sent her a sideways glance out of his pale gold eyes. "Maybe I am the devil."

She stared at him, confused and frightened by the bitterness in that muttered comment. "Look," she said, dismayed to hear her voice trembling, "I really have lost my memory. At least about six years of it. I wish I could remember everything, but I can't. I just know I didn't marry the man in the photo and I'm not the mother of his children. Don't ask me how I know that. I just know."

"So you've said."

''It's the truth. Which is more than you're telling me.''

He glanced at her again but didn't answer.

''You at least owe me an explanation.''

''I don't owe you a damn thing.''

''If you're not my neighbor, then who are you?'' Again she waited in vain for him to answer. They were heading for the mountains, she realized. Already the commercial buildings were dwindling, giving way to long stretches of open road between the occasional fast-food restaurants and gas stations.

She struggled to make sense of what was happening. She'd seen enough movies to know that cops didn't always dress up in uniform and do things by the book. Even so, this one was being just a little too high-handed. Wasn't he supposed to read her her rights or something? She was beginning to suspect he wasn't a cop after all. She didn't like to think of the alternatives.

The sun beat through the window, burning her arm in spite of the cooled air blowing from the vents. Her head ached, and her shoulder hurt where the bruises were just beginning to appear.

Tired of the tense silence between them, she tried a few more questions. ''Why didn't my...husband—'' she almost choked on the word ''—come for me himself? Why did he send you?''

''He had to stay and look after the kids.''

''Why did he ask you? Are you a friend of his? If so, he's not going to be too happy to find out how you manhandled his wife.''

''Lady, if I really wanted to manhandle you, believe me, I can be a lot rougher. Not that you'd complain about that, from what I hear.''

Outraged, she was speechless for several seconds. When she finally got her breath, she practically spat words at him. ''I don't know exactly what you've heard, Mr. Thorne, but

I can assure you, it is far from the truth. You must have me mixed up with someone else."

"How would you know, if you don't remember? A lot can happen in six years."

She tried to ignore the unpleasant sensation in the pit of her stomach. "I only know," she said firmly, "that I couldn't possibly have changed that much."

"And that lady in the photos isn't you...is that what you're telling me?"

She lifted her hands, and let them fall. "I don't know," she said miserably. "I just can't remember."

"Or maybe you just don't want to remember."

Her fingers curled in her lap. "You are quite the most unpleasant man I've ever met. I don't know why I'm listening to you."

"Then don't. Quit asking questions and you won't have to listen to me at all."

Seething with resentment, she glanced out the window. They were climbing now, leaving the dry valley floor spreading out below them. On one side the reddish brown rocks towered above them, while on her side the wide shoulder gave way to a sheer drop.

Even if she could jump clear of the car, there was a good possibility she'd fall over the edge and plunge to her death. The only thing she could do for now was to sit tight and pray that she'd remember something, anything, that would help her get out of this nightmare.

She closed her eyes and leaned back in her seat. The sunlight flashed across her closed lids. Or was it the sunlight? She tensed, striving to see the visions flickering just out of reach.

Alex's voice, warning her. Of what? *The police. Don't tell them anything.* Something else. *Ahmed Sabhad.*

Startled, she opened her eyes again. Had Alex really said the *sheik's* name, or was she confusing her own thoughts with those brief snatches of memory?

Sylvan Springs. Come and get me. Can't drive. Watch out. Don't talk to the police. Don't trust anyone.

Sylvan Springs. So she hadn't imagined it. Was Alex here in the Sierra mountains? If he was on the run, why would he head for Nevada?

Unless Nat had told her the truth and she really was married and living here. That would explain why Alex would come to the Sierra mountains looking for refuge.

Damn the fog that clouded her mind. She'd just have to wait until she got to the mansion. If she was really married to the man in the pictures, he'd have the answers she was looking for.

On the other hand, if all this was a simple case of mistaken identity, then Sabhad—if that was his name—would tell Nathan Thorne he'd made a mistake and Nat would have to take her to the halfway house. Clinging to that hope, Valeri sat in silence as the car climbed the rugged road through the mountains.

She felt Nat's glance upon her a couple of times, but she ignored him. She concentrated instead on her elusive memory, trying to focus in on Alex. The brief flashes she got were not helpful.

She saw herself walking alongside a river thick with boats. She was arm in arm with Alex, laughing at something he said. Obviously they had become close over the past six years. She was glad about that. She'd missed out on a lot, not growing up with a father. It was nice to know she could enjoy being with him now.

They'll be looking for me. Again Alex's voice. He'd called her. Called her where? From where? A brief vision of a bedroom flicked across her mind. A comforter in desert shades covered the bed. Matching curtains hung at a window.

She strained mentally to see out the bedroom window. Buildings. A city. She lived in a city. Not a house on an acreage in the mountains. Damn, why hadn't she thought to try calling directory enquiries in Sacramento? Because Nat's story had thrown her, that's why.

But now she had proof. Her own memory. She was not married to Ahmed Sabhad. She lived on her own in an apartment in Sacramento. She even knew the address. So who was Nathan Thorne and where was he really taking her?

Nat glanced over at his passenger as the little car toiled up the steep climb. She hadn't said a word in twenty minutes, but he could tell she was doing plenty of thinking. The longer he was with her, the more uneasy he became about the whole damn deal.

Sabhad had warned him that Valeri would lie. She'd do anything to avoid going back, he'd told Nat. Yet Valeri's insistence that she was not the mother of twins held a ring of sincerity. And that made Nat uncomfortable.

Sabhad had also told him that Valeri was a loose woman, ready to jump into bed with any man who asked her. That description definitely didn't fit the woman who now sat silently by his side. The way she'd reacted to his deliberately coarse comments—uttered more to shut her up than anything—he'd have said just the opposite.

Either the concussion and her loss of memory had altered her personality, or she was one hell of an actress.

Or there was one more possibility: Sabhad's story about his wayward wife could be a lie. If so, the big question was—why? Right then, Nat would have given a great deal to know which of his scenarios was the right one.

One thing he did know. This whole setup didn't smell right. He could feel a certain tingling in his spine that usually warned him when he was walking into danger. Making a note to stay on guard, he leaned forward to watch for the sign that led to Windridge.

It came up on him suddenly, and he braked to make the sharp turn onto the dusty road. He saw Valeri's hands braced against the dash. They were clenched, the knuckles white.

In spite of his convictions, he couldn't help saying, "Don't worry, he's not going to eat you alive. If you really aren't his wife, we'll get the whole thing straightened out when we get there."

She sent him a look that said plainly that she wasn't holding her breath. Not that he could blame her. What he'd done amounted to a case of kidnapping: a federal offense. It wasn't the first time he'd broken the law, but most of the time it hadn't bothered him. He wasn't sure why it bothered him now.

He knew he didn't like forcing a woman to do anything against her will—not even when she deserved it. And something was telling him that Valeri Richmond did not deserve the treatment he'd handed out to her. It was a little late now to say he was sorry. He could only hope that one day, when she watched her daughters graduate from high school, she'd remember to thank him.

"There's the house, up ahead," he said unnecessarily, as wrought-iron gates, embedded in a ten-foot-high brick wall, loomed ahead of them. The name *Windridge* was worked into the iron like a florid inscription.

To the left of the towering gates, a small hut with a glass window looked out onto the narrow road, which was hemmed in on both sides by smooth-faced reddish rock.

A thick mass of pine trees obscured the house from the road, but Nat knew that the cameras mounted on either side of the gates gave whoever was inside the house a clear view of the street in both directions. The estate couldn't have been better situated for security. The place was a virtual fortress. Sabhad had to be nervous about something—or somebody.

Valeri's apprehension was stamped all over her face as Nat drew up to the gate. An armed guard appeared outside the hut. He wasn't the same man Nat had seen on his last visit to the house. Nat stayed at the wheel and stuck his head out the window.

"Nathan Thorne," he said crisply. "I'm bringing Mrs. Sabhad back to the house."

The guard looked puzzled. "Mrs. Sabhad? She has arrived from Riyadh?" He bent low to peer at Valeri. "Wait, that is not—"

From the speakers on the gates came a furious spate of guttural foreign words. The guard reached for the gun in his belt, just as another guard burst from the hut.

Nat, his instincts bristling like the fur of an angry dog, had already eased the gear into reverse. He slammed his foot down on the accelerator and yelled, "Duck! Hit the floor!"

Valeri obediently crumpled into a ball at his side as the car shot backward, bucking and rocking in a cloud of dust. Bullets zinged past, and he heard a couple of them smack into the body of the car as he twisted in his seat and frantically threw the wheel right and left.

Ever watchful for a way out of situations if necessary, he'd noticed a small clearing on the way up. There would be barely enough room to turn the car, but it was all he had. The gates were already opening up at the house, and a couple of serious black sedans sat with their engines chugging, just waiting to spring into the chase.

"Hold on!" he yelled at Valeri, who was crouched down in front of her seat, her arms held protectively over her head. She never made a sound, and he spared her a second's grudging admiration before concentrating everything on the wild maneuver that would either spin them around in the right direction, or catapult them off the mountain into oblivion.

Chapter 3

The clearing came up fast, and Nat sent up a silent prayer as he swung the wheel hard to the left, his foot clamped on the brake. He could hear Sabhad's cars screaming down the hill, just a few car lengths behind him.

The compact shuddered, and seemed to leap into the air as the back wheels slid in a wild skid. Concentrating on his timing, Nat swung the wheel over to the right and hit the gas. For one bad moment he thought he'd overcompensated as the wheels slid perilously close to the edge. Then the tires gripped and the car shot forward, just as the first of the two huge black monsters rounded the curve.

"Stay down!" Nat yelled at Valeri as he took a sharp bend on two wheels.

She didn't answer, but stayed curled in a ball, half of her body tucked under the dash.

He wondered if she'd passed out or something, but then he saw her rub her eyes with the back of her hand. He relaxed his mouth in a grim smile. So she wasn't as cool as she made out. Not that he could blame her. Thank God she hadn't been able to see out the window when he'd spun the car.

Another bend came up fast, and he concentrated on the road. Sabhad's men must have had orders not to shoot, since there were no more bullets flying. Not that they needed to. With the engines these guys had under their hoods, they could sit on his tail until he ran out of gas—he flicked a glance at the fuel gauge—and by the looks of it, that wasn't going to be too long. He had less than a quarter of a tank.

It was time for another desperate move.

He glanced out the window. They were still too high up to risk going over the edge. He would have to wait for a side road, and hope to take those goons on his tail by surprise. All the time they were going downhill he had the speed, and the Volvo was small enough that he could outmaneuver them to gain a few yards. Once they reached any kind of rise, his advantage would be lost. It had to be now.

He spotted a road coming up on his right. A dirt road winding up into the mountains, little more than a trail that looked as if it went nowhere. It was, however, just in front of another wicked curve, after which the road he was on was blocked from view by a tall outcrop of rock.

Just to make sure, he risked slowing the car a little in a series of short skids, stirring up enough dust to cover his escape. He went into the steep climb sideways, the springs groaning as the car hit gravel, rocks and potholes.

He fought the temptation to look in the rearview mirror. He needed all his concentration now. One split second could mean the difference between making it—or smashing the car against a rock.

As it was, he scraped the side of the car as he rounded one of the huge boulders. He glimpsed Valeri scrunching up even tighter and felt a stab of remorse. "Hold on," he muttered. "We're almost there."

One more boulder and they'd be out of sight. He slid

around it, braked hard and cut the engine. In the distance the sound of screeching tires and revving engines slowly died away.

It seemed incredibly quiet when he cautiously rolled down the window. Not even a bird chirped. Dust still swirled around them, and the sun seared the arm he rested on the window frame. A faint smell of burning rubber mingled with the pungent fragrance of sagebrush and pine.

"Stay there," he ordered quietly, "and don't move. I'm going to take a look around."

She gave him a quick, silent nod, without even looking up.

He eased his long legs out of the car, and stood, ears strained to catch the slightest sound. Trusting that she wouldn't try to make a run for it, he left the car door open. His feet made no noise as he made his way to where he could see the road. It appeared to be deserted.

Satisfied, he trod carefully back to the car. Leaning in through the window, he tapped Valeri on the shoulder.

She started violently, but uttered no sound.

"You can sit up now," he said, and opened the car door wide enough to climb in. "We're okay for the moment, at least."

Her dark eyes seemed huge in her drawn face when she looked at him. "Thank you," she said, as if she were ready to burst into tears.

"For what?"

"For not leaving me there."

He narrowed his eyes and studied her face, his fingers drumming on the wheel. "Lady," he said softly, "I don't know what in the hell is going on here, but trust me, I'm going to find out."

"When you do, please tell me." Her voice sounded shaky, but her eyes rested steadily on his face.

"You're still saying you remember nothing?"

She shrugged, and he had the feeling that she wasn't

telling him everything. He'd been in enough tough situations to sense when someone was hiding something, and this woman was definitely keeping something to herself.

No matter. He'd find out what it was eventually.

"I'm glad you finally believe that I'm not that man's wife." She looked down at the gold watch on her slender wrist. "I'd like to go to the halfway house now."

"Sorry, sweetheart, but you're not going anywhere." He leaned back in his seat and stretched the tension out of his back.

"But…I thought…"

"I know what you thought. You were wrong." He turned his head to look at her, and saw her face filled with dismay. His pang of guilt was becoming persistent. He didn't usually waste time on self-recrimination. Damn her. She had a way of making him feel like some kind of barbarian.

Needing to justify his attitude, he said harshly, "Look, right now I don't know what to believe. I admit, so far Sabhad's score isn't too good. But I was hired to do a job, and once I agree to an assignment I'm obligated to deliver unless there's a very good reason why I shouldn't."

"I would say that sending armed bandits out to gun us down is a clear indication that Sabhad is not exactly welcoming his loving wife home with open arms."

The scorn in her voice was obvious. He didn't like the contempt on her face, either. "If I remember rightly," he said, trying not to grit his teeth, "it was the guards at the gate who shot at us. Probably reacting to the moment. The goons in the car didn't fire one shot, so I assume that Sabhad issued orders that you weren't to be harmed."

"Any fool could see that a man who would go to such lengths to trap his wife is not likely to win the Husband of the Year Award. I'm surprised at you, Mr. Thorne. You seem to be assuming a great deal. So far your score has been dismal."

With an effort he held on to his temper. "Don't push me," he muttered. "I get ugly when I'm pushed too far."

"Really. I would never have guessed."

"Try me. You might get lucky."

She lifted her chin, and he was intrigued to see the dull red flush creep across her cheeks. Whatever this lady was, she was no tramp. That was one big point in her favor. Now, if he could only make out where Sabhad figured in this, he'd feel a lot easier.

He wound up the window and started the engine. "We've got to get out of here. It won't be long before Sabhad's hatchet men realize we've fooled them, and they'll be back looking for us."

She glanced out the window and shuddered, as if realizing for the first time that they were perched precariously on the side of a mountain. "How do we get down without them seeing us?"

"Good question." He leaned across her to open the glove compartment where he kept his maps. She shifted at the same time, and his arm brushed her breasts. The contact sent a jolt through him all the way to his knees. Sheer will power kept him from looking at her. Warning bells clanged through his head, and his body literally tingled with the aftershock. He grabbed the map and opened it carefully, hoping like hell his hands wouldn't shake.

Whatever this woman had, it was potent. He could feel the tension crackling in the car, enough to make his hair stand straight up. Just his damn luck to run into a woman who could get him this excited—a woman he was forced to keep at arm's length.

He pried his mind away from Valeri Richmond and studied the map. "If we could steer this heap over the rise, we could hit a back road and make it to one of these little towns here."

"And then what?"

He folded the map and laid it on the dash in front of him. "Then we hole up until I figure out what to do next."

"I hope you realize that you're breaking the law. Kidnapping is a serious offense."

"Yeah, well, put it on my tab." He had managed to sound indifferent, but the truth was that he was more than a little worried. What she'd said was true. He could be in serious trouble if all this backfired on him. It wouldn't be the first time he'd been in trouble. But it was the first time he could get tangled up with the feds, and that could lead to all kinds of hell.

He'd taken that into consideration when he'd first been offered the job, and he'd almost turned it down. Sabhad had assured him he would take responsibility for any charges Valeri might bring against Nat. But now he wasn't so sure anymore that Sabhad was in a position to back him up.

The only way out of this, as far as he could see, was to find out exactly what was going on, and then to make a judgment. The bottom line in all this was those two little girls. He was going to do whatever was best for them. Period.

What he'd like to do was dump Valeri Richmond into Sabhad's lap, take his money and let them fight it out between themselves. But now that he knew for sure that Sabhad played dirty, he couldn't just abandon her to her fate. He might have lost most of his principles so far in his struggle to survive, but he wasn't that far gone.

He'd seen enough tragedies in his life to know that the underdog seldom wins. He considered it part of his duty in his doubtful profession to avoid contributing to that pathetic state of affairs. Most of the time he even offered a helping hand when the situation called for one.

He let out the brake and eased the compact over a small ridge. One thing he did know: the longer he stayed with this deal, the less he liked it. He had a strong suspicion that someone was making an ass out of him. Nat did not like being taken for a fool.

Right now he was feeling pretty damn gullible. He should have seen this coming. It didn't take a rocket scientist to know that something was not on the level. Valeri was right: normal men did not welcome their wives home with a barrage of bullets. He wasn't sure how they did things in Saudi Arabia, but he was pretty sure they didn't get that drastic there, either.

He should have stayed out of it. He'd broken a cardinal rule by letting his emotions sway his decision when he'd seen those pictures. He should have learned by now, after everything he'd gone through. Now he was paying for his weakness.

He only hoped for Valeri's sake that she wasn't trying to outwit him. He wasn't sure how forgiving he'd be if he found out she was the one handing him a line.

On the other hand, if he had made a mistake by snatching her off the street, then he'd have to remedy it somehow. He had a nasty feeling that it wasn't going to be easy. Judging from the dark looks she kept giving him, he wasn't exactly listed on her dance card.

She sat stiffly in her seat, staring straight ahead with her hands fisted on her thighs. The shirt she wore was made of some clingy material that hugged the lush curves of her firm breasts. He would have liked to linger on the pleasant view, but the bumpy trail claimed his attention.

When he looked back at her, she was still staring ahead with that stony expression. She had a good-looking profile. Her sleek, dark brown hair curved smoothly behind her elegant ears, giving him a clear view of a straight nose and rounded chin. He noticed for the first time a slight dimple at the corner of her mouth.

He wondered what she looked like when she smiled. Without warning, he found himself fantasizing about kissing that dimple. He snatched his gaze back to the road.

"You hungry?" Maybe if he concentrated on food, he'd forget how she affected his hormones.

"Yes."

Her snappy answer warned him that conversation might be difficult. She looked pale, and obviously needed a rest. On top of everything else, she must still be feeling the effects of the accident.

He decided to wait until they were safely tucked away in a motel somewhere, before trying to find out what he wanted to know. Now all he had to do was find somewhere suitable, preferably nearby, and close to a fast-food joint.

Valeri made an effort to unclench her hands as the car bounced and bumped over the rough ground. She was beginning to breathe a bit easier, now that Sabhad's men were out of sight. She was not out of the woods by any means, but right now Nathan Thorne's solid presence at her side was a good deal more comforting than the sight of armed thugs bearing down on her.

Although he'd abducted her and was basically holding her prisoner, he'd made no attempt to hurt her. He had, in fact, saved her from what seemed to be a very dangerous situation. Although she wasn't about to trust him, she did feel fairly confident that he wasn't going to harm her—though she wasn't quite sure how she knew that.

At least one truth had emerged from these past terrifying minutes. She knew, without a doubt, that she had never married Ahmed Sabhad. She would have sworn she'd never even met the man, if it hadn't been for those photos.

And one thing she would swear to. Whoever those children were who held her hands in the picture, they were not hers.

Feeling somewhat comforted by that conviction, she tried to remember where she might have met Sabhad. She thought Alex might have spoken his name, which worried her. There had to be an involvement.

The big question was how Nat fitted into all this. He

seemed to be as confused as she was. Then again, that could be an act for her benefit. What she didn't understand was, if Nat was the enemy, why had he rescued her from Sabhad's men?

If only she could remember where Alex was hiding. He must be desperate by now. She just had to escape at the first opportunity.

Her flashes of memory were happening more frequently, gradually filling in some of the time she had lost. Apparently her business was doing well, and she'd adjusted to living alone.

Alex hadn't married again, either. She knew that now. She was also on very good terms with her father, which made it all the more imperative that she remember the events of the past few days. Apparently she'd been the only one he could trust, from what she could make out from the garbled visions she'd been getting.

Alex was somewhere in Sylvan Springs—she was sure of that. Wherever that was. And how was she going to go about finding him? He'd warned her not to trust anyone. Especially the police.

What she needed were more answers, and right now her best bet seemed to be Nathan Thorne. He must know more about this than she did. Maybe if she could get enough information out of him, it would jog her memory and she'd remember the rest.

The trail had smoothed out a bit, making the ride a little easier. She wasn't sure if the bruises she could feel were a result of the car wreck, or of the rough treatment she'd taken riding over the mountain in Nat's battered Volvo.

"There's a road down there," Nat said, squinting against the sun that was now sinking lower in the sky. "Looks like we'll be off this commando course any minute now."

She'd have preferred not to answer him, but that would not get her the information she needed. "Is it safe, do you think?"

He shrugged. "As safe as any other. I'll feel a lot better once we find a motel."

His words produced a tingling sensation deep in her belly. What was it about this man that made everything he said seem like an innuendo? Maybe it was the way he looked at her, with a kind of primitive hunger in those feline eyes that stirred her blood.

As far as she could remember, she hadn't looked at another man since her divorce. There was no point, since she couldn't give them what they wanted. She'd convinced herself she could be perfectly happy without them.

But now, seated next to this virile, earthy stranger who could or could not be a dangerous enemy, she felt a vibrant, aching restlessness that had nothing to do with her memory loss or her father's problems.

It had everything to do with the sight and the feel and the smell of Nathan Thorne, who was at that moment looking for a motel where, presumably, he intended to share a room with her until one or the other of them sorted out what was going on.

The prospect was frightening and incredibly exhilarating. Valeri couldn't remember when she'd felt so alive, and so vulnerable at the same time.

She had to be mad, she told herself. Allowing a man like this to get under her skin. He could be a cop. He could be something much worse. So far she'd heard nothing to prove he wasn't. She was simply going on gut feeling—which had not proved too reliable in the past, judging by her divorce.

"I want you to stay down when we hit the road," Nat said, reminding her that they were not out of danger, yet.

She slid down in her seat, wincing at the sting of pain from her bruises. She was exhausted and hungry. A cool shower sounded good, too. In spite of her misgivings, she was actually looking forward to getting to that motel.

She felt the car level out, and heard the blissfully smooth

hum of pavement beneath the wheels. She stayed where she was, hoping it wouldn't be long before Nat found a motel. On top of everything else, she was in dire need of a bathroom.

"This looks like it might do," Nat muttered after several minutes of silence.

She wasn't sure if he was talking to himself or to her, but it didn't really matter since the car had swerved to the right and come to a shuddering halt.

"Before we go in," Nat said above her head, "there's a few things we need to get straight. I'm not done with you by a long shot. At this point I don't know what to believe, and until I get at the truth, I'm sticking to you like a burr to a terrier's coat. So don't try anything cute, okay?"

She gave him a look loaded with disdain. "Is it all right if I sit up now?"

"Yes, it's all right if you sit up now."

He'd mimicked her voice and she flushed. How could she ever have considered him attractive? The man was obnoxious. Devil was a good term for him.

She wriggled up in her seat, smoothed her hair back with both hands, then brushed the dust from her shirt. She'd never felt so grubby in her entire life.

Nat wound the window down. "I'm going in to book a room. You stay in the car. If anyone asks, you're my wife. We just got married in Reno."

She avoided looking at him, afraid her discomfort would show in her face. She wasn't about to let him know how much he unsettled her. That would be like handing him a deadly weapon. The best way to handle a man like him was to pretend he didn't affect her in the least.

They were parked outside the office of a shabby-looking motel. The rooms on both floors led straight out into the parking lot. There was only one car—a rusted, mud-covered station wagon—parked outside one of the rooms.

The land around the motel looked flat, dry and barren,

with only a few clumps of coarse grass and wildflowers to break the monotony. ''Nice place for a honeymoon,'' Valeri murmured.

''If there's one thing I hate,'' Nat growled as he climbed out of the car, ''it's a woman with a smart mouth.''

''If there's one thing I hate it's a man without principles.''

His face darkened. He shut the door, then leaned in through the open window. ''Stay there, and don't move. If you try to run, you won't get far, I promise you. And no one is going to believe that dumb story of you losing your memory. If I don't catch up with you, you can bet Sabhad's men will. And this time I won't be around to protect you.''

Valeri flashed him a sweet smile. ''Oh, is that what you're doing?''

She expected him to answer with a sharp retort. Instead, she was disturbed to see his gaze drop to her mouth. ''Don't tempt me, sweetheart,'' he drawled. ''It's been a long time since I've been this cozy with a woman.''

All her good intentions flew out the window. Totally flustered, she sat back in her seat, mortified to feel the heat burning her cheeks. His soft laugh as he strode off did nothing to calm her jitters.

How could she imagine she'd be safe with a man like that? He'd kidnapped her, threatened her, and worked for a man who would obviously stop at nothing to get his hands on her. The best thing she could do was get away from him and try to find Sylvan Springs. Or maybe it would be better if she went back to her apartment. Perhaps there she'd find enough answers to jog her memory.

If only she could go to the police. But Alex's voice, warning her not to contact them, was too strong to ignore. She'd have to try hitching a ride back to Sacramento.

She looked over at the door of the office, but couldn't see anything through the window blind. It was now or never. He'd be back at any minute.

Dusk was drawing in fast. The sun painted the sky a deep red as it drew closer to the horizon, and already the long shadow of the motel crept across the parking lot. It would be dark soon. She wasn't sure she fancied wandering around the desert after dark, but it was better than taking her chances with the devil.

She leaned across the driver's seat—farthest from the motel office—and carefully pulled the door handle down. The door stuck and she had to shove to get it to open. It swung out of her hand and she held her breath, praying it wouldn't slam again.

Valeri slowly slid down until her head was below the level of the window, then crawled across the seat and scrambled out. Keeping her head down, she closed the door again and twisted her head to look around for cover.

The only thing she could see was a Dumpster at the edge of the parking lot. It would have to do for now. Making sure she kept the car between her and the office door, she scuttled over to the metal bin and crept behind it.

She peered over the top of it, knowing as she did so that she was too exposed. She would never escape the eagle eye of Nathan Thorne. She had to move, right now. Even as she formed the thought, the office door opened. Valeri froze.

Nat paused in the doorway, looking back at someone inside who must have said something to him. She didn't stop to think. She bent double and scooted for the parked station wagon.

Darting behind it, she held her breath, waiting for the sound of Nat's footsteps to come pounding after her. Instead, to her immense relief, she heard the Volvo's engine start up. He must have figured she'd headed for the road.

After what seemed an eternity, she heard him drive out of the parking lot. A minute or two later, the roar of the engine died away, leaving only an unearthly silence behind.

Even so, she waited a long time before venturing out

from behind the station wagon. The parking lot was deserted. Hardly able to believe how easily she had hoodwinked Nat, she crossed to the road and looked both ways.

It was almost dark now, with stars beginning to dot the night sky. The road lay flat and straight in one direction, with no glimmer of lights to indicate a car. In the other direction lay the mountains from which she and Nat had driven just a short while ago. That stretch of road looked empty, too.

Valeri was beginning to feel very alone. Her body ached with weariness; someone was hammering nails to the inside of her head; and she was hungry. And she still needed to go to the bathroom.

She looked longingly back at the motel. It would be so blissful just to open one of those doors, climb into a refreshing shower and then sink into a soft, clean bed.

Impossible, of course. In the first place, she had no credit cards. In the second place, Nat would probably come back to the motel when he couldn't find her. In the third place, she needed to get home to her apartment.

Her best bet, she decided, was to walk down the straight stretch of road. It was probably safer than the mountains. That way she could see if anything was coming—long before it got to her.

She started walking, not too steadily, into the inky blackness that lay ahead. Keeping her eyes on the narrow white strip to guide her, she concentrated on putting one foot in front of the other. She was dying of thirst. She kept imagining tall frothy glasses of soda, or huge carafes filled with sparkling spring water.

Her mouth felt so dry she could barely move her tongue. With every step she took she felt as if her feet were sinking into a marshy bog, instead of the hard surface of the road. The heat of the day had vanished, leaving a biting chill behind. She shivered violently as she trudged along, making it even more difficult to stay on her feet.

When she heard the purr of a car engine behind her, she didn't even bother to turn around. She didn't have the energy left.

She wasn't really surprised when Nat's voice asked pleasantly, "Enjoying your walk?"

She stopped dead, watching the road sway back and forth in front of her. Even if she'd had the strength left to run, there was nowhere to go. She lifted her face to the sky, and watched the carpet of stars tilt crazily, then sweep toward her in a brilliant flash of color.

Nat swore as Valeri collapsed in a heap on the road. He'd read her wrong. He'd figured on her doubling back up the mountain. Actually he'd figured on her staying in the car. He wouldn't make that mistake again.

Worried now that he had a sick woman on his hands, he scrambled out of the car and bent over her. Her pulse was erratic, but strong. Her skin felt cool, though a faint sheen of perspiration covered her face. She must be exhausted. Probably dehydrated. He had to get her back to the motel and get some liquids into her.

She was like a fragile bird in his arms. Her perfume reminded him of orange blossoms, tangy and exotic. Her head lay back against his arm, exposing the long line of her throat. Mad as he was at her, he wanted to bury his lips in the soft hollow beneath it.

There was no way to ignore it any longer. He wanted her in the worst way. He had ever since he first set eyes on her in that hospital bed, her enticing body naked except for a flimsy gown that left little to the imagination. He'd wanted to crawl in there with her, and make love to her until she begged him to stop.

He wanted to saturate himself in her warmth and sensuality, take what she had to offer and give back every atom of his roaring passion until he had finally eased the tormenting ache in his loins.

What the hell was she doing to him? How could he let

her get under his skin like this? The chances were good that she was married, and worse, had abandoned her kids—something he could never forgive.

Yet he couldn't seem to get her out of his mind. She was driving him crazy, and the longer she was with him, the worse it was likely to get. How did a woman like this get mixed up with someone like Ahmed Sabhad? Nat shook his head. How the hell had he managed to get himself mixed up in this?

Now, more than ever, he wanted to get to the bottom of this crooked deal. But first he had to get her back to the motel where she could rest. Gently, he laid her down on the back seat, then headed back down the road, trying to forget how the feel of Valeri Richmond in his arms drove him wild.

When Valeri opened her eyes, it took her a moment to realize where she was. She'd expected to wake up in her bedroom, not this drab, faded motel room in the middle of nowhere.

Everything came back in a rush. She'd run away from Nathan Thorne and he'd caught up with her. She'd more or less expected it. Her attempt had been more bravado than anything. If she were honest she'd admit she was actually rather glad to see him. Better him than Ahmed's thugs.

At least she was reasonably comfortable now. She was lying on a double bed in the middle of the room, snuggled under a comforter. Her face flamed when she realized she was wearing only a bra and panties. Her entire body reached meltdown when she realized the person who'd removed her clothes must have been Nathan Thorne.

The sound of a toilet flushing brought her head around. The door on her left opened, and a man's figure appeared in the doorway.

''So, you're awake,'' Nat drawled.

She opened her mouth to speak, but could only manage a dry croak.

"Wait, you need to drink before you try talking." He moved over to a table, poured something into a glass clinking with ice, then handed it to her.

She propped herself up on an elbow and almost snatched it from him. The soda burned her throat, but she didn't stop drinking until it was all gone.

Silently, she held the glass out to him.

"More?"

She nodded gratefully, and gulped another half a glass down before pausing to take a breath.

"Feel better?"

"A little." She noticed her clothes lying on a chair next to the TV and snatched her gaze away.

Nat, as usual, missed nothing. "Since that's all you've got to wear, I figured you wouldn't want to sleep in them."

Not knowing where to look, she said unsteadily, "I need to use the bathroom."

He waved his hand at the door. "Be my guest."

She measured the distance from the bed to the door. At least ten feet, possibly more.

"I could carry you, if you wanted."

She sent him what she hoped was a look of pure contempt. "Thank you, I'll manage." She sat up, taking care to pull the comforter up with her.

Nat leaned against the wall, watching her as if prepared to enjoy the show.

She stared at him in disgust. "A gentleman would at least turn his back."

"Maybe. But then—I'm no gentleman."

Her heart began to pound. He had that hungry look in his eyes again. She was reminded, potently, of the fact that should he make a move, she'd be helpless to stop him.

What really worried her, though, was the knowledge that deep down, a small part of her wouldn't really want to stop him. And that was the part that shocked her more than anything else that had happened so far.

Chapter 4

Valeri jumped when Nat let out an exaggerated sigh and turned his back on her. "I don't know what the hell you're worrying about," he muttered. "I've already seen what you're showing, and it isn't any more than I've seen a thousand times at the beach."

He was right, she thought as she slipped nervously and not too steadily out of the bed. But being half dressed and alone in a motel room with him was a whole different proposition than being one of many on a crowded beach.

She made it to the bathroom and, with a sigh of relief, shut the door behind her. At least now she had a few seconds to collect herself and decide what to do next.

Her body still ached, but the pounding in her head had stopped. If only she could get some food inside her, she thought as she watched warm water run over her hands, she'd feel a good deal better.

She eyed the miniature shower stall tucked in the corner. That would help. After making quite sure the door was locked, she turned on the faucets and slipped out of her underwear.

The water felt so good cascading over her body. She washed her hair with the little pouch of cheap but surprisingly fragrant shampoo she'd found, then scrubbed her body until her skin tingled.

Now she was starving. The thought of a hamburger and a plate of hot fries made her feel faint. Rubbing herself dry with the rough towel provided, she wondered if Nat had already eaten. If so, she was in for a miserable night trying to sleep on an empty stomach.

Her hands stilled as another thought occurred to her. There was only one bed. It didn't seem feasible that Nat would leave her alone in the room. Not after she'd already tried to escape.

That was a mistake. She should have played along with him, led him into a false sense of security. Then the minute he'd turned his back, she could have made a break for it.

She wound a towel around her hair, and pulled a face at herself in the mirror. And go where? She'd already tried that once. They were miles from any kind of civilization.

It looked as if she'd just have to tough it out for a while until she could remember where Alex was. Obviously, Nat knew more than he was telling her. He worked for Sabhad and must know something about what was going on. Yet, he'd helped her escape.

Nothing made sense, and wouldn't until Nat told her what he knew. So far, she hadn't made much headway in that direction.

Which brought her back to the subject of the bed. Something would have to be arranged, even if she ended up sleeping on the floor. Anything was preferable to spending the night sharing a bed with the devil.

Reluctant to put her underwear back on, she washed her bra and panties in the sink, then hung them over the towel bar to dry. She was beginning to wish she'd thought twice about the shower. Now she had to get back to the bed dressed only in a towel.

She wrapped it around her and tucked the ends in firmly before venturing to open the door. Through the narrow gap, she could see Nat pacing up and down in front of the window. Whatever was bothering him, it had to be painful to put that look of agony on his face.

Taking a deep breath, she walked out of the bathroom. She saw Nat turn to look at her, raking his gaze over her body from head to toe. She felt hot and cold at the same time. She was actually responding to this obnoxious man. A kind of wild excitement seemed to be thrumming through her.

It had to be lack of food, she told herself as she walked over to the bed, doing her best to appear indifferent. Either that, or she'd had some interesting experiences in the past six years that she'd forgotten about. Certainly Dan had never made her feel this way.

Nat's voice sounded unusually gruff when he spoke. "I take it you feel better."

"Much, thank you." She'd allowed her voice to soften just a tad. If she was going to get the answers she needed from him, she would have to mellow out a little. After all, honey caught more flies than vinegar.

"Good. Now I guess it's my turn. But first—"

Her entire body tensed when he reached for his belt. Her heart began thumping painfully against her ribs as she watched him flip open the buckle and draw the length of wide leather through the tags on his waistband.

She'd underestimated him, after all. Prepared to fight for her life, she raised her chin and stared defiantly at him.

He ran the belt slowly through his hands as he walked toward her, his gaze hot and intent on her face.

She wanted to plead with him, beg him not to hurt her, but she couldn't say a word. Somewhere deep inside her, something curled into a tight knot. In spite of the towel she felt naked, exposed and scared to death.

"Get on the bed," Nat ordered quietly.

She clamped her lips together. No matter what he did to her, she wouldn't yell. Something hot and liquid suddenly poured through her veins. Her throat felt tight, her heart hammered so badly she felt dizzy. She was going crazy. The thought of his hands on her sent sizzling streams of excitement all through her body. She had to be out of her mind.

Very slowly, she sank onto the edge of the bed. She could see a pulse beating furiously just below his left ear. If only he'd say something, anything....

"Hold out your hands."

Trembling, she did as he asked.

"I'm sorry to have to do this," Nat murmured thickly, as he wound the end of the belt around her wrists, "but you leave me no choice. I can't take a chance on you making a break for it again, and I really don't think you want to get in the shower with me."

Stunned, Valeri watched him loop the other end of the belt around the bed rail and fasten the buckle.

"Not too tight?" He seemed to be having trouble looking at her.

She shook her head, amazed at her sense of disappointment.

"Did you leave me a towel in there?"

She tried to speak, had to clear her throat, and tried again. "There were only two."

"Then I guess I'll need one of yours."

Her heart seemed to give up the fight and stop beating. It started up again when he reached for the towel covering her hair and unwound it. "This will have to do, I guess."

"Sorry."

"Yeah. Me too. Believe me." He dropped the towel on

the floor. Before Valeri realized what he was doing, he tugged the shirt from his jeans and pulled it over his head.

His body was tanned, smooth and sinewy. Dark hair sprinkled down his chest, stopping above his hard, flat stomach. Obviously Nathan Thorne believed in working out.

Aware that she was staring, Valeri jerked her gaze to his face.

He was watching her beneath hooded lids, his hands at the waistband of his jeans.

For long seconds time stood still in that musty, stark motel room. It was as if she were communicating with him on a level she didn't understand—mind meeting mind, will contesting will, need sensing need.

Then, as if surfacing from a deep, deep lake, Nat shuddered and took a long breath. "I'll be back," he muttered, and reached for the towel before practically leaping for the bathroom door.

Only then, after he'd disappeared from view, did she feel anger at the way he'd left her tied up to the bed like a dog. It certainly helped to dispel the erotic sensations she'd been experiencing.

She tried twisting herself free, but only succeeded in tightening the straps that bound her. Nathan Thorne knew his job. Obviously he'd had plenty of experience.

She relaxed against the bed rails, trying her best to figure him out. He'd lied about being her neighbor—that much he'd admitted. Apparently Sabhad had hired him to bring her back, telling him she was his wife. But why? The obvious conclusion was that it had something to do with Alex...though she couldn't imagine why her father would have any dealings at all with a man like Sabhad.

She closed her eyes and tried to concentrate. She could hear Alex's voice on the phone, begging her to be careful. What had he said about Sylvan Springs? *Campground.* That was it. He'd mentioned a campground. It had to be somewhere in Sylvan Springs. Excited to have remembered something important, she frowned at her bound wrists. How was she going to get there?

Her attention was caught by the sound of rushing water in the bathroom. Nat was taking his shower. She tried not to imagine him standing naked under the flow of water. But it was impossible to concentrate. Every time she tried, the image of him got in the way.

If only she could tell if he was the enemy or a potential ally. If only she could trust him with what she knew so far. Maybe he would help her. After all, he hadn't hurt her. He hadn't touched her...and heaven knows he had had enough opportunity. He'd actually risked his life to save her from Sabhad's men.

On the other hand, here she was trussed up like a chicken because he didn't trust her not to run away. In other words, she was technically his prisoner. He could decide at any time to take her back to Sabhad and hand her over.

The big question here was, what did Sabhad want with her? Information? What did she know that Sabhad needed? Where did Alex fit in? Who was murdered, and by whom?

The questions chased around and around in her head until a dull ache began behind her eyes. She was so hungry. If only she could eat she'd be able to think better.

The water shut off in the bathroom, and gurgled down the drainhole. She heard a lot of splashing in the sink, then Nat emerged wearing only his jeans, his dark hair curling on his head.

"Hungry?" He leaned down to pick up his shirt from the floor.

"I was the last time you asked me—hours ago," Valeri said pointedly.

"Well, if you hadn't run off into the desert, we could be eating by now."

"What would we be eating? I didn't see a restaurant around here."

"We passed a hamburger joint on the way in. You were on the floor and didn't see it."

"Hamburgers?" Her stomach growled in anticipation.

"Yeah. I'll go get us some. Shouldn't take me longer than twenty minutes or so."

She tugged on the belt. "You're not going to leave me here tied up, are you?"

"Yep."

"I promise I won't run."

"Like I'm going to believe you."

She lifted her chin. "I don't break promises. Of course, you wouldn't understand that, would you."

His eyebrows lowered. "I like you a lot better when you're not snarling at me."

"You should have thought about that when you decided to kidnap me and put my life in danger."

He gave her a long look. "Take my word for it, had I known what I know now, I'd have stayed a hundred miles away from anywhere you were."

Her heart skipped a beat. "What do you know now? What does Sabhad want with me? What did he tell you?" She resisted the urge to ask about Alex. If her father was involved in this mess, the less she appeared to know, the better.

Not that she was going to get anywhere. Nat wore that closed expression that told her he didn't intend to answer any of her questions. He really could be infuriatingly stubborn.

He turned to leave and had his hand on the door handle when she said plaintively, "My wrists are hurting."

With a quiet oath he came back to the bed and reached for her wrists. "If you'd quit wriggling around so much, this wouldn't tighten up on you." He loosened the strap and stood back. "Now just stay put until I get back. I'll be bringing back a couple of hamburgers and a bag of fries.

I'll even throw in a milk shake. Now, isn't that worth hanging around for?''

She glared at him. ''I'd rather have a soda.''

''All right. I'll bring you back a soda.'' He leaned over and switched on the TV. ''That should keep you entertained for a while.''

''How do I switch channels?''

He grinned, sending that annoying sizzle of response through her again. ''Nice try, sweetheart. You don't. I guess you have to take what you can get until I get back.''

She had a strong urge to stick out her tongue at the door closing behind him. Deciding, however, that she might as well make the best of it until he got back with the food, she squirmed under the comforter and stretched out her legs in front of her.

A segment on the national news was coming up, but Valeri was only half listening. Her mind was on Nat, and the promise of hamburgers. After she'd eaten, she decided, she'd tackle once more the problem of getting him to open up.

Up until now she'd had very little success. There had to be a way to break through those tough defenses. If only she could think of it. Appealing to his sense of chivalry certainly didn't work. It was doubtful he knew the meaning of the word.

She had to meet Nat on his level. Maybe if she tried being really nice to him.... He'd made it pretty obvious he didn't exactly find her unattractive. If she really tried, she might just get him to relax enough to tell her what she wanted to know.

It wouldn't be easy to be nice to him, of course. The man was crude and obvious, without an ounce of sensitivity in his body.

Thinking of his body conjured up the vision of him standing in front of her, naked to the waist, his hands on the waistband of his jeans. For a moment she actually sat there contemplating what it would be like to make love with a man like Nathan Thorne. Then, with a start, she pulled herself together.

She was beginning to worry about herself. Men like Nat had never appealed to her.... She had never been attracted to that kind of earthy, blatant sexuality reeking of male chauvinism. She had always hated caveman tactics, perhaps even been a little scared by them. She had certainly hated Dan's aggressive advances.

She shivered at the thought. The memory of her problems with Dan were all too clear in her mind. Six years might have passed since her divorce, but it seemed to her to be just a few short months.

She could still remember the tension that had gripped her during those nights of lovemaking—the aching longing to feel something...anything, the anxiety to get it over with, and the dreadful frustration when Dan finally rolled away from her, leaving her feeling dead and useless inside.

She couldn't...she just couldn't....

Without warning, she was jolted back to the present in a violent rush. The news anchor's droning voice had mentioned a name she knew well.

"The police are no further along in the case and are still trying to establish the whereabouts of Forrester, who is apparently in hiding. Alex Forrester, a noted scientist working for the government, was due to appear in Washington, D.C., this morning in order to request a grant to continue his studies on a revolutionary new process that could replace oil as a major fuel source. This latest development has been a great shock to his peers."

Not to mention his only daughter. Valeri leaned forward, eager to learn more, but to her intense disappointment the announcer smiled at the camera and said, "Turning to the local news..."

She leaned back against the pillows, churning this latest information over in her mind. She didn't remember anything about Alex's work. Since he worked for the government, a lot of his projects were top secret, and he had never talked much about them.

She was still trying to understand what this latest news meant when she heard the key in the lock. She tensed, torn between the hope that it was Nat with the hamburgers and the even stronger hope that it was someone else coming to rescue her.

Nat's muscular body seemed to fill the doorway as he paused to look around the room.

Valeri watched him, intrigued by his cautious attitude. She'd seen that stance before, as if he were in the habit of thoroughly casing a room before entering it. It would seem Nathan Thorne was used to walking into danger, and was skilled in the art of avoiding it.

Her curiosity about the man was growing by leaps and bounds. Somehow she had to get the truth out of him. If he was as experienced in avoiding hazards as she suspected, it wouldn't be easy to get through his defenses. She had one shot, and that was to charm her way through.

She wasn't sure at this point whether she could pull it off, having had no practice in that area. She only knew she had to try. Even if it meant embarrassing herself. She wasn't sure if she was looking forward to it, or dreading it.

Nat's gaze rested on her briefly before he crossed the room and laid the brown paper sack on the table. The delicious smell of grilled hamburger and onions made Valeri's mouth water.

"I brought a couple of beers along with the soda, in case you wanted one," Nat said, pulling a six-pack out of the sack.

"They sell beer at a fast-food place?"

"This was a restaurant. Take-out at one end, sit-down at the other—complete with a full bar."

She should be grateful he hadn't come back with a bottle

of Scotch, she thought, as she watched him unbuckle her wrists. That would have made her task even more difficult. As it was, now that he was back in the flesh—so to speak—she wasn't at all sure she could be nice to the man, after everything he'd put her through.

"You'd better eat this now while it's still hot," Nat said, walking back to the table. He picked up her pants and shirt from the chair and brought them back to her. "Put these on first," he added gruffly.

When she looked up at him, his gaze slid away from her. "I don't think my underwear will be dry."

"Then don't wear any." He dropped her clothes on the bed, then went back to the table and sat down heavily in the chair.

After a moment's hesitation, she slid out of the bed, grabbed her clothes and headed for the bathroom. Her panties were almost dry except for the waistband, but her bra was still damp. Hanging next to them was a pair of dark blue briefs. Apparently Nat wasn't wearing underwear either.

Damn that sizzle down her spine.

She dropped the towel and pulled on her chinos and shirt. She'd never gone without a bra before. It was an odd sensation. Actually, she rather liked it. Gave her a sense of freedom. Though what her mother would say, she shuddered to think. Thinking about her mother made her want to cross her arms over her chest. She opened the door and did her best to stroll nonchalantly over to the table.

Nat had already started on his hamburger. Out of the corner of her eye she saw him staring at her. She was unnerved when he took a bite of his hamburger, choked on it and had to reach for his beer to take a long gulp.

She sat down hurriedly in the chair and grabbed one of the hamburgers. Sinking her teeth into the bun, she forgot her embarrassment. It tasted absolutely wonderful. She hadn't realized just how hungry she was until the first bite hit her stomach. She didn't speak, or even think about anything else, until every bite was gone.

"You enjoy that?" Nat asked dryly.

She nodded, grabbing a napkin to wipe her mouth. The fries tasted just as delicious, and she ate a pile of them before sitting back with a sigh. "That was the best meal I ever tasted."

"It's amazing what hunger can do for the taste buds." Nat picked up a beer and snapped open the lid. He handed it to her, and she took it, deciding she needed a little help if she were going to go through with her plan.

Now that the moment had arrived, she didn't know quite where to start. "Where did you meet Sabhad?" she asked, trying to sound as careless as if she were asking him the time.

He pushed the end of a fry in his mouth and bit off the end. "How did *you* meet him?"

"I don't remember ever having met him."

Nat pursed his lips and slowly nodded his head. "Back to square one."

"I might be able to remember if you told me more about him."

"I don't know any more about him than I've already told you. You know him a hell of a lot better than I do."

"But I don't remember."

"So you keep telling me."

"You work for him. You must know more than you're telling me."

He narrowed his eyes to slits. "Maybe I do, maybe I don't."

Valeri looked down at her napkin, which she was slowly tearing to shreds. This wasn't working. She wasn't being nice enough.

She made herself relax, pasted a smile on her face and said pleasantly, "You must have a very interesting job."

He deliberately ignored that, and shifted his chair around so that he could watch the TV.

She had to be doing something wrong. She had to think of a way to get his attention.

Leaning forward on her elbows, she looked up into his face. "How long have you worked for him?"

His gaze flicked down to the open neck of her shirt, then away. "I don't work for him. I work for myself."

"Then why are you helping him abduct me?"

Nat shoved his chair back. "Quit with the questions, all right? I don't have all the answers, and even if I did, it's very doubtful I'd tell you. So you're wasting your time."

She noticed beads of sweat forming on his brow. Either she was getting to him, or the thermostat was turned up too high. "Okay," she said, getting up from her chair. "Then let's talk about something else. Are you married?"

The second the words were out of her mouth, she wished them back again. She hadn't meant to ask him that. She didn't know what on earth made her ask him that. She didn't care if he was married or not. He could have three wives for all she cared.

He was studying her now, his eyes hooded and glinting with suspicion. "What difference does that make?

"It doesn't. Er...I mean, it was just a casual question. I was just trying to make conversation, that's all." Feeling as if she needed support, she reached behind her for the table.

Nat's gaze dropped to her breasts. "I'm not in the mood for conversation."

His voice sounded strained. Remembering she wasn't wearing a bra, she straightened up at once. This wasn't what she was aiming for. She might have known he'd misunderstand. Of course he wouldn't know when a woman was just being nice to him. More than likely the women he associated with couldn't wait to drag him into bed.

"You'd better get to bed. You've had a busy day."

Startled at the similarity to her thoughts, she stumbled over her answer. "I'm not tired. You go ahead."

"And let you creep out of here the minute I close my eyes? I don't think so."

"I'm not going to run." Suddenly she was tired after all. Tired and beaten. She couldn't remember something as vitally important as where her father was hiding, injured and helpless. She was with a man who could possibly give her the answers, and she couldn't get him to utter a word.

She had no money, no ID, no driver's license and no car. She was at least two hundred miles from her home and had no idea why. Alex was depending on her, and she couldn't even get this big ox to help her. To her annoyance, a tear slipped out of her eye and down her cheek.

"You're not going to cry, are you?" Nat asked in a gruff voice.

"No," she said stiffly while tears spilled down her cheeks, "I'm not going to cry."

"Then what the hell are you doing?" He strode to the bathroom, coming back a minute later with a handful of tissue. "Here, use these."

"Thank you." She sniffed, took the tissue from him and loudly blew her nose.

Nat sat on the edge of the bed and patted the space next to him. "Come and sit down. You look as if you're about to fall down."

She did as she was told, taking care not to sit close enough to touch him.

"Look, I'll make a deal with you." He paused, tapping his thighs with his fingers. "I'll tell you what I know, if you'll tell me what you know."

"I don't rem—"

"Just tell me what you do remember, all right?"

Maybe it was the way he'd brought the tissue to her. Maybe it was his softer tone of voice. Maybe it was her worry over Alex. Or maybe it was just everything she'd been through that day, and the effects of the bump on her head.

Whatever it was, she suddenly felt a craving to be held, to be comforted by someone stronger than she was. She turned her head into his shoulder and began to cry softly.

Nat uttered a quiet oath. "God, I hate it when women cry."

He shifted his arm and wrapped it around her. "Go ahead, if you must. It will probably make you feel better."

His arm felt heavy on her shoulders...heavy and comforting. She could actually hear his heart beating beneath her ear. He smelled of soap and the same shampoo she'd used for her hair. She felt guilty, remembering how little of it she'd left for him.

She made an effort to pull herself together. She couldn't afford to let her guard down like this. She couldn't allow herself to trust him. Alex's safety could depend on it.

She sat up and blew her nose again. "I'm okay," she said, her voice muffled.

"Let me see." He put his fingers under her chin and tilted her face up to him. "You've got a stray eyelash. Hold on."

He took the tissue from her hand and gently wiped the corner of her eye. "There."

"Thank you," she whispered.

His eyes darkened immediately. She froze as his gaze dropped to her mouth. He brushed the corner of her lips with his thumb—a soft, tantalizing gesture made all the more erotic by his roughened skin.

She couldn't have moved now if her life depended on it. She watched his face as he let his gaze wander down to the gap in her shirt. She couldn't breathe. Her lungs ached with the effort. A thousand thoughts sang through her mind.

She wanted him to touch her. She wanted to know what it was like to be kissed by him. She would die inside if he didn't kiss her now.

As if reading her thoughts Nat leaned in, opened his mouth and gently covered hers.

She was drowning in pleasure. His lips tasted salty, warm and sweet. She returned the pressure eagerly. A second later shock rippled through her as his tongue touched hers. Now she felt confused, excited and afraid at the same time.

His hands were on her arms, drawing her closer. His mouth grew more intense, more urgent. Alarms started going off all over her body as she felt herself responding.

She couldn't do this. She mustn't do this. She tried to draw back, but he held her closer, one hand reaching for the back of her head. For a second or two she let herself enjoy the heady delight of knowing she'd aroused him. Then she felt his hand move toward her breast.

Her body reacted instantly, jerking away from him. She raised both hands and pushed against his chest, struggling to draw back.

To her relief he let her go at once. He didn't say a word, just got to his feet, moved over to the table and picked up his beer. He drained the can and flipped open another.

She didn't know whether she was angry at him or at herself. He didn't seem to be at all affected by the kiss. She felt a surge of irritation when he sat down again in front of the TV. He was deliberately ignoring her.

After a while she couldn't stand his silence any longer. Throwing caution to the wind, she asked loudly, "Where is Sylvan Springs?"

If she'd expected some reaction from him, she was disappointed. He simply shrugged, his gaze glued firmly on the baseball game playing on the TV. "Down the road a ways. That little town we came through on our way out here. If you blinked you probably missed it."

She stared at him, trying to figure out whether he really didn't attach any significance to the name, or whether he was just very good at hiding his reactions.

"You were going to tell me why you're working for Sabhad," she reminded him.

He sighed, leaning forward to put his head in his hands. After a moment or two he switched off the TV. "All right," he said, getting to his feet. "If you want to talk, then we'll talk. But I've got a few questions of my own. I don't buy this story of you not remembering anything. I think you've been remembering plenty these last few hours."

She started to deny it, but he held up his hand. "Lady, sooner or later I'm going to get to the bottom of all this. If you're not married to Ahmed Sabhad, as you claim, I want to know why he lied to me, and why he's willing to pay a great deal of money to get his hands on you."

"I don't know—"

"I also want to know what it is you're hiding from me."

Caught off guard, she stammered, "I...I don't know what you mean."

"Oh, I think you do." He walked toward her, his eyes narrowed, his expression hard and dangerous. "I've had the feeling you've been hiding something ever since we left the hospital, and if you want to get out of this mess with that cute little butt of yours intact, then now would be a real good time to tell me about it."

Chapter 5

If Nat had meant to frighten Valeri, he'd certainly succeeded. He almost felt sorry for her when she shot off the bed with a kind of wild, desperate look in her eyes.

"I keep telling you," she said, her voice low and tense, "I don't remember. I've never met Sabhad, I'm not married to him and I'm not the mother of his children."

Somehow he believed that now. Out of all the things she didn't remember, it seemed that this was the one thing she was certain about. He wasn't going to get anywhere, however, unless she told him what she was hiding.

He was pretty sure now that she'd remembered something important, and was intent on keeping it to herself. Maybe it was time he told her his side of the story. If nothing else, it could jog her memory enough that she'd give something away.

Deciding that it was in both their best interests if he stayed on the opposite side of the room from her, he backed off and sat down.

"All right. Let's get back to our deal. If you like, I'll go first. I'll tell you what I know, then you can do the same. Maybe then we can both figure out what's going on."

She sank on the side of the bed, watching him warily. "I don't know if I can tell you anything else."

"We'll take it one step at a time. I got the call real early yesterday morning. The message said only that I was needed at Windridge for an interview with Ahmed Sabhad. I was to be there before noon."

He saw her expression change, and wondered what had triggered that look of apprehension. He was surprised when she asked in a low voice, "Are you some kind of cop?"

He found that very interesting. Apparently Valeri Richmond didn't want to get tangled up with the cops any more than he did. That made him feel a little easier. If he had made a big mistake in grabbing her, she wouldn't be in a hurry to sic the law on him. What he wanted to know now was why she wanted to avoid the police.

He made his voice sound reassuring. "I'm not a cop. I promise you."

"A private investigator?"

"Not exactly."

"Then what?"

He sighed. "If you must know, I'm what most people call a soldier of fortune."

Her face mirrored her disgust. "A mercenary. No wonder you don't have any principles. What I don't understand is why you rescued me from Sabhad just to hold me prisoner."

He shrugged. "There might be some things I've done that I'm not particularly proud of, but there's no way I'd dump a woman into what could be a sticky situation without making damn sure she's not going to get hurt."

"Pretty high morals for a mercenary."

"I prefer to think of myself as an adventurous entrepreneur."

"Think of yourself how you like, you're still a paid killer."

That stung. He didn't usually bother to defend his profession, knowing that most people simply wouldn't understand, but for some reason he felt compelled to say something this time. "Anything I've ever done in the call of duty has been in self-defense, or in defense of innocent people. There are some real problems in this world that can't be taken care of with conventional methods. Without people like me there would be a hell of a lot more innocent deaths to mourn—women, children...even babies."

For a moment his throat closed, then he shut his mind down from the memories. In his job, he couldn't afford sentiment.

She watched him, her dark eyes brimming with suspicion. "You said that Sabhad called you. How did he get your number?"

"I didn't say Sabhad called me. I said I got the call. Sabhad called the organization."

"What organization?"

"That, I'm afraid, comes under the category of top secret."

"You mean it's unofficial."

"If you like."

"And illegal?"

He sighed, wondering how he'd allowed her to lead him off the subject. They could use someone like her in the organization. "I mean," he said carefully, "that it's an association that isn't listed in the *Yellow Pages*. Call it a sort of employment agency."

"For itinerants."

His eyebrow twitched. "You're beginning to bug me, lady."

"So what did Sabhad want when you met with him?"

He closed his eyes briefly, picturing the scene: the gold damask drapes at the long windows; the sunlight casting a shadow across a magnificent Persian carpet; huge bowls of flowers everywhere, scenting the air with an almost sickly sweet fragrance; Sabhad in a long white shirt tied with a red sash, his dark, somewhat cruel features set off by a white turban. He'd looked spectacular, imposing and dramatic, as if he'd just stepped off a *Desert Song* movie set.

"He was very upset," Nat said, remembering the man's wild, black eyes. "He told me that he loved you very much, even though he knew you had married him for his money. He didn't mind that you didn't love him, he said, because you had given him such beautiful little girls."

"That's a bunch of lies," Valeri said scornfully.

Ignoring her, Nat went on, "He said that you had become bored, though he couldn't understand that, since he had given you everything that money could buy."

"Except freedom, apparently."

Nat raised an eyebrow. "So you admit you could be married to him?"

"I admit no such thing. I'm generalizing. So go on, what else did he say? So far I've heard nothing really convincing."

He had to hand it to her, she stuck to her guns. If she was lying, she was doing one hell of a job. "Sabhad then showed me the photos of your two daughters—"

"Of someone else's daughters."

"—and told me that he'd agreed to give you a divorce on the condition that you signed for joint custody. He wanted to be sure that both of you remain in the girls' lives. You had refused to sign the papers. He was afraid that you'd disappear and never see the girls again. He couldn't bear to see their little hearts broken that way. He begged me to find you and bring you back. He was hoping that once you saw how miserable your children were without you, you'd have a change of heart."

"And you believed all that garbage."

"I did when he played the tape. The cries of those kids were heartwrenching."

"He played a tape?" She sounded disgusted. "Boy, he must have really laid it on thick to get to a tough nut like you."

He probably deserved that, Nat thought ruefully. He hadn't exactly been too sympathetic toward her. Even if he'd felt it.

Valeri, it seemed, was now on a roll and didn't intend to quit. "If you are so experienced in all this low life, why would you take the word of a man like Sabhad? Why would you accept money to force an innocent woman into doing something she obviously didn't want to do? That's kidnapping, and even you can't be above the law. This is not Saudi Arabia, it's a free country, and if I wanted to leave my husband I'd have every right to do so."

He watched the toe of his boot tapping on the floor. There was no way he could make her understand. "It was the kids," he said quietly. "I agreed to do it for the sake of those little girls. I was hoping you'd change your mind about leaving them once you heard them crying."

He wasn't about to tell her that he'd been attacked by pangs of guilt from the moment he'd shoved her into his car. He couldn't afford to give an inch, just in case he was wrong about her. He'd made enough misjudgments over this deal.

His first indication that he was in real trouble had come when he'd taken off her shirt and pants. His intentions had been decent enough. He figured she'd be more comfortable, and would prefer not having to wear clothes that were any more creased and crumpled than they already were.

The minute he'd started unbuttoning her shirt he'd been helpless to prevent his mind from conjuring up all kinds of erotic images. He'd been sweating by the time he was through.

And just now she was sitting here almost completely

destroying his will. She looked so damn sexy in that clingy shirt which left absolutely nothing to the imagination. When she'd looked at him with that warm, soft invitation in her eyes, he'd been utterly unable to resist tasting her inviting mouth. After all, that's what any red-blooded man would have done.

He'd actually been stunned by the soaring excitement he'd felt the moment his lips had touched hers. Considering his suspicions about her, he'd have liked to think that if she hadn't put a stop to what was happening between them, he would have. But if he were totally honest with himself, he had to admit that he couldn't be sure.

The knowledge had shaken him more than he cared to admit.

"You took the word of that...monster, over mine."

He looked up. "So why don't you start explaining how come he has pictures of you cozying up to him and the kids?"

She shook her head, looking as if she were about to burst into tears again. "I don't know. I wish I did. I must have met them at some time...but I don't remember...." Her beautiful dark eyes pleaded with him. "Think about it. Do you honestly believe that a man would bring the mother of his children back at gunpoint? What kind of father is that?"

"A desperate one, I'd say. Who knows how they go about things in Saudi Arabia? All this could seem very normal over there."

"Then all I can say is, I'm really glad I'm not married to the man. I'd last about six seconds with him."

Nat could believe that, at least. "So how about sharing with me what it is you've remembered? If you tell me, maybe we can wrap this up tonight and we can both go home."

She looked as if she were fighting whatever was going on in her head. For a moment he thought she would actually say what she was thinking. Then, as if coming to a decision, she gave a quick shake of her head. "The only thing I've remembered is where I live in Sacramento. I don't remember anything else."

Frustration made him curt. "All right, then. I'm tired, and there's not a lot I can do tonight. Maybe when we've had some sleep we can both think more clearly." And maybe, he added silently, after an uncomfortable night she might just be ready in the morning to tell him why she was afraid of the cops and what it was she was fighting so hard to keep a secret.

Valeri felt all the strength draining out of her as Nat got up abruptly from his chair and strode over to the bathroom. He threw words over his shoulder as he reached for the door. "Don't move. I'm only going to be a second and I'd catch up with you before you reached the road."

She didn't doubt that. She'd never felt so tired in her life. Her head ached again, and she thought longingly about the unfilled prescription in her pocket.

Remembering the envelope she'd been given, she pulled it out and ripped it open. Inside was a small note wishing her luck, and five twenty-dollar bills. The hospital staff had been generous. At least she had some money. The knowledge brought her a smattering of peace. She wasn't totally helpless.

Just as soon as she got away from this brute, she'd hitch a ride to the nearest town. From there she'd have to find a way to get to Sylvan Springs.

The bathroom door opened again before she had time to think about anything else. She wasn't prepared to see Nat, clad only in his dark blue briefs, emerge briskly from the bathroom and head for the bed.

"I suggest you change into your underwear," he said, sliding under the comforter. "You'll be more comfortable and you'll look more presentable in the morning."

Valeri hoped fervently that her expression wasn't giving away her confusion. There didn't seem to be anywhere to look without seeming as if she were trying to avoid staring at him.

He'd thrown her into a tumult of emotions, none of them familiar. He affected her in a way she would have described as immoral if anyone else had described it. He seemed to reach a strange, primitive level of her being that she hadn't even suspected existed until now.

Instead of being repelled by him, which would certainly be more appropriate given the circumstances, she seemed driven by this wild sense of desire that she didn't associate at all with the Valeri Richmond she knew.

Could she have changed that much in six years? She didn't think so. There was nothing in her memory so far that would indicate such a drastic alteration in her personality. No, it was the man himself. He literally exuded a raw kind of animal magnetism that was impossible to ignore.

Everything she had been taught while growing up dictated that she should stay as far away from this downright sexy male as she could get. Yet feelings and cravings she didn't understand were begging her to find out what it would be like to make love with a man as erotic and primitive as Nathan Thorne.

It was as if her mind were at war with her body. Her mother would have turned over in her grave if she knew the torrid fantasies racing through the mind of her refined, conventional daughter.

"Well?"

The tenseness of the word startled her. "Sorry?"

Nat scowled. "Are you going to sit there all night glaring at me, or are you going to get undressed and into bed? I'm tired and I need some sleep."

She was going hot and cold again. Sleep with him? Practically in the nude? No way. No damn way. "I'll sleep here," she said, indicating the broken-down armchair in the corner of the room.

"Uh-uh, sweetheart. I need to know where you are if

I'm going to relax enough to get some sleep. Which means you get in this bed right next to me."

"You can tie me up to the armchair," Valeri suggested, a little desperately.

"Right. And you'll get a whole lot of rest that way. Believe me, you're gonna feel a whole lot better in the morning if you lie down and go to sleep."

She pressed her lips together in an unconscious gesture copied from her mother.

Nat stared at her a moment, then cursed. "You don't have to worry, I'm not going to touch you again. I've never had to force my attentions on a woman, and I'm not about to start now. Especially with someone who could be leading me into a nice little trap."

Her voice sounded thready when she answered. "Trap?"

"Yeah." He propped himself up on one elbow to look at her. "How do I know this isn't some story you and Sabhad have cooked up between you to get me into the mansion?"

She looked at him in astonishment. "Why in the world would I want to do that?"

"I don't know," he said grimly, "but I have a lot of enemies out there. Sabhad could be working for one of them."

Valeri sat up straighter. "I can assure you, Mr. Thorne, there is no way on this earth that I would ever be involved with your revolting cloak-and-dagger affairs."

He pursed his lips. "If I didn't know better, Miss Richmond, I'd say that you are a prude."

"If conducting my life with a certain amount of decency and respect is considered prudish, then I guess I am."

"Decency and respect, huh?"

She lifted her chin. "Yes."

"Then why are you so damn afraid of the cops?"

His accusation took her completely by surprise. She stuttered, "I...I'm not afraid of the police. Why would I be?"

"You tell me."

She made a wild effort to recover her composure. "Look, I'm tired, my head hurts and I just can't think straight anymore. So I'd appreciate it if you'd just stop bullying me."

He narrowed his amber eyes to slits, but his voice was softer when he answered, "Then get into bed and stop arguing with me. We both need some rest."

"I prefer to sleep here."

"You'll sleep here if I have to come and get you."

He threw the comforter back and she got up hastily from the chair. "All right. But I'm keeping my clothes on."

He shrugged. "Suit yourself."

She walked warily over to him and sat down on the edge of the bed. He didn't move, and after a moment she slid her legs under the comforter, balancing herself on the very edge of the mattress.

"Wait a minute." He leaned over the side of the bed and came up with his belt in his hands.

"You're not going to tie me up again?"

"Believe me, this hurts me more than it hurts you."

"I sincerely doubt that." She watched in rebellious silence while he fastened one end of the belt to both her wrists and wrapped the other end around his arm.

"There. Is that comfortable?"

"About as comfortable as a ride on a three-legged mule."

For a moment she thought she saw a flash of sympathy in his eyes. Then it was gone. With a muttered "Good night," he stretched out an arm to switch off the bedside lamp and immediately fell asleep.

At least, she thought he was asleep. She wouldn't put it past him to fake it, just to see if she'd try to make a break for it. He needn't have worried. She was far too tired to even think about running away.

Even so, she lay in the darkness, listening to him breathing beside her, painfully aware of the warmth radiating from his body. Her mind was wide-awake, her body tingled all over.

She hadn't even known she'd been capable of such feelings, but what really shocked her was not so much the nature of the sensations rocketing throughout her body, but the source of her turmoil. Her tastes must have changed considerably in the past six years.

She lay for some time staring into the darkness, struggling to replace the lost time. Visions wafted across her mind, some hazy, some more defined. None of them suggested that she'd had any kind of relationship since her divorce. Nothing that would account for the way she reacted every time Nathan Thorne so much as looked at her.

Nor could she remember any more about the recent days, and what had brought her to Carson City, Nevada. She must have been looking for her father. That seemed the most likely scenario, but it still didn't explain what part Sabhad played in all this, and why he had found it necessary to hire a mercenary to bring her to his house.

One thing seemed fairly certain now. Nathan Thorne was apparently as much in the dark as she was. Though that didn't make him an ally, exactly, it did suggest that he wasn't the enemy she had at first thought him to be.

Much as she longed for someone she could trust to help her find Alex, she still couldn't afford to confide in Nat. He may or may not know about the accusation of murder against her father, and she couldn't quite shake the suspicion that he might be a cop, and that his story of being a mercenary was simply a cover-up. In any case, he almost certainly would turn a suspected murderer in to the police—if he found him.

Valeri closed her eyes. Poor Alex. If only she knew he was all right. He'd been injured, she knew that much. She didn't know how and to what extent. She could only hope and pray that he was safe and not too badly hurt. Tomorrow, she would have to make a run for it. She couldn't wait any longer. She had to find him before the police did. Each day that went by could make things worse for him. Even now, she didn't know how long it had been since he'd called her.

Though the accident had happened last night. If she *had* been on her way to look for him, it was possible he'd called her sometime yesterday. She was still trying to figure out a way to escape from Nat's clutches when she drifted into an uneasy sleep.

Nat awoke with a start, coming wide-awake in an instant, a habit he'd learned a long time ago. It was just starting to get light outside, the pale dawn filtering through the thin window curtains.

He moved his head just enough to confirm that Valeri was still beside him, her bound wrists snuggled under her chin as she slept. Her dark hair was spread across her pillow, and her face looked flushed from a slight sunburn.

In sleep, she looked utterly defenseless, and incredibly sensuous. He wondered what she'd say if he laid his hand on her soft breast.

She'd probably sock him in the jaw.

He looked away, forcing his mind off his erotic thoughts. He'd woken up twice in the night, reminding himself just how long it had been since he'd been in bed with a woman. It hadn't been easy, ignoring the demands of his body.

He hadn't felt this urge in a good many years. Something about Valeri Richmond stirred up his blood and made him forget all the promises he'd made to himself to stay away from her.

He still didn't trust her, though he was inclined to believe her when she said she didn't remember much of the last six years.

What he had to do was jog her memory enough to get it working again. And that's exactly what he intended to do. One way or another, he would get the truth out of her.

Because now, more than ever, he was convinced that there was a great deal more going on with Sabhad than he'd realized at first. And the stakes had to be pretty high if the man was using armed thugs to achieve his objective. Whatever that was.

Obviously Valeri was mixed up in it somehow. Her apparent fear of the police indicated as much. The thought depressed him. He had begun to think she was a completely innocent party in all this, dragged into it by accident. Now he wasn't so sure. And he had better be sure before he made his move, he told himself, or he could land them both into more trouble than he could handle.

Valeri opened her eyes, startled to see a strange window across the room. A movement at her side paralyzed her. For a moment she thought she was back in bed with Dan. The thought was nauseating.

Then she moved her hands, and it all came flooding back. She was in some dingy motel room with a madman who'd taken her prisoner. Alex was somewhere in a place called Sylvan Springs, wounded, wanted by the police and waiting for her to rescue him. She had to go and get him. But where was he? For heaven's sake, where was he?

"Sleep well?"

The husky voice close to her ear sent a hot rush of awareness through her veins. Without turning her head to look at him, she murmured, "I think so."

"Oh, that's right. You have trouble remembering anything."

She flushed at the sarcasm in his voice. "I really don't care if you believe me or not. It makes no difference to me. It's not going to matter once I get out of here, anyway. Just as soon as I get within earshot of anyone, I'm going to have you arrested for kidnapping."

"It's nice to know you've got your spirit back. I was beginning to worry."

She turned her head, then wished she hadn't. His face

was inches from hers. A grim smile tugged at his mouth, and his pale gold eyes were warm and intent on her face.

She sat up and swung her legs over the side of the bed. "I'd appreciate it if you'd untie me. I'd like to go to the bathroom."

"Anything to oblige a lady." He scooted over to her and slipped the leather noose from her hands.

Ignoring him with all the disdain she could muster, she fled for the bathroom and closed the door. The shower felt good, and she tried to wash off all memory of her night in bed with a merciless kidnapper. That was one thing she'd be glad to forget, she told herself, as she scrubbed herself dry.

She towel-dried her hair, then hung both towels on the rack before climbing into her clothes. Her pants were creased, but her shirt looked fine when she slipped it back on. Feeling a lot more secure now that she was clothed again, she clawed her fingers through her tangled hair. Maybe Nat had a comb in his pocket. Her gaze fell on his jeans and shirt, hung over a towel rack. She felt guilty, running her hands through his pockets, but when her fingers closed over the car keys, she felt a little stab of excitement.

She might not be able to run from him, but she sure could drive. She'd be out of the parking lot before he knew what had hit him. Hardly daring to breathe, she eased the keys into the pocket of her chinos.

She found his comb in the back pocket of his jeans, and quickly raked it through her hair. She didn't need him coming in to grab his clothes before she was ready.

After a quick inspection in the mirror, she replaced the comb, then opened the door and stepped back into the room.

Nat stood at the window, his back to her. His legs were long and tightly muscled, his hips firm in the dark blue briefs. His sinewy back was tanned a deep bronze, several shades darker than his legs.

He turned to face her as she closed the door of the bathroom, and she steered her gaze away from him toward the TV. "It's all yours," she said unsteadily.

She'd seen the belt in his hands, and resigned herself to being tied once more to the bed while he took a shower. She was surprised when he crossed the floor to the bathroom, saying, "I'll be right back."

She was just congratulating herself on her easy escape when he turned at the door and said, "I've decided to trust you. I'd appreciate it if you don't let me down."

She glared at the door as he closed it behind him. That wasn't fair, appealing to her conscience. She had a duty to escape, for heaven's sake. Alex needed her. She couldn't tell Nat about him. She couldn't tell anyone. That was one of the few things Alex had said that she remembered. *Don't talk to the police. Don't trust anyone.*

She waited until she heard the rush of water from the shower before creeping to the door. After all, she assured herself as she eased the door open, she hadn't asked to be kidnapped at gunpoint outside the hospital. Nat was the one breaking all the rules.

As far as she knew, she'd done absolutely nothing to deserve all this trauma she'd gone through since she'd woken up in the hospital with a gap in her memory. He'd had no right to force her into his car. And she had every right to try to escape.

The desert had begun heating up already when she stepped outside into the balmy air. The sun felt hot on her bare head and the dazzle from the light pavement hurt her eyes.

She left the door slightly ajar for fear of making a noise if she closed it. Crouching almost double to avoid being seen from the window, she crept over to the car.

The Volvo looked even more dilapidated than it had yesterday. She hoped it would at least get her to the closest town. Wherever that was. She might even be lucky enough to hit Sylvan Springs on the first try.

Her hand shook when she tried to fit the key in the lock, and she used her other hand to steady it. The click of the door handle when she turned it seemed as loud as a gunshot in the still, quiet air.

The inside of the car was stifling, and she rolled down the windows before slipping the key in the ignition. At the first roar of the engine, Nat would come running. Valeri wondered if he'd stop to put some clothes on first.

The vision of him running naked out of the room was so potent that she took a moment or two to get her mind back on track.

All that was important now was to find Alex and get him to a doctor. She had to put Nat right out of her mind.

Unfortunately, she thought ruefully as she fastened her seat belt, forgetting him might be a tad difficult for a while. It was necessary, however, if she was going to get out of there. She needed all her concentration, and Nathan Thorne had a disconcerting habit of throwing her off balance.

She toyed with the idea of going back into the mountains, but the possibility of meeting up with Sabhad's men made that move unwise. She'd be better on the open road, she decided. Sooner or later she'd have to come to a town.

Grasping the key, she braced her shoulders. This would have to be done in an instant. Engine on, brake off and foot on the accelerator. She looked down at the gearbox. There was just one small problem. She'd never driven a stick shift in her life. She pulled in a deep breath. She couldn't let a little thing like that stop her now. Closing her eyes, she turned the key. The engine sputtered…then died.

One glance at the fuel gauge told her why. The stupid car was probably out of gas.

She could have cried with frustration. Resting her head on her folded arms, she tried to think.

The gun. Of course. Nat had a gun. He'd said as much

when he'd first forced her into the car. If she could get her hands on it, she'd make him take her into town. But where would he have hidden it? It certainly wasn't with his clothes.

She darted an anxious look at the motel room. Maybe she still had time to get back into the room and look for it before he finished his shower.

Climbing out of the car, she marveled at her daring. Her six years of independence must have strengthened her nerve. The Valeri she remembered would have fainted dead away at the thought of holding a gun in her hands, much less actually threatening someone with it. Now she couldn't wait to get her hands on it and bring the hardheaded, insolent devil in there to his knees.

She just hoped she knew how to hold the darn thing. She'd seen movies in which someone released a safety catch before pulling the trigger. Maybe Nat wouldn't notice if she couldn't find it to release it.

She scurried back across the parking lot and carefully opened the door. Luckily, she'd left it open. She stepped inside, grateful for the cool air in the darkened room.

She could still hear water cascading in the shower.

So far so good. Maybe the gun was under his pillow. That seemed the most likely place. She hadn't actually seen him put a gun there, but then she hadn't been watching his every move.

She crept across the room and around the side of the bed. Turning her back on the bathroom door, she lifted Nat's pillow. There was nothing underneath. Darn it. He must have hidden it somewhere else.

She looked around the room.

Then it hit her. Of course. It was still in the car. Probably the glove compartment. Why hadn't she thought of that? She turned to creep out again, and was halfway across the room when a gust of wind caught the open door and slammed it against the chair behind it.

Valeri froze.

She heard the bathroom door open, then Nat's voice, asking a little too pleasantly, "Going somewhere?"

Now she was in trouble, Valeri told herself. She was going to need more than luck to get out of this one.

Chapter 6

Valeri turned to face the bathroom. Nat stood propped against the door frame, water dripping from his bare chest, his towel clutched strategically in front of his belly. His dark hair lay plastered to his head, and in the light from the doorway his gold eyes seemed almost feral.

She lifted her chin. "I was just going out for a breath of fresh air. It's getting real stuffy in here."

"I see. You were taking my keys for a walk, is that it?"

Unnerved, she decided her best defense was to attack. "What did you expect? You kidnap me and hold me in this miserable motel against my will, and I have no idea why. Just give me one good reason why I shouldn't run to the nearest cop and turn you in."

He didn't move a muscle, but stood there watching her like a tiger ready to pounce on his prey. After a nerve-racking pause, he said quietly, "Why don't you? The phone's right there. As far as I know, it works just fine. Go ahead, call them."

She almost expected him to add, "Make my day." She

glanced at the phone, then back at him, unable to think of a single thing to say that wouldn't get her into more trouble.

"That's what I thought." He pushed himself away from the wall and walked toward her, his hand outstretched. "My keys."

She backed up a step and fished the keys from her pocket. Dropping them into his open palm, she tried very hard not to notice the expanse of bare flesh exposed on either side of his towel. Her mouth felt dry, yet her palms were damp. She couldn't have looked him in the face right then if her life depended on it.

"Not that they'd have done you any good." He threw the keys onto the bed with a careless gesture. "I took the distributor cap out last night when I brought you back. You couldn't even start the engine without that."

"So you didn't trust me after all." She didn't know why that should matter, but it did.

"Lady, there isn't a woman alive I'd trust. And believe me, you are no exception."

She did look up at him then, stung by his superior tone. "And you're completely trustworthy, of course. A hired killer without principles."

His scowl warned her she'd overstepped the line. She was suddenly aware of her vulnerability. He was close enough that she could feel the steam rising from his skin. In spite of the soap and flowery shampoo, there seemed to be a subtle maleness in the fragrance surrounding him. She noticed tiny droplets of water clinging to his dark chest hair, and felt an insane urge to catch them with her tongue.

Her heart raced. She took a step backward, and came up against the wall. He moved closer, his damp, near-naked body towering over her as he muttered harshly, "I warned you once before not to push me too far. Just be thankful I'm not what you think I am, or you'd be flat on your back trying to fight me off right now. And I can promise you one thing. You'd lose."

With that, he turned his back on her and strode back to the bathroom, apparently oblivious of the fact that he was giving her an unobstructed view of his buttocks.

Valeri's knees gave out completely, and she sank onto the chair, feeling as if all the breath had been squeezed from her lungs. She was trembling from head to foot, and somehow she didn't think it was from fear. Whatever that man was, there was no doubt he knew how to rattle a woman.

She'd never been treated like that in her life. What was even more disturbing, she'd never been so erotically aware of a man, either. He was the most outrageous, blatant man she'd ever met and she resented the way her treacherous body responded to him.

She didn't want to feel this way about him. The man was dangerous, in more ways than one. She could only hope he never tried to carry out his threat.

She lifted her face to the ceiling and closed her eyes. If she were truly honest with herself, the mere thought of him throwing her onto the bed and covering her with his body thrilled her to the bone.

And the real reason she didn't want him attempting it was not because she didn't find him attractive, but because she knew full well what would happen if he did try anything. She'd freeze, as she always did. No matter how badly she wanted to participate. And if there was one thought she couldn't bear, it was for Nathan Thorne to find out that she was sexually inadequate.

The water shut off in the bathroom, and she got hurriedly to her feet. It was too late now to search for the gun. Not that she had any illusions as to how that would turn out, even if she did try to threaten him. More than likely he'd just lean over and take it out of her hand, making one of his suggestive remarks.

She moved over to the TV and switched it on. She needed something to occupy her attention. She'd have liked to turn to the news, just in case there was more word on Alex, but she was afraid Nat would hear it and put two and two together. The police must know by now that she was missing, too. They could even be out there looking for her, assuming she would lead them to her father.

That's what worried her most of all. If Nat was a cop, he could have grabbed her from the hospital knowing that she would eventually lead him to Alex. Maybe all that stuff with Sabhad was to frighten her into trusting him. This whole thing could be a setup, with Nat waiting to grab Alex as soon as he found out what she knew.

That would certainly explain why he rescued her from Sabhad, and why he was so intent on holding her prisoner, so persistent in wanting to know what she remembered.

She just had to stay on guard, and the last thing on earth that she could do was let him seduce her into trusting him.

The door opened abruptly, and she looked up warily as Nat came into the room. He was fully dressed, she was thankful to see, except for his feet, which were still bare.

He sat down on the edge of the bed to pull on his socks and boots, and seemed to be ignoring her.

She waited until he'd finished dressing, then asked him quietly, "So what happens now?"

He looked at her, his strange eyes giving away none of his thoughts. "We're going to try to jog your memory. We're going back to where you live in Sacramento. Maybe being around something familiar will help you remember something else."

She felt a leap of excitement. He was actually going to take her home. She'd never heard more welcome words in her life. Once she got back to her apartment, she was positive she'd find out more about Alex. It was certainly better than roaming around Sylvan Springs not knowing what she was looking for.

Of course, she still had to get away from Nat. That was a major hurdle she'd have to think about on the way home.

Remembering her escape attempt that morning, she recalled something else. "There's no gas in the car. The fuel gauge is on empty."

He gave her a brief nod. "I know. There's still a couple of gallons in there. I always carry another two in the trunk. That should get us to the gas station. We passed one on the way in."

"We're going back over the mountain?" All of a sudden her newly found excitement vanished. "What about Sabhad's men?"

Nat shrugged and crossed to the door. "We'll just have to keep an eye out for them. You ready?"

Now she felt uneasy again. He didn't seem unduly worried about running into the thugs who'd tried to run them down. Could that be because he knew he had nothing to fear from them? Once more her anxiety surfaced.

She followed him out the door and got into the car. She'd left the windows rolled down, but even so, the air felt stuffy inside the small interior. Nat lifted the hood and fiddled with the engine for a moment, then slammed the lid down with a bang that echoed across the dry desert.

He climbed in beside her and started the engine. "Fasten your seat belt," he said, his voice calm and matter-of-fact.

She did as he ordered, her pulse skipping nervously. Maybe he was expecting trouble, after all. She sat back in her seat, feeling the tension creeping over her again. She still had a long way to go. She wasn't out of the woods by any means.

Nat spoke no more than brief snatches of sentences as they climbed the steep slopes. They stopped briefly for gas, largely ignored by the bearded old man who took Nat's money. In a broken-down shack next door, Nat bought some bitter coffee and a bag of tough donuts. It wasn't much of a breakfast, but it satisfied the hunger pangs.

The sun climbed high in the sky, doing its best to overpower the air-conditioning in the little car as they traveled over the mountain. Valeri concentrated on keeping an eye out for the black sedans, now and then distracted by more vague snatches of memory.

She must have kept in close touch with Alex over the past six years. She seemed to remember opening gifts with him under a Christmas tree, even playing volleyball with him on the beach.

She thought she remembered moving into her new apartment. It didn't seem to be that long ago, but it was hard to tell if that was her memory playing tricks again. Maybe all these memories were nothing more than dreams.

She wondered if she'd left a message for her secretary when she had left the apartment after Alex had called. She seemed to remember telling someone she'd been called away on business and would be in touch.

She sat up straighter when she realized this was a new memory. She remembered hanging up from Alex's call, and frantically dialing the office number.

"Remember something else?"

She jumped. She'd almost forgotten about Nat. He didn't miss a thing, she thought ruefully. "Just the move to my new apartment."

"You have a job?"

Her pulse leapt. Of course. If she owned a business in Sacramento, she could hardly be living in the mountains as Sabhad's wife. He'd have to believe her now. "I own my own business in the city. I'll take you there. Anyone there can tell you I'm not married."

"Where is it?"

She frowned, wondering if her office was still on Eleventh Street. No, it couldn't be. She'd called her office from the hospital and reached an entirely different business. She tried to visualize herself dialing the number of her new office, but couldn't see it.

"I...I'm not sure. But it has to be listed in the *Yellow Pages.*"

"What kind of business?"

"Public relations. I arrange for advertising, promotions, fund-raising events, among other things, for various businesses in Sacramento. There are several people who can vouch for me."

"And the name?"

"Richmond Enterprises. At least it was. I might have changed the name when I changed the office."

"You don't remember?"

She shook her head. "It's all a blank."

"Well, if you're as well-known as you say you are, there should be no problem in finding it."

She felt a pang of apprehension. What if she ran into someone she knew and they asked her about Alex? Everyone must know by now that he was wanted on a murder charge.

So far, Nat hadn't mentioned anything about her father. If his story was true about Sabhad hiring him, he wouldn't connect her to a scientist on the run. On the other hand, if he was a cop he'd certainly know who she was.

She'd just have to plead ignorance. After all, if Alex had called her just before the accident, it was feasible she wouldn't know about the murder charge. Or didn't remember. There was a lot she could hide behind a lost memory.

She tried to relax. Her head was beginning to ache again, as it always did when she tried too hard to remember. "You never did tell me how the accident happened," she said, as Nat swept the car around a curve. "If I knew how it happened it might help me remember something."

Once more the valley spread out below them, she noticed, and this time she could see the highway winding into the distance, the sunlight glinting now and again on the miniature cars that traveled the road.

After a moment or two, she realized that Nat hadn't answered her. She sent him a quick look and was disconcerted to see him scowling at the road ahead. At first she thought he'd seen Sabhad's cars, and was immediately afraid. They had the road to themselves, however, and it was impossible to see around the many bends.

"What's the matter?' she demanded sharply.

"Relax." His voice sounded gruff, not at all reassuring. "So far we're in the clear."

"Then why didn't you answer me?"

He sighed. "You asked the question I was hoping you wouldn't ask."

Her heart began bumping again. "Why?"

"Because I guess it's my fault you cracked up the car."

She thought about that. "You were driving? I thought I was."

"You were."

"Then how—"

His voice was curt when he cut in. "I wasn't in the car with you, Valeri. I was following you. You took off across the desert without lights, hit a gully and overturned the car. Luckily I was close enough to drag you out before it blew up."

Her heart lurched in panic. She'd been running from him. He could be a cop, after all—following her to where Alex lay in hiding. "Why were you following me?"

"I told you why. Sabhad told me about the children crying for their mother. I took the job. I drove back to Sacramento and went to the address he gave me, just in time to see you leave. I didn't know where you were going, but I figured it was to a bar or something. I figured I'd make your acquaintance, get you in my car and take you back to Sabhad."

"I see." She frowned. "How did Sabhad know where I live?"

He sent her a sardonic glance. "That's one of the reasons I bought his story. He knows a hell of a lot about you for a stranger."

She sighed. "I must have met him at some time. I just wish I knew where."

"Maybe there's something in your apartment that will tell us. Maybe then we can figure out what's going on."

She had to admit that "we" sounded very comforting. Much as she hated to acknowledge it, working alone in the dark—without her memory to rely on—was pretty terrifying. It would be so wonderful to have someone she could trust to help her. Someone strong, capable and experienced like the man at her side.

She took a hold of herself. There she went again. She was in this on her own, she reminded herself, until she was good and sure she wouldn't be betraying Alex by revealing what she knew. No matter how little that was. She couldn't afford to trust anyone. Least of all Nathan Thorne.

She managed to keep the conversation on mundane matters during the long drive to Sacramento. When they finally approached the city limits, she began to recognize street names, and things started clicking into place.

She had pretty much all of it now, except the crucial hours just before the wreck. Alex's voice kept fading in and out of her mind, leaving those annoying gaps in the conversation. If only she could remember. She sat up suddenly and leaned forward. "Didn't we just pass the entrance to my apartment block?"

"We did." Nat's face was set like stone.

"Why didn't you go in?"

"I have a suspicious nature. There's a cop car sitting in front of the main entrance. Something tells me there's probably another one around the back."

She caught her breath. "I should have thought of that."

Nat swore. "Lady, you've got some explaining to do. I think you'd better start talking, right now. Or—I could take you back and let you talk to the cops."

"No! I mean—"

"I thought so." He swung the wheel so hard she banged

her elbow on the door. For several minutes he said nothing as they sped along Arden Way; then he pulled off and headed into the parking lot of a shopping mall. Finding a space between two trucks, he pulled the little car in and cut the engine.

Valeri's heart pounded again as she faced him. He was furious. She could see it in the hard glint of his eyes, and in the pulse that twitched in his jaw.

"Now, you and I are going to get a few things straight," he said, his voice dangerously quiet. "You are going to tell me why you have a police escort waiting for you to come home. You are also going to tell me where Sabhad fits into all this. And I don't want to hear any more baloney about a lost memory."

She tried a desperate bluff. "The police could be trying to find out who kidnapped me. After all, I'm missing from the office. Someone could have called them."

"After two days? I don't think so. That was a stakeout I saw, not an investigation. I've been around them enough to know the difference."

He sounded like a cop. But he wasn't a cop. She wasn't sure how she knew that, but she did. Maybe it was the way he'd looked when he'd driven by the apartment. As if the last thing he wanted was to talk to the police.

That left Sabhad. She believed now that Nat knew no more than she did. She looked down at her hands, struggling with uncertainties. She needed help if she was to find Alex. Without her memory, she couldn't do it alone. If the police were guarding her apartment—and probably her office—she couldn't go back there. She couldn't delay much longer. Every hour that she waited could mean more trouble for Alex.

She thought about the way Nat had rescued her from Sabhad's men. Without knowing what was going on, his instincts had been to save her. He'd come after her down that long, dry road, and had taken her back to the motel to take care of her. He'd slept in the same bed as her all night and hadn't laid a finger on her.

She had been wrong about him. He had principles. Enough to get angry when she accused him of not having any. She had to start trusting someone. And Nat was all she had.

She looked up. "All right. I'll tell you what I know. On condition that you swear you won't make any contact with the police."

He stared at her for a long time, while her nervousness grew. Finally, he let out his breath on a long sigh. "You've got a deal."

"I want your word on it."

He raised an eyebrow. "I was under the impression you didn't think much of my word."

She met his gaze head-on. "I'm prepared to change my opinion."

The smile began in his eyes but faded before it reached his mouth. "I suppose I should be grateful for that."

"Under the circumstances, I consider it a miracle."

His mouth twisted in a wry grimace. "I'll apologize, if necessary, once I get the truth."

"And your word?"

"I'll leave the police out of it. That, I can promise you."

She'd felt fairly safe in that respect. After all, he would have a tough time explaining why he'd kidnapped an innocent woman from the steps of a hospital. Nevertheless, it seemed important that he promised.

She leaned back in her seat, not quite sure where to begin. "When I woke up in the hospital, I had no memory at all of the past six years. It's all been coming back gradually over the past two days. Now I think I remember just about everything, up to the day before yesterday. Those last hours are still a complete blank."

"And you are not Sabhad's wife."

She shook her head. "To be honest, that part has me

really puzzled. I swear I've never met the man. All I can think is that the woman in the pictures is my double."

"More like your identical twin. On the other hand, people can do amazing things with computers these days."

"Of course. Morphing." Why hadn't she thought of that? "I've seen software advertised that can do that. With the right equipment you can blend any image into another picture."

"Right," said Nat. "Even put someone's face on another body. They've been doing it in movies for quite a while."

Valeri sank back against the seat in relief. "So that's how he did it."

"We assume that's how he did it. Now, what I want to know is why?"

She shrugged. "I really don't know. It seems like an awful lot of trouble to go to, just to get me to his house. It must have something to do with my father."

"Your father?"

If she'd had any doubts left, they were swept away by the bewilderment in his voice. Praying that she was doing the right thing, she said hesitantly, "I don't suppose you've heard much of the news lately. My father is Alex Forrester. He's a scientist working for the government. When I tried to call him from the hospital, I was told that he's wanted for questioning in connection with a murder."

Nat's breath hissed out through his teeth. "No wonder the cops are waiting for you to turn up. What the hell have I walked into here?"

She shrugged her shoulders. "I wish I knew. All I know is that Alex couldn't possibly have killed anyone. I'd stake my life on it."

"You might very well have to before this is over." The look on his face told her he wasn't joking.

"Go on," he said grimly, "tell me everything you know."

She examined her fingernails. "Alex called me. I'm

pretty sure it was two days ago—the day I crashed the car. Anyway, he sounded terrible. I can't remember everything he said, but I do remember him saying that he was hurt. I think he told me where he was. He told me not to talk to the police and not to trust anyone."

Nat was listening closely, his gaze intent on her face. "Anything else?"

She frowned. "I think he mentioned Sabhad by name, though I'm not sure about that. He said something about Sylvan Springs...and a campground." She laid her hand on Nat's arm. "That's all I remember. I have to find him, Nat. He's injured, holed up somewhere all alone. He could be seriously hurt."

She felt his arm flinch slightly beneath her touch. He looked down at her fingers resting on his bare skin, as if he'd only just noticed them. After a moment he drew in his breath. "Okay, take it easy." He looked up at her again. "What about your mother? Could she know where he is?"

She shook her head. "My mother's dead. In any case, they were divorced a long time ago."

"Brothers or sisters?"

"There's only me."

For a second she saw something in his eyes—a flash of pain—then it was gone, leaving her wondering what she'd said to trigger a reaction in him.

"Did your father say anything about the murder?"

She shook her head. "If he did, I don't remember. The first I knew of it was when I called from the hospital."

"Called where?"

"His office at the lab where he works. A policeman talked to me."

Nat groaned. "What did he say?"

"Just that Alex was missing, and I was to contact them if I heard from him."

"Did he know you were calling from the hospital?"

"I guess so. Though he didn't know which one."

"And you don't remember anything else?"

"Nothing. Except..." She hesitated, then decided it was common knowledge anyway. "Last night, when you'd gone for the hamburgers, I was listening to the news. The anchor mentioned Alex—that he was wanted for questioning and was still missing. I guess he was supposed to be in Washington, D.C., right now, reporting on some project he's working on. Something to do with fuel."

Nat's gaze sharpened. "Fuel? What kind of fuel?"

"I don't know," Valeri said miserably. "If I know about it, I don't remember it."

"That's real interesting," Nat said, almost to himself.

Valeri watched him, alerted by his thoughtful expression. "What is?"

Nat smiled, and despite her anxiety she felt little sparks of pleasure set off down her spine. "Fuel. Your father's project."

"I don't understand."

"Oil, for instance. From Saudi Arabia."

She caught her breath. "Sabhad."

"Sabhad is right. My guess is that Sabhad cooked up his abandoned kids story to get you to his house. I'd say it's a safe bet that it isn't you he wants, but your father. One sure way to smoke him out is to kidnap his daughter."

"But how would Alex know I was at Sabhad's house?"

"Maybe Sabhad doesn't know Alex is hurt. He probably figures you're hiding him. In which case, your father would sure know if you went missing. It wouldn't be that tough to figure out where you went."

Valeri nodded. "I've thought all along that Sabhad might be involved with Alex's disappearance. Though I couldn't figure out why."

"More than likely it has something to do with the fuel project. And a murder."

"You think he's responsible?"

"The only way we're going to find out for sure is to find

your father. And we'll find him if we have to search every campground in the area.''

She could have hugged Nat. "Then you'll help me?''

He sent her one of his sidelong glances. ''Don't get too grateful. This is my neck here, as well. One of the reasons I've stayed alive this long is because I know how to protect my own tail.''

His voice had been gruff, as usual, but she had the distinct feeling that he wasn't entirely thinking of himself. They were working together now instead of against each other. They were on the same side, and that thought gave her the first real assurance she'd felt since she'd woken up in the hospital with a frightening blank in her memory.

They still had a long way to go. They still had to find her father, find out where Sabhad figured in all this, and possibly solve a murder. But Nat had agreed to help. He finally believed her. He wasn't fighting her anymore. And right now, that was all that mattered.

''Do I have time to buy a change of clothes first?''

He sighed. ''Now isn't that just like a woman. I guess we'd better grab something to eat as well while we're here.''

He followed her into a chain store, and made some purchases of his own while she bought a couple of cotton shirts, a pair of jeans and a change of underwear.

Back inside the car, he surprised her by tossing a pair of sunglasses in her lap. ''I never wear them,'' he said, when she thanked him. ''But I thought they might help your headache.''

Her headache had disappeared earlier, but she wasn't about to spoil his kind gesture. Maybe she'd misjudged him, she thought, sitting the glasses on her nose. He wasn't totally without sensitivity, after all.

''I bought a newspaper, too.'' He handed it to her. ''I thought there might be something in there about your father.''

Once again he'd surprised her. She scanned it eagerly, and found a small story near the back of the main section. It was brief, and said little more than what she'd heard on the radio.

As they turned onto the business loop, Valeri voiced the question that had been bothering her for some time. "What I don't understand," she said, "is why Sabhad hired you to pick me up instead of sending one of his own men."

"He probably couldn't afford to take the chance. Kidnapping is a pretty risky operation. If something went wrong, he couldn't afford to have one of his men involved. Whereas I'm expendable."

"How would he know you wouldn't reveal who'd hired you?"

He gave her a sardonic smile. "I wouldn't live long if I did. Men like Sabhad have a long reach. In any case, he was pretty confident I could pull it off."

"I thought you'd never met him before."

"I hadn't."

"Then how could he be so sure?"

He grinned at her. "Because my reputation speaks for itself. I'm good. You have to admit that."

She rolled her eyes in disgust. "That's not the word I would have chosen. If I hadn't been recovering from a bump on the head and wrestling with a lost memory, you wouldn't have stood a chance of getting me in this car."

"Oh, yeah?" He slowed in front of a gas station and pulled up in front of the pumps. He cut the engine, then leaned toward her. "You were lucky—I treated you nice because you'd just come out of hospital. You should see me when I really get tough."

She gave him a sweet smile. "I'm sorry I missed the experience. I'm sure it would have been memorable."

"Well, just in case, I'd better warn you. Double-cross me, and you'll find out how memorable I can be."

Dismay wiped the smile from her face. "I thought you

believed me now. Isn't it time you started trusting me? After all, I'm trusting you enough to tell you everything I know about my father."

"So you said." He opened the door and swung his legs outside.

She felt a flash of irritation. What was wrong with the man, anyway? "You mean you still think I'm lying?"

"I don't think anything. It's safer that way." He closed the door before she could answer.

She sat in resentful silence while he pumped gas, then watched him stroll over to the store to pay for it. The view of his back reminded her vividly of when he walked away from her in the motel room, naked and unconcerned.

He was the crudest man she'd ever met, and the most infuriating. Just wait until they found Alex. Her father would soon set the man straight. Then she'd see that Nathan Thorne ate his words, if it was the very last thing she did.

Chapter 7

After paying for the gas, Nat climbed back into the car and reached across Valeri for the map in the glove compartment. She shrank back, making it clear she was trying to avoid any contact with him.

He knew he'd upset her. He was sorry for that, but the questions kept buzzing around in his head like angry flies. Her latest bombshell had been a real doozie. Not only was he involved in kidnapping, but he was also mixed up in a murder.

If he had any brains at all, he thought darkly as he unfolded the map, he'd dump this woman back in front of her apartment, hightail it out of town, and forget he ever heard of Valeri Richmond or Ahmed Sabhad.

Except he couldn't do that. He couldn't let a helpless women walk into a hornet's nest like that. The cops would be all over her, and they wouldn't give up until they'd squeezed her dry.

They'd find her father, arrest him and he wouldn't stand a chance against someone like Sabhad. Which was probably why he was still in hiding. Whatever he knew about Sabhad obviously wasn't strong enough to protect him.

That's if Sabhad's target was Alex Forrester and not Valeri, which seemed to be the most probable scenario given that Valeri couldn't remember ever meeting the man.

If she was telling the truth.

Nat frowned as he studied the map. So many damn *ifs.* He didn't like being mixed up in a murder case. The whole story was so wild that it was hard to believe. There were too many holes, too many unanswered questions. Maybe if he asked her a few, he could fill in some of the gaps.

Much as he wanted to believe her, his instincts were too strong too ignore: never accept anything without proof. So far he had little else to go on except her word. Any proof they might have found in her apartment or office was inaccessible now, thanks to the police.

"It looks as if there are three campgrounds around the Sylvan Springs area," he said, refolding the map. "I guess we'll take them one by one."

"All right."

Her voice was tight, and he winced. It wasn't often he cared about stepping on someone's toes, but in this case he genuinely regretted his bluntness.

He drove out of the gas station and once more headed for the highway back into Nevada. After several long minutes of tense silence, he glanced at his passenger.

She sat stiff-backed, staring out of the window as if she'd like to demolish every living thing out there. Knowing he was responsible, he felt a twinge of guilt.

"We should be there in a couple of hours," he said in an attempt to open the conversation.

She nodded, but didn't look at him.

He tried again. "So how come you got divorced?"

This time he'd startled her into looking at him. "What?"

He shrugged. "Just asking. You don't have to tell me if you don't want to."

"I don't want to." She looked back at the road.

"Okay. So tell me about your father."

He thought at first she wasn't going to answer him, then she said in a resigned voice, "What do you want to know?"

"I don't know. Anything that might help us track him down. What does he like to do? What is he good at?"

"A lot of things. I can tell you one thing, though. Alex is no camper. He's a city man, through and through. The closest he comes to roughing it is spending a night in a motel room."

"Well, that's a great help."

"It tells me that he wouldn't be caught dead in a campground, unless he had no choice."

He glanced at her. Little lines of tension creased her brow. As he watched, she caught her bottom lip between her teeth and chewed on it for a moment before letting it go. "You're really worried about your father," he said quietly.

She took off her sunglasses and laid them on the dash in front of her. Her voice wasn't quite steady when she said, "He's all I've got. I never knew him when I was growing up. They were divorced when I was five. My mother never let me see any of the letters he wrote, or the gifts he sent. We lost so many years...if anything happens to him now...I—"

"Nothing's going to happen to him," Nat said fiercely. "Not if I've got anything to do with it. We'll find him."

He surprised himself at how sincerely he meant that. He realized that he no longer doubted the truth of her words. Whatever the game was here, her father's disappearance was genuine—and definitely not part of the plan.

"I hope so."

She lapsed into silence for so long that he thought she'd drifted off to sleep. Then she startled him by saying, "I guess you must do a lot of traveling around in your job."

He didn't answer her at first, unsure of how much he could tell her without arousing her contempt again.

She must have thought he was ignoring the question because she added, "You don't have to talk about it if you don't want to."

His mouth twitched. He enjoyed the way she had of getting back at him. It wasn't often someone scored the way she could. "I don't mind talking about it. I'm not sure you'd find it all that interesting, though."

She shrugged, pretending indifference, but he noticed her fingers playing with a loose thread on her seat and knew she was wound as tight as a guitar string.

"I've seen pretty much every part of the world—the good and the bad," he said, squinting against the shimmering heat that created imaginary lakes in the middle of the road.

She must have been turning that over in her mind. After a while, she spoke again, her voice deceptively casual. "That must make it hard to establish friendships."

He almost laughed out loud. "Men in my profession don't make friends. Only enemies."

"That's sad."

"It's sensible. That way I only have myself to worry about." He glanced at her, and felt his body quicken. She was watching him with a look in her soft brown eyes that made him want to crawl between cool sheets with her and take her until his passion was exhausted.

Women had looked at him that way before. Experienced women, who knew full well what they were doing. With Valeri it was different. Now that he knew her better, he was willing to bet that she wasn't even aware she was giving away her thoughts with that hot invitation in her eyes. He wondered if she knew what that could do to a man.

That's what made her so exciting. He ached to show her. His body cried out to answer that challenge, to watch her writhing beneath him, caught up in her own rising tide of passion.

He jerked his gaze back to the road, reminding himself again why that would be a bad idea. He'd almost given in to his need in the motel room, and she'd stopped him. Judging from that look in her eyes now, she might not do that the next time. He couldn't afford a next time. Not with this woman.

"Didn't you ever want to get married and settle down?"

The question unnerved him. He took a moment to answer. "From what I hear, marriage could be a worse hell than anything I've ever gone through."

He risked another look at her. She was slumped in her seat now, with an expression on her face that reminded him of a dog he'd found injured on the roadside. He'd never forgotten the look in its eyes. Valeri had that same look on her face. She'd been hurt. And badly.

He wanted to stop the car, hold her close and promise her she'd never be hurt again. What was he, crazy? He was the last person in the world who could promise her that.

Nathan Thorne, the man who'd never stayed the entire night with a woman in his life. The man who'd locked up his heart against emotions long before he was old enough to really understand what it was all about.

Uncomfortable with his thoughts, he leaned forward and switched on the radio, tuning in to a country station. There was something about Valeri Richmond that made him look deep into his soul, and that was something he would rather not do.

For the next hour or so, he kept the conversation down to the odd comment or two. Valeri seemed perfectly content to sit there, gazing pensively out the window. He would have given a great deal to know what she was thinking.

Finally they passed the sign he was looking for, and he pointed it out to her. "The campground should be about a mile or so down the road."

She sat forward, her hands pressed between her knees. "I hope Alex is there. I just hope he's all right. I keep trying to remember the last time I saw him—" She broke off with a little gasp.

Nat tightened his hands on the wheel as they took a curve. "Remember something?"

"Yes…I think so."

When he looked at her again, she sat with her fingers pressed against her forehead. He kept quiet, giving her time to wrestle with her erratic memory.

"It's gone again…." she said at last. "But I seem to remember something about computer disks."

Nat pursed his lips. "Wonder if that's got anything to do with Sabhad's pictures of you."

"I don't know." She uttered a growl of exasperation in the back of her throat. "Oh, why can't I remember?"

"Because you're trying too hard." He leaned forward to peer at another sign. "You know how sometimes someone asks you a question, and you're certain you know the answer but you just can't think of it, no matter how hard you try? Then when you're not thinking about it at all, up it pops in your mind."

She nodded. "I've done that. Sometimes I'll say the answer out loud when I'm in a store or something, and people think I'm talking to myself."

"Exactly." He stepped on the brake, slowing the car. "Well, just stop thinking about your memories and they'll come back when they're ready."

She leaned forward. "Is this the campground?"

"It's the closest one to Sylvan Springs." He turned off the road and drove up a steep trail that wound around a murky-looking lake. A handful of boats was tied up at the long deserted dock. At the top of the rise a narrow dirt trail—barely wide enough to accommodate a boat trailer—plunged sharply down to the lake and ended at a weathered, run-down boat ramp.

"It doesn't look that busy," Nat said, pulling up at the top of the slope.

She looked down to where campers were dotted around a clearing in the sparse trees.

"I guess we could just drive around and see if there's anything worth checking out."

She nodded, eyeing the trailers parked below. "He could be in any one of those."

"Maybe. But if he told you not to talk to anyone, I doubt if he'd ask strangers for help."

"He could be in an empty one."

Nat sighed. "I guess we have to start asking questions. I was hoping to avoid that." He cut the engine and wound down the window. Blue jays screeched at each other in the dried-up branches of a pine tree, and somewhere a dog whined for its master. Otherwise, nothing seemed to be moving in the entire camp.

The sun was losing its power as it crawled toward the horizon, and the first cool chill of the approaching night brushed Nat's arms as he climbed out of the car and stretched his legs. "You'd better stay here," he said, shielding his eyes from the glare of the sizzling sunset. "I'll go down and ask around. What does your father look like?"

He bent down to hear her answer through the window.

"He's five-eleven, kind of rugged looking. Thick gray hair, tanned face, stocky build, glasses—" She broke off, her hand going to her mouth. "He broke his glasses," she finished in a near whisper.

Nat pulled the door open again and climbed in. "Go on. What else?"

She blinked, staring at his face as if he weren't there. "Alex...stole the disks back. He was injured trying to get away. He called me. He said he wasn't badly hurt, but he couldn't drive. He was wounded in the shoulder and couldn't use his arm, and he'd smashed his glasses and he couldn't see."

"He stole the disks from where?"

She shook her head with an impatient gesture that at any other time would have made him smile. "Not stole them. Stole them *back*. They were his disks."

Nat frowned, trying to make sense of it all. "Did he keep his work on disks? Like the fuel project, for instance?"

She grabbed his arm, her fingers digging into his flesh. "That's it! The project. Someone stole the disks and he had to get them back."

Nat eased her fingers off his arm. "Someone like Sabhad, for instance?"

She looked down at the imprint of her fingers in his flesh. "Sorry."

"That's okay. I liked it."

That conjured up a tiny smile. "So that's why Sabhad wants my father. He wants the disks back again."

Nat nodded, sobering at the thought. "And he's willing to kill to get them."

Valeri's eyes widened. "Kill my father?"

"Possibly. Think about it. There was a murder. If your father didn't do it, then someone else did."

"Sabhad."

"Or one of his men. I assume someone got killed when the disks were stolen in the first place."

"But there was nothing on the news about the stolen disks."

"Maybe no one knows they were stolen."

"Except Alex and Sabhad."

"Right. Sabhad's not going to tell anyone. And your father can't."

Valeri sat up with a look of alarm on her face. "Nat...if Alex was injured while he was trying to get away from Sabhad, he must still be close to the house. He couldn't have gone far on foot. He might even have called me from the house."

"You don't remember where he was when he called?"

"No, I—" She broke off again, her eyes growing wider. He thought she'd remembered something else. He was about to ask her, when she pointed a shaky finger down the road behind them. He followed the direction she was pointing. Creeping up the slope toward them were two big, black sedans.

Cursing himself for his carelessness, he grabbed the wheel and twisted the key in the ignition. As he did so, two more cars burst out between the campers on the road below them, and headed straight for them.

Nat didn't have time to think. There was only one avenue of escape and he took it. He wrenched the wheel around, stepped on the gas and pointed the car straight at the lake.

Valeri didn't utter a sound as the car careened down the bumpy slope, but Nat caught a glimpse of her terrified face as he fought the wheel. With one foot hovering over the brake, he waited for the precise moment to slam it down.

He spared one quick glance in his rearview mirror and saw the sedans parked at the top of the rise. One of them was already backing out, probably to head back down the road to cut them off.

Nat smiled. He had no intention of trying to reach the road.

The water seemed to race toward them as the Volvo headed for the boat ramp. Valeri's hands were on the dashboard, fingers curled in a tight grip. "Hold on," Nat muttered, and slammed on the brake, turning the wheel just enough to bring the rear wheels around.

The little car rocked violently, paused on two wheels, then skidded another twenty feet. They came up just short of the edge of the ramp, facing away from the road.

Ahead of them were trees, rocks, slopes and God knows what else. He couldn't worry about that. Already the sedans were circling the lake. This was the only way out, and he had two minutes start at most.

He stomped on the accelerator and the Volvo leapt forward. He heard a tiny sound from Valeri, that was all. Then they were bouncing and crashing toward a line of trees.

He scraped through somehow, taking twigs and leaves with him. Behind him, he could hear the angry jays screeching in fury as they soared into the air. The roar of a car engine echoed across the lake, and again he smiled. They would have to come off the road to follow him, and he didn't think they'd risk it in those black monsters.

It was only a matter of time before the thugs picked up his trail, however. He had to get out of there—and fast—or he could run into an ambush farther up the rise.

He glanced at Valeri. She still sat clutching the dash, her eyes shut tight and her lips a thin, pale line. "Relax," he said, feeling sorry for her. "I've done this before. We'll be okay."

She opened one eye to look at him. "If that's supposed to reassure me, it's not working."

"Sorry." He twisted the wheel again as a jagged rock rose up in front of him. "We don't have much choice at this point."

He bounced past the rock, wincing as he heard the sound of scraping metal. He'd probably left a few square inches of paint behind to point the way.

To his immense relief, he saw a paved road ahead over the next rise. If he could just make that, he told himself, he might just have enough head start to make it out onto the main road.

The car creaked and groaned with every jolt, until finally the wheels hit firm terrain and they could race along the smooth, winding curves without danger of losing their teeth.

Valeri sank back against the seat with a little sigh. "Where did you learn to drive like that?" she muttered. "The Andes?"

He grinned. "Monte Carlo. In my rebellious youth I raced cars."

She nodded. "I should have known."

"The experience has come in handy a couple of times."

"Did you ever win?"

"What?"

"The Monte Carlo."

"Oh. No. I was usually bombed out on Scotch before the end of the race."

"I should have known that, too."

"I quit after I smashed up my third car."

"The racing or the drinking?"

"Both. It took me a few years longer to give up smoking. Now I have no objectionable habits."

She gave him a look that showed she clearly disagreed, but she wisely refrained from answering. After a long pause, she asked, "How do you think they found us?"

"Sabhad's goons? They could have spotted the car when we came into the area. Or they might have had someone posted close by your apartment, seen us drive by and followed us."

"All the way here?"

"As long as we were heading in the right direction, why stop us?"

He saw the main highway up ahead and braked to a halt at the stop sign. He barely hesitated before turning the car left, heading into the setting sun.

"So where are we going now?"

"Back toward Sabhad's mansion. I'm going to scout around and hope I can pick up a few clues as to where your father might be."

She looked alarmed. "Isn't that dangerous? They're bound to still be looking for us."

"I'm sure they are. But I don't think they'll figure on us going in this direction."

She didn't look convinced, and he added, "Quit worrying. I know what I'm doing."

"I hope so. I just wish I knew—"

"Damn." He stared into the rearview mirror.

"What's the matter?"

He caught the urgency in her voice and wished he could reassure her. "We've got company."

She looked over her shoulder, her eyes fearful as she obviously caught sight of what he saw in the mirror—four black cars, one behind the other, kicking up dust about a half mile behind them. "Can we outrun them?"

"Not a chance. We'll have to do a little cross-country jogging again."

"Great. I'd just got my heart rate back to normal."

He took another look in the mirror. "Well, fasten your seat belt tighter, sweetheart, because we're off again."

The cars were close enough now for the drivers to see him veer off the road. He had to pick his spot. He saw it when he was almost on it—a rough trail leading up behind a crop of large rocks.

He plunged onto it, skidding and sliding, and then the tires grabbed and they were once more playing mountain goat up the steep slope.

This area was even rougher than the terrain around the lake. Without the trees and the water to soften the ground, the wheels had less traction, and the car bucked and kicked like a wild rodeo bull.

Nat clung to the wheel, hoping like mad that his hard-won skills wouldn't let him down. After several minutes of tortuous progress, he saw a small rise ahead. He couldn't see beyond it, and prayed there wasn't a drop on the other side.

There just wasn't anywhere else to go, except to turn back. By now Sabhad's men were too close to make that a feasible choice. He aimed the car at the rise, his gaze fixed on the uneven horizon.

They hit the top, and bounced over. Nat swore. He could see nothing but sky—hell, his luck had finally run out. He felt the wheels leave the ground, and knew it was out of his hands now. All he could hope was that the drop wasn't too deep and that they landed squarely. They might be shaken up a bit but they'd be all right.

Two seconds later, they hit with a bone-jarring thud. For a wild moment he thought he had it under control. The car rocked, bounced and hit again. This time the off-side wheels came down first. Before he had time to catch a breath, the car flipped over on its side with a deafening, splintering crash that echoed across the canyon like thunder.

His upper body slammed into Valeri before being jerked back by his seat belt. He hung above her, concerned to see that she was unconscious. She must have hit her head on the dash.

He had to get them out of there. He sniffed the air, but so far he couldn't smell smoke. Even so, he couldn't waste any time. If an explosion didn't get them, Sabhad's men probably would catch up to them soon enough. They must have heard the crash for miles.

He opened the door above him and shoved it open. Then, wedging his foot against Valeri's seat, he undid his belt. It took him longer than he liked to get her out of her harness and up through the door. By then, to his immense relief she showed signs of coming around.

He slid off the car and eased her to the ground. Her dark hair covered her eyes and he brushed it back, careful not to touch the darkening bruise from her first wreck. She was going to have one hell of a headache when she woke up.

She whimpered then, and opened her eyes. She moved her lips, moistened them with her tongue, then whispered, "What happened?"

"We flipped. Are you okay?"

She nodded, then winced. "My head."

"You banged it again. Sorry."

"I'm getting used to it."

"Can you sit up?"

"I think so."

He helped her sit upright, and she looked over at the car. "I guess we're not going anywhere in that now."

He grinned, relieved that she seemed to be all right. "You guessed right. We'll have to go the rest of the way on foot. But we'll have to move it. Those goons can't be far behind."

She nodded, started to get up, then sat back down with a thump.

Worried now, Nat crouched down beside her. "What's up? Are you dizzy? You didn't get another concussion, I hope."

"I don't think so." She peered up at Nat, looking as if she were peering through a thick fog. "Where are we going?"

"To Sabhad's mansion to find your father."

She shook her head. "No, we don't need to. He's not there."

Nat let his breath hiss out. "You've remembered where he is."

"Yes." She smiled, dazzling him for a moment. "I've remembered everything."

"So where is he?"

He hoped she'd tell him that her father was safe with friends. But she looked around her as if expecting to find him tucked behind a rock somewhere. "He's back at the lake. Or near it, anyway. There's an abandoned gas station just down the road from the campground. He's waiting there."

Nat held out his hand. "Good girl. Let's get going." He pulled her to her feet.

She staggered, and might have fallen if she hadn't grabbed onto him. He closed his arms around her in an instinctive move to catch her.

For a moment she tensed, then relaxed against him. Her eyes met his, and immediately he could feel the tug in his groin. For the space of a heartbeat, the world disappeared and there were just the two of them, floating in a haze of hot need and unspoken promise.

He knew she understood the question that had to be burning in his eyes. He saw the answer in her face, and his elation at the prospect tied him in knots. But not now. His time with her would have to wait. And it would be all the more worthwhile for the waiting.

It was with real effort that he grasped her upper arms and moved her away from him. "Can you walk?"

"Yes, I'll be fine. I just want to find my father now."

"Okay. But the minute you start feeling faint, you let me know. All right?"

Valeri nodded, passing her hand across her forehead in a little gesture that told him her head was hurting. The evening breezes were already making their presence felt, cooling the earth. If they didn't find her father soon, they'd have to hole up somewhere for the night. It was a long walk back to the campground, and he wasn't sure she could make it even that far.

She stood for a moment, looking around her, then she walked over to the car. "I need the clothes I bought," she said, peering into one of the windows.

Nat sighed. "Hang on, I'll get them for you," he muttered, and clambered up onto the car. They'd been lucky, he thought, as he lowered himself through the door. This car hadn't burned like the last one—which was a miracle, considering the amount of gas spilling from the ruptured fuel tank.

He grabbed up two plastic bags, then hauled himself out of the car again and back to the ground. "I'll carry them," he said when she held out her hand. "You just concentrate on staying on your feet."

She gave him a tired smile. "Thanks."

"Sure." He knotted the bags together and threw them over his shoulder. "Okay, let's go. We may have some climbing to do before we get to the lake. I want to avoid the roads and trails as much as possible.''

''What about my sunglasses? They were on the dash.''

''They fell off. They're broken.''

She looked as if she were about to cry.

Nat felt an odd pang of helplessness as he watched her. ''I'll get you another pair as soon as we hit town,'' he said gruffly.

''It's okay.'' She started to move ahead of him, but he held up his hand.

''I'll go first. Just step where I step, okay? There shouldn't be too many rattlers around, but you never know.''

Valeri followed him without a word, and for the next hour he led her over some grueling terrain while he concentrated on cutting the trek as short as possible.

She kept up with him, but he could tell she was getting gradually weaker as she scrambled over boulders and down gravel slopes with treacherous footing. In spite of scraped hands and a grazed knee, she kept going without one word of complaint. His admiration for her grew by leaps and bounds.

It was almost dark by the time he spotted the lake, partially hidden by the surrounding trees. ''There it is, up ahead,'' he said, nodding in that direction. ''Now, where's that gas station?''

''All I know is that it's not far from the entrance to the campground.''

''Well, we didn't pass it on the way in, so it has to be a bit farther on.'' She stumbled and he caught her arm. ''You all right?''

''Tired.'' She gave him a weak smile.

''How's the headache?''

''Brutal. I should have filled out my prescription while we were at the store.''

"If you had you'd have been surrounded by cops before you got outside."

She looked startled. "I hadn't thought of that."

"You'll feel better once you get some rest and some food inside you."

"That sounds wonderful."

He gave her an encouraging smile. "Almost there. You'll think it was worth the hike when you see your father again."

"I just hope he's still there. It's been at least three days. He might have given up and gone somewhere else."

"He doesn't have anywhere else to go—unless he hitched a ride, and I doubt he'd risk that."

She looked scared. "What if he's gone without food and water all that time?"

"We'll cross that bridge when we come to it." He tightened his grip on her arm. "Come on, lean on me. It's not much farther now."

Together they made their way down the last hundred yards, with Valeri leaning more and more of her weight against him, until finally, by the time they reached the road, he was supporting her with his arm around her.

She seemed to do better on flat ground. Even so, he kept his arm about her as they trudged around the bend. He didn't want to admit he enjoyed the pressure of her warm body against him.

She gave a little cry as they rounded the curve and saw the deserted gas station. A rusted pump stood forlornly in the middle of an empty yard beneath a large sign declaring the station closed. A phone box, its glass panes shattered, stood nearby.

The sight seemed to revive her. She pulled away from him and hurried down the road to where the door hung open on the run-down wooden shack.

He called out a warning, but she ignored him and disappeared inside. He was right behind her, every nerve tensed for whatever might be waiting.

He needn't have worried. One glance inside the building told him that it was empty. There was nowhere to hide in that barren room. If Alex Forrester had holed up in this place, he wasn't here any longer.

Chapter 8

Valeri slumped against the wall, unwilling to believe that all their efforts had been for nothing. She heard Nat's step behind her and didn't even bother to turn around. "He's not here," she said dully.

Nat slung the bags onto the ground and looked around. "I can see that. Are you sure this is the place?"

She nodded, barely able to make the movement count. "I'm positive. He described the campground, with the lake and the boat ramp. He must have called me from that phone outside. He described the gas station and he said it was just down the road from the sign that said Sylvan Springs."

Nat sighed. "I guess this is it, then."

She made the effort to look at him. "What do you think happened?"

Nat shrugged. "Hard to say."

She watched him prowl around the room, peering at the floor and out of the grimy window at the back. "There's no sign of any scuffle, and no blood. He either walked out of here on his own, or he went willingly with whoever was with him."

She hated to voice the question, but she needed to know. "Do you think Sabhad's men have got him?"

He lifted his head, but it was dark now and she could barely see his face. She couldn't read his expression, but his voice held conviction when he answered her. "No, I don't think so. Otherwise they wouldn't be so anxious to get their hands on you."

"Then where could he have gone?"

"My guess would be the town. He probably got tired of waiting for you."

She was exhausted. Her head hurt and she was dying of thirst. The crushing disappointment of finally reaching the gas station only to find her father gone seemed overwhelming. Even so, she was determined not to let herself admit defeat. "So what do we do now?"

"You hold on here. I'm going to look around. There's a bathroom out back. I'll take a look at it."

She nodded, barely able to keep her eyes open. How she longed for a soft bed to lie down on. Even the memory of that motel bed, with her wrists tied, was appealing.

Nat disappeared, and she slid down the wall until she could sit on the floor. It felt good to get the weight off her feet. She leaned her back against the wall and closed her eyes. The place smelled of fungus and rotting wood. The damp seemed to creep down her arms, raising goose bumps on her sunburned skin.

In spite of her discomfort, she had almost dozed off when the squeak of the door told her that Nat had returned. She opened her eyes and found him bending over her.

"You okay?"

She nodded. "Just tired. Did you find the bathroom?"

"Right outside. It's even got running water. At least we'll be able to wash up and have a cool drink."

"Wonderful. I feel better already." She made an effort

to smile, even though she knew he probably couldn't see it.

"Here." He thrust her bag of clothes into her hands. "You go first. Get into some clean clothes. You'll be surprised how much better you'll feel."

She took them from him. "How far do you think it is to Sylvan Springs?"

"Too far for you to get there tonight. We'll stay here the night and leave first thing in the morning."

"Can't we hitch a ride?"

"You really want to take that chance? The cops have probably got an APB out for you by now. And Sabhad's men could be anywhere."

She wanted to argue, but she didn't have the strength. He was right. Even if she could make it there without collapsing, she didn't have the energy left to search for her father tonight. She needed rest, sleep. Though how much sleep she'd get on the bare floor of a cold and drafty shack, she shuddered to think.

She left the door open in the bathroom so that she could see what she was doing. Moonlight flooded the area, giving her enough light to see her faint reflection in the cracked and filthy mirror.

She looked a little wild. Her hair was tangled and windblown, and she wished she'd thought to buy a comb in the chain store. She'd have to ask Nat to borrow his again.

The sink was chipped and stained, but water flowed from the faucet. She washed her hands, then cupped them to get a drink. The water tasted slightly metallic, though it was cold and wet—the two main essentials right now. She drank it down greedily.

It took a while to satisfy her thirst, drinking that way. When she was through, she filled the sink with water, rinsed it out, then filled it again.

She stripped off her clothes and dropped them onto the floor, then bathed as best she could in the narrow space.

The water chilled her skin, and she shivered as she dried herself with her chinos before pulling on the clothes she'd bought earlier that day.

She wished she could have washed her hair, but that would have to wait. It was enough to feel at least marginally clean and refreshed. Even her head felt better now that she was out of the sun. If she could just have something to eat, she'd feel almost human again. She picked up the clothes she'd discarded and stuffed them in the bag.

When she returned to the shack, it was so dark inside that for a moment she thought Nat had left.

Then he moved and she saw his silhouette framed against the window. "Feel better?" His low voice, coming out of the shadows, sounded strained.

"Much better." After a slight pause, she added, "Is something wrong?"

"You mean other than being holed up like animals in a decaying woodshed—hunted by carloads of armed thugs, not to mention the cops? I certainly hope not."

She scowled in the darkness. His sarcasm could be so irritating. "I hope Sabhad's men don't come poking around here. There isn't any place to hide."

"I think we're pretty safe for the night, at least. They probably figure we've holed up for the night somewhere, and they're sitting out there waiting for us to make the first move."

She felt him brush by her on his way to the door. "Just in case, lock this door behind me—that's if that rusty old lock still works—and don't open it again until you hear my voice." He stepped outside and she closed the door, struggling with the lock for several minutes before she finally got it to turn. Fumbling around in the dark, she spread out the plastic bag as a liner, then laid her clothes on top of it.

She'd have given anything for a sleeping bag, she thought as she lowered herself onto the makeshift bed. She could feel every seam in the wood through the meager padding. Still, she had to admit it was better than lying on bare floorboards. Barely.

Nat was probably used to roughing it this way, but she seriously doubted if she'd be able to sleep at all. The cold water wash had woken her up, and although her body still ached with weariness, her eyelids no longer felt heavy.

She wondered if hunger would keep her awake. She was almost hungry enough to suggest to Nat that they try to make it to Sylvan Springs that night.

She seemed to wait a long time for him to come back from the bathroom. Now and then she heard a car whiz past, and she held her breath until the sound had died away. If only they could chance hitching a ride. She'd give anything for a warm bed and something to eat.

She wondered what it was that made a man choose a life like this; always on the edge, always looking over his shoulder. On the other hand, it was impossible to envision Nat in suburbia, dressed in a coat and tie, leaving every morning for the drive into the city. Some men, like most animals, just weren't cut out to be domesticated.

Maybe that's why he affected her so much. That element of danger about him—the reckless adventurer—appealed to her imagination. He was the kind of man fantasies were built around—certainly not real life. Men like Nathan Thorne did not settle down with a wife and family. What was it he'd said? *From what I hear, marriage could be a worse hell than anything I've ever gone through.*

She wondered whom he'd been talking about. His parents? Friends? Maybe a brother or sister? Considering she'd spent so much time with him, she knew very little about him. She probably never would. Nat did not like questions. That didn't mean she was going to stop asking them. For much as she tried to deny it, the deep need to know what made him tick was too powerful to ignore.

Outside, Nat paused for a moment at the bathroom door, breathing in the cool night air. He'd hoped that drenching his body in ice cold water would cool down the craving that had ravaged him ever since he'd caught a glimpse of Valeri's naked body bathed in moonlight inside the bathroom doorway.

He hadn't meant to spy on her. He was no Peeping Tom. He'd checked both windows, just to make sure they hadn't been followed. He didn't need the police or worse, Sabhad's men, creeping up on their unstable refuge.

He'd seen her standing in the doorway, arms raised to give him a clear view of her jutting breasts and small, rounded buttocks. The heat of his response had threatened to suffocate him.

He'd turned away at once, fighting the almost irresistible urge to stay glued to the window until the very last second when she was fully dressed again. He'd recovered some measure of control by the time she'd come back to the shack, but in spite of the cold water he slapped over his body he had not been able to rid himself of that erotic image.

Now he had to go back to her in that dark, intimate room, with nothing to separate them except a bag of clothes. And he was still hard. He ached with the need to satisfy the craving that would not let him go.

He stood for a moment longer, his face raised to the star-sprinkled sky, reminding himself of all the reasons why he shouldn't just give in to his insatiable urges.

Then he lowered his chin. She wanted it to happen. He'd seen it in her eyes when she'd looked at him, in her body language every time he got within two feet of her. He'd been around enough to recognize the signals, even if she didn't know she was sending them.

It was time she did know. He was positive now that she wasn't a married woman. She was free to do what she wanted. What they both wanted. It was time they stopped pussyfooting around and got down to it. Who knew when they'd have another chance? Tomorrow she'd find her father, they'd get this whole mess sorted out and she'd be back to her life in Sacramento. He'd be off to whatever part of the world his job took him next.

Tonight was theirs.

He patted the back pocket of his jeans, where he always kept his store of protection, more out of habit than the need for them. It had been a good many years since he'd felt this kind of earthshaking need. But he'd denied his body long enough. Tonight he was going to do his damnedest to make it pleasurable and memorable for them both.

Valeri would give him something to remember in the future, when he was crawling through the brush in the sultry heat of a forest somewhere on the other side of the world. He liked to think she'd remember, too, and think of him now and again.

Now that his mind was made up, the thrill of anticipation crawled all over his body. He pulled in a deep breath and headed for the shack.

The loud rattle, followed by a thump on the door, jolted Valeri to her feet. She crept across the room, every nerve quivering, until she heard Nat's muffled voice. "Okay, open it up. It's cold enough to freeze my buns out here."

She fumbled with the lock, struggling to get it open. Finally it turned, and she pulled the door open.

"It's cold as hell out there." He strode past her, and she closed the door again, shutting them both in the darkness. She heard the bag he'd carried plop onto the floor.

She wasn't sure she could find her way back to her own bed. The moon wasn't shining directly through the window, and she could see nothing but that small square of glass.

Nat must have hunkered down because she couldn't see him at all. She edged toward the left side of the window, where she'd left her clothes. She took two steps, then bumped into something soft and warm.

She backed up hastily, muttering a low, "Sorry. I can't see in the dark."

"Yeah, that's too bad. We can't risk a light, though, even if we had one. It would show up for miles."

"I guess." She sidestepped around where he stood and felt along the floor with her foot until it hit her pile of clothes. His voice halted her, making her skin tingle.

"Where are you?"

Her own voice shook a little when she answered him. "Over here, in the corner. I thought it would be warmer."

"Hold still, I'll bring my stuff."

Her heart thumped. "Your stuff?"

His voice was much closer when he spoke again. "We'll be warmer and a good deal more comfortable if we combine the clothes and make one bed."

What he said made sense. After all, it was no different from sleeping with him in the motel room. Except this bed would be a lot narrower. They'd have to sleep practically in each other's arms. The thought made her mouth go dry.

"All right," she said, wishing she didn't sound so nervous. After all, except for that brief kiss in the motel, he hadn't made a pass at her. Even if he did, she felt certain she could handle the situation. He'd said himself he wouldn't force himself on a woman. She believed that. So why was her heart pounding hard enough to put a hole in her chest?

He bumped against her, and she had to make herself breathe again. When he spoke, his voice was at waist level. "I don't know how good this will be in the dark, but we'll make the best of it."

He was shuffling around at her feet, and she stooped to help him spread out the clothes. His hand brushed hers, stopping her heartbeat. Her eyes were adjusting again to the darkness. She could just about make out his outline. His rugged profile looked less forbidding now that the edges were softened by the shadows.

Her heart skipped another beat. The sense of yearning came from nowhere, quickly escalating into an urgent need. She wanted to touch his face, to hold it in her hands. She wanted, in the worst way, to fasten her mouth to his and never let go.

She wanted to feel his hands on her, to feel his body covering hers. She wanted to have him inside her, to know what it was like to be loved by this man. If only he would touch her....

He shifted his body and sat down. His face was a blur now; she couldn't make out any of his features. Her mouth felt dry, her palms damp. If she didn't move away from him, she thought frantically, she'd do something really stupid.

"Come here."

The soft command froze her.

"Valeri?"

She forced her lips to move. "Yes?"

"Come and sit down here, next to me. It's not a feather bed, by any means, but I've slept on worse."

She had to get a grip on herself. She couldn't let him know how he affected her. She patted around with her hands, then edged herself onto the makeshift bed until her arm touched his.

She cleared her throat. "I...I'm not sure I'll be able to sleep on an empty stomach."

"We don't have to."

She heard the rustle of paper, then he said, "Hold out your hand."

She did so. His fingers touched hers, and he laid something cold and hard in her palm. "I picked these up when I was in the store."

"What is it?"

"Granola bar. When you've been in as many primitive places as I have, you learn to be prepared."

For some reason she seemed to have lost her appetite,

but she unwrapped the treat anyway, and bit into the crunchy bar. She had to admit, the chewy, nutty flavor was wonderful. Taking tiny bites to make it last, she finished the whole thing in silence.

"Thank you," she said, brushing the crumbs from her chest. "Now I feel better."

"Want another one?"

"Please."

He handed her a second bar. "I think it's time you filled me in on everything you've remembered."

"There's not a whole lot more." She unwrapped the bar and took a bite, doing her best to concentrate on what she knew. "I don't know anything about the fuel project Alex is working on. He doesn't talk much about his work. All I know is that he called me two days ago, shortly after I got home from the office. He said there'd been some trouble at the lab. That someone had stolen some important disks and he'd had to get them back."

"Did he say anything about the murder?"

She hesitated, then decided it was a little late to start worrying about trusting him again. "He said one of his assistants had been shot and he'd been framed for the murder. That's why he couldn't go to the police. He'd stolen the disks back during the night, but he'd been hurt while trying to get away."

"From Sabhad."

"Alex didn't say so at the time, but I guess it must have been. He told me his shoulder was injured and he'd smashed his glasses. He said he'd had to abandon the car and that it had taken him all day to get to this gas station. He asked me to come and get him."

"Did he say anything about Sabhad?"

"Only that I was not to trust him." Valeri took another bite of the granola bar, chewing it slowly before swallowing it. "He told me I was to talk to no one, especially the police. He told me not to trust anyone. But especially not

Sabhad. I asked him who Sabhad was, but he said he'd tell me everything when I got here."

Nat sounded tired when he said, "Sabhad must have called the organization early that morning, after your father had stolen back the disks. It took me four hours to get out there. That would have given Sabhad plenty of time to morph the pictures of you onto his own."

"But what I don't understand is where he got pictures of me."

"From your father?"

"Could be, I guess."

"Anyway, I drove straight back to town to find you."

"And meanwhile Alex called. I was on my way to him when you got there."

"You must have realized I was following you."

"I did." She closed her eyes briefly, remembering her terror when she realized the Volvo had been on her tail since she left Sacramento. "I saw you on the freeway, jumping lanes. It irritates me when people do that. That's how I noticed you. Then, when I was almost into Carson City, I saw you again. I might not have noticed you even then, if it hadn't been for the warning my father gave me. I was on the lookout for someone following me."

"If I'd known that, I'd have been a good deal more careful. I thought you were taking off to meet someone." He paused, and she heard the rustle of paper again. "You took me by surprise when you shot off the road into the desert."

She shuddered. "I didn't know what else to do. I thought if I could outrun you without lights, I'd lose you. The last thing I remember is the ground spinning away from me."

"Then I had to put you through it all again when I turned over my car today."

"Well, one good thing came out of it. I got my memory back. Though what good will it do us if we can't find Alex?" Her voice faltered, and she cleared her throat.

"We'll find him. He can't have gone far."

"Unless he's hitched a ride back to Sacramento."

"Then we'll find him there."

"I just wish I knew he was all right."

She felt Nat move, shifting his position. "Try not to worry. You'll be surprised how much better things will look in the morning when you've had a chance to rest."

"I hope so." She folded her wrapper and laid it on the floor. "Right now everything seems pretty bleak. Alex is missing, wanted for murder, hunted by the police and Sabhad."

"We're not much better off."

She sighed. "I have to tell you, Nat, reassuring people is not your strong suit."

"Sorry. I believe in facing the facts. It's the best way to deal with them."

A cold draft wafted across her shoulders and she shivered.

"Cold?"

Nat's husky voice sounded close to her ear. His arm closed around her shoulders, and her heart started thumping again. "It's so drafty in here," she said, trying to sound matter-of-fact.

"I know. That's why we have to stick together."

He pulled her against his chest, and she forgot about being cold. His fingers stroked her cheek, then, very gently, he lifted her chin.

When his lips found hers it seemed the most natural thing in the world. She knew she'd been waiting for this moment—longing for this moment—ever since he'd kissed her in the motel.

She melted against him, reaching up to clasp her hand behind his neck. Her fingers tangled in his thick hair and the heat raced through her veins when he nudged her mouth open.

His chin felt scratchy against her cheek, but it didn't

seem to matter. The bare boards bit into her shoulders when he eased her down onto the floor. She was oblivious to the pain. All that mattered was his mouth on hers, and the pressure of his body setting fire to her soul.

His hand moved slowly up her arm, over her shoulder, then down to her breast. She tensed.

"Valeri."

His voice was a sensual whisper in the darkness. She tried desperately to relax. She wanted this. Her mind wanted this. Why was her body fighting it?

"It's all right, Valeri. I won't hurt you, I swear. I'll take it easy. I won't do anything you don't want me to do. Just relax."

More than anything in the world, she wanted to relax. She wanted to enjoy what was happening. She wanted to be free of all her inhibitions and just make love with total abandon. Just once she wanted to throw away everything she'd ever been taught, and drive this man out of his mind with wild, unbridled passion.

She forced her muscles to ease their tension. Eagerly she sought his mouth, deliberately arching her back to thrust her breasts against his chest.

His fingers closed around her arm. How she loved the way he kissed. Persuasive, persistent and so in command, it was the most exciting sensation she'd ever known. She could love this man, if only—

His hand moved to the buttons on her shirt. Her fingers curled in his hair. She wanted this. She wanted him to touch her. Her body longed for him to touch her.

She felt the buttons give, one by one, while his mouth traveled down her neck. His voice, thick and husky, seemed to come from a long way off as the blood pounded in her head.

"You are beautiful, Valeri. I want to see you, to hold you, to kiss every inch of your gorgeous body."

His lips touched the curve of her breasts, while his hand

slid inside the opened front of her shirt and moved to her back.

With an expert flick of his fingers he unsnapped her bra.

No. She couldn't do this. It was no good, she just couldn't. She should never have let him get this far—

"What's the matter?"

She pulled away from him, clutching the edges of her shirt together in front of her. "I'm sorry. I just don't think we should be doing this."

"Valeri, I have protection, if that's what you're worried about."

"It isn't that. I'm sorry." She was perilously close to tears. She scrambled to her feet, fastening her bra as she did so. "I didn't mean to let you think—"

"What did you mean?" His breathing was harsh, his voice brittle.

"I'm sorry, you don't understand...."

"Try me."

She turned her back on him, blinking back tears. How could she explain to him something she didn't understand herself? This wasn't Dan, with his clumsy attempts to get her aroused. This man was everything she'd ever fantasized about...experienced, gentle and considerate.

Why couldn't she go through with something that promised to be the most incredible experience of her life? Why did she have to let that wonderful feeling get lost in a stupid maze of panic and guilt? It wasn't fair. It just wasn't damn fair.

"Valeri, if it was something I did...."

Her embarrassment and frustration got the better of her. Her tone was clipped when she said, "Forget it, Nat. I just can't sleep with a man I'm not ready to trust. That's all."

The pause seemed to go on and on, while she listened to the steady thump of her heart.

Then Nat said steadily, "I see. My mistake. I apologize for misreading the signals."

She pressed her lips together so hard they felt numb. She wanted to tell him that it wasn't his fault. That he was the most exciting man she'd ever met. That his touch could set her soul on fire, and his kiss could make the world and everything that was wrong in it disappear.

She wanted to tell him that she hated herself for not being able to respond the way she wanted to, for not being the woman he thought she was. She might have even found the courage to tell him, if he hadn't chosen that moment to say, a little stiffly, "Let's get some sleep. We both need some rest. You can lie down here. I won't touch you again. That's a promise."

She started to say awkwardly, "I'm sorry—"

He cut her off. "You don't have to apologize. It was my fault. I should have known better. Now get some sleep."

The moment had passed, and it was too late to say anything now. In a way, she was glad she hadn't tried to explain. Now he would never have to know that she was frigid.

She slept little that night, torn between worrying about her father, and wondering how she was going to face Nat in the morning. She was conscious of his warm body next to hers, alert to every movement that he made.

A dozen times she silently berated herself for letting things go too far before she called a halt. The problem was, Nat could do things to her that just blew her mind, making her forget everything except sheer pleasure.

She knew she'd wounded his pride. That hurt her more than anything. It was the last thing she had intended to do. Until now, she hadn't thought it was possible to get through that thick hide of his. But in one area at least, like most men, Nathan Thorne was vulnerable. He would probably never forgive her.

She finally drifted off to sleep, and awoke sometime later to find Nat shaking her gently on the shoulder.

"It's almost light," he said when she opened her eyes.

"I'd like to get off the road and out of sight before the sun gets too high."

She groaned as her sore muscles reminded her of yesterday's hike. "We're not going mountain climbing again, are we?"

"No, we'll stick close to the road. It's only a couple of miles, and we should be in town before Sabhad's men can wipe the sleep from their eyes."

He turned his back on her and went to the window, rubbing at the dusty pane before peering through. He wore the clothes he'd bought at the store: a yellow T-shirt that stretched tight across his shoulders, and black jeans. "It's all clear to use the bathroom before we leave—if you want to go first." He sounded brusque, the way he had the first day he'd forced her into his car.

Miserably, she busied herself with the task of gathering up the clothes. She reached for her chinos, and as she did so something caught her eye.

She moved closer, her pulse quickening as she read the letters scrawled on the wall. It had been too dark to see them last night, but with the first rays of the sun already creeping through the window, the inscription jumped out at her.

Forgetting the tension between them, she turned to Nat. "Look what I've found."

He gave her a cursory glance, as if reluctant to look at her. She pointed to the wall, and waited while he peered closer to study the scratches.

In a puzzled voice, he read the words out loud: "'Tinkerbell. Gone into town for POP.'" He looked back at Valeri. "So?"

Valeri smiled. "Tinkerbell is what Alex used to call me before he left us. He used to read *Peter Pan* to me every night."

Nat raised his eyebrows and looked back at the wall.

"Look at the word *POP*. It's spelled out in capitals. It's what I call him, sometimes."

Nat's gaze came back to her face. Her smile faded at the cool expression in his eyes. "It looks like our search is almost over. All we have to hope now is that he waited long enough in Sylvan Springs for you to catch up with him."

There was such a sense of finality in that flat statement that she felt like crying. She scolded herself as she visited the bathroom. Nat was the kind of man who would never belong to any woman. She couldn't lose something she'd never had. Even so, she knew it would take her a very long time to get Nathan Thorne out of her system. Maybe forever.

Chapter 9

He had no idea why Valeri was sending him mixed signals, Nat mused, as he led the way across the rough, dry ground with one eye on the distant road. He must be losing his touch. It had been a long time, sure, but there was no way he could have mistaken that look in her eyes. He'd seen it too often.

What had she called him? An *itinerant.* The word had a sordid ring to it.

One thing was for sure. It would be a cold night in hell before he tried anything like that again. There were too many women around to waste regrets on one who didn't know what she wanted. She could send him all the hot looks she liked. She wasn't going to burn him again.

He looked back at the road, squinting against the shimmering haze of sunlight. They were skirting the highway by about half a mile, but the flat, bare terrain made them easy to spot if anyone cared to look hard enough. He knew, full well, that if Sabhad's men came charging at them across the desert in their big machines, he and Valeri wouldn't stand a chance. There was just nowhere to run.

In the distance he could see the sun glinting on low-lying buildings. Sylvan Springs was a very small town—which again would make them easy to find. Actually, it also would make Alex Forrester easy to find. Nat felt surprised that Sabhad hadn't picked him up already.

Or maybe he had. That could be why he'd not seen any sign of Sabhad's men since yesterday morning. He glanced over his shoulder at Valeri, who trudged a little way behind him in the hot sun, her face flushed and grim.

He paused, waiting for her to draw level with him. "Not long now," he told her, nodding at the glimmering buildings. "Think you'll make it?"

She flicked a glance at him, then away. "I'll make it."

He felt sorry for her. She obviously wasn't used to this kind of trekking over rough ground. It had to be telling on her. She was limping slightly, and he didn't know if it was from the car wreck yesterday, or if the ridiculous canvas shoes she wore had rubbed a blister in her heel.

Either way, there wasn't much either of them could do about it until they reached town. She'd probably be thankful to see the last of him.

Even so, he intended to stick with her until she found her father and got this mess straightened out.... He was the one who'd screwed things up for her. If he hadn't stepped in and whisked her off in his car, she might have been reunited with her father days ago. Now it was up to him to see that they got back together again.

After that, once he knew where Sabhad figured in this, he'd chalk it all up to experience and be on his way. One thing he was pretty sure about: Sabhad wasn't going to pay him for taking off with his bait. Not that he cared if he ever saw that bastard again. All he wanted now was to satisfy himself that he'd done everything he could. Then he could leave and forget the whole damn thing.

He could forget most of it, anyway. Once more he glanced at the slender woman struggling along gamely by his side. Something told him it would take longer than he cared to think about to forget Valeri Richmond.

She was limping badly by the time they reached the outskirts of town. Nat would have preferred to leave her while he checked out a few places, but he wasn't sure she'd be any safer there alone. In any case, he was sure she'd refuse to let him go in by himself.

Now that they were actually in the town, she was in a real hurry to search the place. "He's probably in a motel," she said, doing her best to speed up her uneven stride.

"We have to take it easy," he told her, understanding her impatience. "First you need to take care of that foot."

She scowled down at it. "It's only a blister. It will heal."

"Not for a long time if you don't get a bandage on it. Look, there's a drugstore across the street. I'll get you something."

"I have some money left." She started across the road, and he almost smiled at her show of independence. Suddenly a black car eased around the corner, and he tensed, ready to dash across the street and throw her to the ground if need be. But he relaxed when he realized the driver was an elderly woman with white hair.

Valeri disappeared inside the drugstore, and Nat took his time following her. When he got there, he heard her asking a man behind the counter if he'd seen her father.

The assistant, his deeply grooved face creased in a perpetual frown, listened while she described Alex Forrester.

"There was a fella in here a couple of nights ago," he said when she paused for breath. "Could have been your father. Bought some painkillers and a pair of them magnifying glasses, as I recall."

Nat watched Valeri's face light up. "Did he say where he was staying?"

The man shook his head. "Ain't that many places to stay

around here, anyways. A couple of motels, or a room one of the townsfolk rent out, maybe. That's about it, I reckon. Don't get many visitors in these parts. Most folks camp out at one of them campgrounds. Otherwise they're in Reno, or Tahoe."

"Well, thank you, anyway." Valeri took the small white bag from him and handed over her money.

"Whereabouts are these motels?" Nat asked pleasantly.

The man peered at him over rimless glasses. "Well, there's the Cactus Motel down the road a ways—give you a room real cheap, I reckon. Though if it were me, I'd be inclined to go to the other end of town. The Sunset Inn. Friend of mine runs it. Tell him Jim sent you, he'll give you a good rate."

"That's very kind of you. Thank you." Valeri turned to go, but the man stopped her with his next words.

"Funny thing, someone else was asking about your father a couple of days ago, if that's the same guy. Sounds like it, from the description."

Valeri's face turned white, and Nat said hurriedly, "Probably friends of ours. We're all supposed to meet up here for a reunion."

"Ah, that explains it." The man nodded, smiling at Valeri.

She managed to smile weakly back at him and hurried out of the store.

Nat lifted his hand in a gesture of thanks, and strolled out after her.

"It must have been Sabhad's men," she said in a low urgent voice when he reached her. "What are we going to do?"

"Go on looking for him. They didn't find him or they wouldn't still be looking for us."

"I hope you're right." She looked scared and flung a look over her shoulder.

More to distract her than anything, Nat took the bag out

of her hand. "I hope you got some antiseptic for that blister," he said, opening up the bag to look inside.

"I did. Now all I need is somewhere I can take off my shoe."

"How about there?" Nat nodded at a one-story building with a sign that advertised breakfast for less than five dollars. Faded yellow checked café curtains hung in the murky windows, and the walls were in desperate need of a coat of paint. Cheap and cheerful, Nat thought. As long as it was clean inside, and he could get some hot coffee, he didn't really care.

Valeri looked at the building without much enthusiasm. He could tell she'd rather be down the road looking for her father.

The problem was, he figured the chances of finding Alex Forrester right now were pretty slim. She'd be able to deal with that a lot easier if she had some food inside her.

"I don't know about you," he said, stepping out into the street, "but if I don't get something in my stomach soon, I'm going to die of malnutrition. I'll order breakfast while you fix your foot."

She followed him with obvious reluctance. "I'm not hungry."

"Eat anyway. It could take a while before we find your father."

She sighed. "All right. I guess we would think better on a full stomach."

"I do everything better on a full stomach."

He hadn't meant that to sound the way it did. She sent him a look that clearly said she wasn't interested. As if he didn't know that already.

The smell of fried bacon reached his nose the minute they pushed open the door, jangling a bell somewhere in the rear of the dining room. He followed her into the restaurant, his stomach growling in anticipation.

The place was empty except for a surly-looking man who

sat at a table near the window. He looked up as Valeri limped in, then looked her over with an insolence that balled Nat's hands into fists.

He fought the urge to shut the man's eyes with his knuckles. Instead, he deliberately moved between him and Valeri, blocking the man's view. "Still serving breakfast?" he asked. He'd kept his voice pleasant, but he put all his antagonism into his eyes.

The man dropped his gaze, shuffled the newspaper he'd been reading into a clumsy pile and got to his feet. "What'll it be?"

"Breakfast for two." Nat glanced at Valeri. "Eggs and bacon all right?"

She nodded.

"Pancakes?"

"No pancakes," the man muttered. "Just hash browns."

"That will do. And coffee." Nat led the way across the room to a table at the back that still afforded him a view of the street between the bedraggled curtains.

He pulled out a chair and sat down.

Valeri hesitated, looking around the room. "Can you see a bathroom anywhere?"

"It's probably out back. I'll ask Sunshine when he comes back."

For a minute there, he thought she was going to smile. She sat down, wincing as she settled herself on the chair.

"Still sore, huh?"

She flicked her glance across his face. "I've collected a few bruises lately."

He felt uncomfortable, aware that it was his fault. "You'll need to soak in a hot tub. Does wonders for sore muscles and bruises."

She didn't answer him.

Her silence hit a nerve. After all, she'd been the one sending him the wrong signals, dammit. He was only human. Despite all his efforts to keep his thoughts to himself, he said a little testily, "We're not going to get far if you intend to keep me at arm's length with that holier-than-thou attitude. We need to work together on this thing."

"I wasn't aware I had any kind of attitude. I'm worried about my father and I'm anxious to find him, that's all."

He waved his hand in the air in exasperation. "We've got to eat. You said yourself that we'd do better on a full stomach."

"I know I did. I'm just not sure I can eat."

"Well, try."

She looked at him the way a schoolteacher looks at a rebellious student. "Do you bully every woman you meet, or are you just trying to be obnoxious because of what happened last night?"

That hurt. He leaned forward, keeping his voice low. "What happened last night was as much your fault as mine. How was I to know you were going to blow hot and cold? Was it my fault you couldn't make up your mind what you wanted?"

A red stain spread over her cheeks. Her magnificent eyes glittered with fire. She lifted her chin and leaned forward until their noses were almost touching. In a low, furious voice, she muttered, "Oh, isn't that rich. You abduct me on the steps of a hospital, where I wouldn't have been in the first place if it wasn't for you. Then you almost get me shot—"

He opened his mouth to protest, but she gave him no chance to speak.

"—As if that wasn't enough, you charge all over the mountains in that pile of junk you have the nerve to call a car until I'm covered in bruises, you tie me up to a bed all night, you nearly kill me when you finally wreck the stupid car—"

"Wait a minute—"

"Then you drag me on foot all over another mountain until I'm ready to drop and then—"

"Hey, I—"

"And then," she said fiercely, "you expect me to be panting to make love to you on bare floorboards that haven't seen a mop since the turn of the century."

He was gathering all his forces to deliver a knockout retort when, above his head, someone cleared his throat.

Nat sat back and met the accusing eyes of their waiter, who stood with a steaming mug of coffee in each hand, obviously having been witness to Valeri's entire tirade.

Nat did the only thing he could do under the circumstances. He looked the man in the eye, shrugged and said, "Hey, at least I offered her protection."

Not a muscle in the guy's face moved. He put the coffee down, muttered something about their order and lumbered off to the kitchen.

Nat looked at Valeri.

Her face was scarlet, her eyes mirroring her embarrassment. "You are unbelievable," she said in a hoarse whisper.

He couldn't help it. He felt the grin tugging at his mouth and gave in to it. "The poor guy looks as if he could use a little excitement in his life. He's probably back there right now, scribbling it all down for future reference."

The resentment in her eyes slowly died. Her mouth twitched. "He doesn't look the type."

"To use protection?"

"To play swashbuckler in the mountains with a captured maiden."

"Ah." His grin widened. "You have to admit, things got a little exciting."

"That's a tad more excitement than I care to deal with."

Her reluctant smile warmed him far more than the coffee could ever do. "Come on, admit it," he said softly. "You'll miss me when this is all over."

The smile stayed on her face, but he was pleased to see

a hint of regret in her eyes. "Don't push your luck, Mr. Thorne."

He held her gaze for a long moment, then offered her his hand. "Truce?"

She smiled and clasped his fingers. "Truce."

He held her hand in his for as long as he dared, then reluctantly let her go. He watched her pick up her coffee and breathe in the fragrance before taking a sip.

"You know," she said, setting down her mug, "as much as I hate to admit it, I really think Alex is going to like you."

Pleased with the comment, he said lightly, "He's not going to be too happy to hear that you could have been here two days ago if I hadn't abducted you."

"I think he'll forgive you, under the circumstances."

"I hope so. I know I'm going to like him. Any man who can father a woman like you is my kind of man."

"I'll take that as a compliment."

"It's meant as one."

She met his gaze. Although the smile still lingered on her face, there was a certain reservation in her eyes now that hadn't been there before. He felt sad. He had the feeling she'd decided to stay on her side of the line from now on. He was going to miss those hot invitations in her eyes.

When the food arrived, they fell into a comfortable silence, which lasted while they ate. The breakfast was surprisingly good, although the service could have been a little more gracious. Their disagreeable waiter slapped plates down as if he couldn't wait to see the back of them, and studiously ignored their empty coffee mugs.

Nat cleaned his plate, and was happy to see Valeri do the same. He hoped the meal had improved her well-being as much as it had his.

The bathrooms, it turned out, were outside the restaurant, and he waited for her, leaning against the wall in the sunshine. When she emerged, she appeared to be walking a little easier.

He would have to do something about a car, he thought as they set off down the road toward the motel. It was doubtful he'd find anything to rent in this one-horse town. He'd probably have to buy an old heap and hope it would get them back to Sacramento.

Remembering Valeri's comment about the Volvo, he almost smiled. She wasn't going to be too happy with his next purchase, either. He never spent much money on cars. Most of his traveling about was done overseas, and he was used to making the best of whatever transport was available at the time.

They reached the first motel, and Valeri would have rushed inside if Nat hadn't stopped her with a hand on her shoulder. "Wait a minute, we've got to be careful. They could have been Sabhad's men asking about your father, but they could also have been the police. We can't just go in and ask if Alex Forrester is registered here. The others could have left word to contact them if anyone asks for him. In any case, it's doubtful he'd use his real name."

She looked up at him with a helpless expression, reminding him potently of how good it felt to kiss her. "What are we going to do, then?"

"Leave it to me. I've done this before. Wait for me by the door."

He was happy to see that the receptionist was female and middle-aged. He leaned an elbow on the desk and gave her his sexiest smile. "I wonder if you'd mind helping me," he murmured, his gaze intent on the flustered woman's face. "I'm supposed to meet a client here, and I've lost the guy's card. Can't for the life of me remember his name. I know he was supposed to check in here sometime during the last three days. That's all I do know, I'm afraid."

The woman's eyes took on a glazed expression as Nat leaned closer. "Uh...what does he look like?"

Nat smiled, and propped his chin on his elbow. He let his gaze wander down to the woman's mouth and linger there. A dull flush spread over her sallow cheeks.

"I've never met the guy," he said softly. "But maybe we can narrow it down. How many people have checked in here during the last three days?"

The receptionist reached for a thick bound ledger, and stared at it. "Three people, I guess," she said at last.

"Good. Did you happen to be here when they checked in?"

She glanced at him, blushed again and looked back at the book. "Only one of them. A Mr. Wilkins. Then there's a Mr. and Mrs. Carsini, but I didn't see them."

"Ah. Then how about Mr. Wilkins? How old would you say he was?"

"Oh, he's just a teenager." She looked shyly back at Nat.

He looked deep into her eyes. "A teenager?"

"Uh-huh."

"You're sure?"

"Mmm, hmm. I'm sure. He didn't look any older than my youngest son, and he's nineteen."

"Well." Nat straightened, and gave her one more smile. "I guess I must have the wrong motel, after all."

"There's one down the road." The woman pointed eagerly out the window. "The Sunset Inn. Six blocks away."

"Thank you, ma'am. I'm much obliged." He backed away, still smiling at the receptionist who grinned foolishly back.

Behind him, Valeri said caustically, "You deserve an Academy Award for that performance."

He grinned at her. "Jealous?"

She made a sound of exasperation in the back of her throat and marched out the door.

She seemed subdued as they headed out to the second motel. Nat chatted on about nothing in particular, trying to keep her mind from dwelling on her father. She had begun to limp again by the time they reached the Sunset Inn. She couldn't go much farther without a car.

The desk clerk at the Sunset Inn was younger, prettier and less susceptible than the first woman. Even so, Nat managed to get enough information out of her to confirm that Alex was not at that motel, either.

Valeri did not take the news well. For a moment she looked as if she would question the clerk herself, and Nat gently took her arm and guided her across the foyer to the front door. "Don't make too much of a fuss," he said as he ushered her outside. "We don't want people remembering too much, just in case someone should come in asking questions later."

She looked up at him, and his fingers tightened on her arm when he saw the desperation in her eyes. "Where are we going to look now?"

"Every available room in Sylvan Springs. Just as soon as I buy some transportation."

"He could have gone back to Sacramento."

"He could have. You could call your apartment and see if he's left any messages. Though I can't imagine he'd do that if the police are looking for him."

She looked down the street, her misery mirrored in her face. "I don't know what to do. Even if he's in Sacramento, I wouldn't know where to begin looking for him."

"There's also the question of how he'd get there." Nat shaded his eyes to look down the street. "For what it's worth, it's my bet he's still here in town."

"You think so?"

He heard the hope in her voice and hated himself for putting it there. What he actually thought was that it was very likely Sabhad's men had found Alex and whisked him off to the mansion. That was the best scenario.

The worst was that once Sabhad had the disks back, Alex would be dispensable. Since he was already on the run, it wouldn't be that difficult to dispose of him. The police would simply think he was still in hiding.

Nat couldn't bring himself to voice either possibility. He glanced at Valeri's set face. They had to at least search the entire town. There was still a slight chance that Alex had found somewhere safe to hole up, and was waiting it out until Valeri found him. Until he'd exhausted every avenue, Nat promised himself, he wasn't going to destroy her hopes.

"We passed a garage a little way back there," he said, taking hold of her arm again. "Let's go see if they've got something we can drive that they're willing to part with."

"What will you do about your old car?"

"Collect the insurance, I guess. Maybe it'll be enough to cover the cost of another one."

"I'll have to do the same when I get back to Sacramento."

He felt guilty, knowing it was his fault she'd wrecked her car. He had a lot to make up for, one way or another. Maybe finding her father would help settle the score. Even if he had to go back to Sabhad to find him.

At first Valeri thought the garage was deserted when she walked onto the forecourt with Nat, but then a door in the side wall opened with a loud squeak and a wizened little man came hobbling toward them.

"Morning, folks," he said in a scratchy voice that sounded as if he had a bad cold. "Need some help?"

"I need some transportation," Nat told him. "Where can I find something that's cheap and still goes?"

The old man scratched his white head, looked at Valeri with curious gray eyes, then gave Nat a toothless smile. "How desperate are you?"

Nat shrugged. "As desperate as my wallet can afford."

"Well, I might have something for you. Come on round the back. It hasn't been driven in quite a while, but it should get you wherever you're going."

He ambled off to the back of the building, and Nat looked at Valeri. "You want to wait here?"

"No, I'll come with you." She didn't want to be left alone on the street. She had the creepy feeling that Sabhad's men were waiting around every corner ready to pounce on her.

She followed the men around the building to where a decrepit-looking pickup sat next to a motor home that looked as if it had been partially destroyed by a fire.

"You folks doing some traveling?" the old man asked, his eyes darting to Valeri again. "We don't git many visitors in this town."

"Honeymoon," Nat said, giving Valeri a lecherous wink. "We wrecked the car, and we need something to get us home until we can collect on the insurance."

"Not a good way to start a marriage, I reckon." The old man leered at Valeri, who valiantly resisted the urge to kick Nat in the shin.

"Oh, we've managed, haven't we, hon?" Nat said cheerfully.

The old man chuckled. "Reckon you would at that."

Valeri glared at Nat. "I thought we came in here to buy a car."

"Oh, I ain't got no cars, missy." The man waved a hand at the pickup. "This here's all I got, unless you want that old camper over there. Got pretty well gutted out inside, but it runs pretty good."

Nat strolled over and peered into the shattered window of the camper. "What happened to it?"

"Stove caught afire. Damn fool kids playing around with it. The owners traded it in on a station wagon."

Valeri crossed her fingers behind her back, praying Nat wouldn't take the camper. Compared to that, the Volvo was a luxury.

Nat walked around the pickup and kicked the tires. "What about this one?"

"It runs okay. Rattles a bit, but gets better mileage than that gas-guzzler."

"How much?"

Nat nodded at what seemed to Valeri to be ridiculously high for a piece of junk. "I'd like to take it around the block," he said, peering in through the window.

"Hold on a jiff, I'll get the keys." He rushed off, obviously delighted to have a potential sale.

"It's not much," Nat said, running a hand over the hood, "but it will get us back to Sacramento. That's if I can get him down to my price."

In spite of her worry, Valeri felt like laughing. "Somehow I don't think you'll have too much problem. You could charm the rattler off a snake."

He lifted an eyebrow. "Dare I assume that's a compliment?"

She managed a casual shrug. "Some people might think so, I guess."

He started to answer her, but the old man reappeared, a set of keys chinking in his hand. "You drive," he said as he unlocked the door. He looked at Valeri. "Keep an eye on the place, will you? I don't like to leave it open as a rule. You never know these days."

"Sure." She watched him disappear around the other side of the pickup.

Nat winked at Valeri. "I'll be back before you have time to miss me."

"That could take forever." She watched him climb up into the cab, knowing that wasn't true. She was going to miss him. More than he would ever know.

The engine coughed a few times, then finally caught. Valeri closed her eyes against the choking dust as the pickup lurched forward, then rattled and banged its way out of the yard.

If Sabhad's men knew they'd bought that old wreck, she

thought as she listened to Nat's noisy progress down the street, they'd be able to hear them all over the mountains.

The noise had barely died away before she heard the pickup coming back. It bounced into the yard and came to a shuddering stop. Nat climbed down from the cab, shook his head at Valeri, then waited for the old man to join him.

"That thing's going to fall apart before it gets ten miles," Nat said, handing the keys back to their owner.

"I never said it was in tip-top condition," the old man said, sounding indignant.

"The way that thing runs, I doubt if it was ever in tip-top condition." Nat frowned, his fingers rubbing his chin. "I'll give you half what you're asking."

"Half?" The man's voice rose to a squeak. "It's worth a hell of a lot more than that."

Valeri sighed. For some reason men really seemed to enjoy haggling over car prices.

The old man argued, but he was no match for Nat. After practically halving his original price, he led Nat into his office to sign the papers.

Balanced on a rickety chair, Valeri listened with half an ear as Nat fielded the man's questions. The room was too warm, and smelled of gasoline and stale tobacco. Engine parts, piles of cans, torn upholstery and half-empty cartons cluttered every conceivable space, leaving a small square in one corner for a battered desk and a couple of chairs.

She watched the man scribble on the form in front of him with a shaky hand. Papers littered the desk, falling out of a tray that obviously held weeks of work waiting to be filed.

Idly she glanced at the top sheet. The company logo at the top caught her eye. She leaned forward to take a closer look, and almost choked.

She was looking at it upside down, but there was no mistaking the scrawl at the bottom of the page. She'd often teased Alex about his flamboyant signature. Now she was sitting in this squalid little office, staring right at it.

Chapter 10

Valeri glanced at Nat, who was intent on watching the old man scribble down the figures. There was no way she could see what Alex had signed without being obvious. Unless she could somehow knock the sheet of paper onto the floor.

She leaned forward, pretending to look over Nat's shoulder. He looked at her in surprise when she laid her hand on his back as if to steady herself.

"How much longer, darling?" she said sweetly. "It's awfully warm in here."

"I'm almost done," the old man muttered.

Nat gave her an odd look. "You want to wait outside for me?"

She smiled at him. "I think maybe I will." She straightened, sticking out her elbow as she did so. "I... Oh! Excuse me." She pretended to stare in horror at the pile of papers she'd just scattered on the floor. "How clumsy of me."

She stooped to pick them up, her hands hidden from the sight of the old man, who hadn't even looked up. Shuffling the papers together, she picked out the one with Alex's signature and looked at it. It was dated two days earlier.

Scanning the lines, she realized it was a rental agreement. According to the form, Alex had rented a room at the garage for one week. His scrawl was shaky and totally illegible to anyone who didn't know it, but she had no doubt it was his.

They could have searched for him all week and not found him. And now, presumably, here he was in a room right above her head.

She picked up the pile of papers and laid them neatly back in the tray. When she looked at Nat, he was staring at her with narrowed eyes. She couldn't resist giving him a grin of triumph.

She'd found Alex. That's if he was still here.

She couldn't wait for Nat to finish the transaction. Finally, the doddery old man handed over the keys and a copy of the papers.

It took another five minutes of idle chatter before Nat could finally unlock the door of the pickup again and give her a boost into the front seat. She fought the urge to look up at the window that overlooked the yard. Maybe Alex was watching them right now, she thought with a little surge of excitement.

The smell inside the cab made her wrinkle her nose, and the heat almost suffocated her. In a fever of impatience, she wound down the window and waited for Nat to climb in beside her. Finally he slid onto the seat, still answering one of the old man's questions. He slammed the door, and wound down the window.

"No air conditioner, I'm afraid," he said as he fitted the key into the ignition. The engine sputtered, and then died. Nat swore, and tried again. This time the engine gave a weak cough, sputtered again and caught.

Valeri struggled to keep silent about her discovery until they were safely out of the yard.

Nat looked at her as he pulled out into the street. "Okay," he said quietly, "you want to tell me what that little display was all about back there?"

She grinned happily at him. "I found Alex."

He looked startled. "Where?"

She told him about the rental agreement. "I didn't say anything back there because I didn't know if we could trust that man."

Nat pulled over in front of a real estate office and parked. "I think the old fool's harmless enough. He probably doesn't know who he's got there. I doubt if anyone has been looking for your father in that rattrap. Did he sign his real name to the agreement?"

"It's hard to tell. Alex's signature is impossible to read at the best of times. I didn't see his name at the top."

"He might have paid cash for the room, in which case I doubt that he gave his real name."

"So you think he's safe there?"

"As safe as anywhere, I guess."

She shook her head. "We might never have found him if I hadn't seen that rental agreement. He certainly picked the right place to hide. No one would think of looking for him there."

"Smart move. Now all we have to do is figure out a way to contact him. We can't just go back and tell that old guy we want to see the man who rented his room. He's curious enough about us as it is."

"You think he'll call the police?"

"He just might mention us to the local sheriff the next time he passes through. I'd prefer not to take that chance—at least until I know what's going on with your father."

"I wonder if Alex saw us through the window."

"If he did, he'll have enough intelligence to know that we have to wait for the old man to leave before we can go up there. The old guy doesn't seem to have anyone else working for him, so he'll probably lock up the place when he leaves."

Valeri sighed.

"I hope he doesn't take long. Do you have any idea how I feel, being this close to Alex and not able to go to him?"

Nat patted her hand. "Take it easy. You've waited this long—one more hour or so won't make that much difference."

As it turned out, they had to wait two hours. Nat had parked the pickup down a side road behind a Laundromat, and Valeri insisted on washing all their clothes. She had left Nat to keep watch, and had barely returned with the clean laundry when they saw the stooped figure of the garage owner hobbling down the road to the tavern.

"We'll wait a few minutes," Nat said as he pulled her back out of sight. "He might have called in at the tavern just to pick up something."

Hardly able to contain her impatience, Valeri agreed. They were so close now that it would be terrible to be stopped before they had a chance to speak to Alex.

Finally, Nat seemed satisfied that the garage owner had decided to stay awhile in the tavern. "Come on," he said, propelling Valeri forward with a light hand on her shoulder. "Let's go meet your father."

Heart thumping with excitement, she hurried up the street with him toward the garage. Now that the moment was near, she started worrying again about Alex, wondering how badly he was hurt.

If he was still in the room—and she prayed that he was—that meant that he was too sick to make it back to Sacramento on his own. Which meant that he could be too sick to move. In which case, they would have another problem on their hands.

Nat paused when they reached the forecourt of the garage. "We'll check the door round the back first. If it's locked, we'll try a window."

"What if we can't get in?"

"We'll get in. There isn't a building yet that I haven't found a way into somewhere. This should be a breeze."

She followed him around the back of the building, hurrying to keep up with his long stride. He reached the door and rattled the handle, while she stared up at the upstairs window, unable to see anything beyond the grimy glass.

"It's locked," Nat muttered in disgust. "I might have known."

Valeri watched him anxiously as he prowled around the lower window, studying it before trying to pry it open. It, too, appeared to be locked.

"What do we do now?" she asked him, looking anxiously behind her. The old man might decide to come back any minute.

"We break in," Nat said cheerfully. "The lock is a fairly new one, but it's not a dead bolt." He fished in his back pocket and pulled out his wallet. Extracting a credit card, he slid it between the doorjamb and the lock. After a second or two of fiddling with it, he pulled it out and tried the handle. The door swung open.

Valeri shook her head in disbelief. "Is there no end to your talents?"

Nat grinned. "I've got a few more tricks up my sleeve."

"I just bet you have."

She took a step forward, but he stopped her with a hand on her arm. "Me first. I don't think there's an alarm, and I didn't hear a dog bark anywhere, but you never know."

She fell back and let him step past her into the gloom of the garage. He looked around, his body as still as a rock, then beckoned her to follow him. She stepped inside and closed the door behind her, shutting out the sunlight.

Nat raised his finger to his lips in a subtle warning not to speak. He nodded at the left side of the garage where two parked cars sat in front of a wooden staircase. It led up to a glass-fronted room overlooking the entire area.

His feet made no sound as he moved lightly toward the stairs, and Valeri did her best to creep after him without making any noise. The faint scuffle of her shoes seemed to echo in the vast emptiness of the building.

Nat reached the steps and signaled for her to wait. She felt sick with apprehension as she watched him climb the stairs—each step, it seemed, creaking loud enough to wake the dead. Any minute she expected men to jump out at him, waving guns and yelling at him to put his hands up. Whether she expected Sabhad's men or the police, she couldn't be sure. Right then it didn't seem to matter.

Nat reached the top of the steps and tried the door to the glass-fronted room. It opened easily.

Valeri put her foot on the bottom step, but again Nat signaled at her. He disappeared inside the room, and she waited—hardly daring to breathe—for him to call her up there.

She waited so long that she was on the point of disobeying him and going up to see what had happened, when he reappeared in the doorway. He motioned for her to come up and, forgetting the need to be cautious, she rushed up the steps, almost shoving him aside in her haste to get into the room.

It was a workshop, the long benches strewn with auto parts and tools. There was no sign of anyone in there. She was about to speak when Nat pointed at the end of the room. A door stood slightly ajar. Her heart began thudding with expectation.

She asked the question with her eyes, and he nodded at her to go forward. She did so, stepping only on her toes, until she could see into the room.

A TV set sat on a low table in front of a vacant armchair. A chest of drawers stood against one wall, next to a window—obviously the one that overlooked the backyard. On the other side of the small room, a narrow bed had been pushed up against the wall.

A figure lay on the bed, his left arm flung across his face, his chest rising and falling in the regular pattern of deep sleep.

Valeri made a small sound in the back of her throat, then crept toward the bed. "Alex," she whispered. She touched his shoulder, half afraid that he was unconscious instead of merely sleeping.

The man stirred, mumbled something and lowered his arm. Dark brown eyes raked her face, then his look of despair turned to relief. "Thank God," he muttered. "I was so afraid—"

Valeri bit back her cry of dismay as she knelt beside him. His eyes looked sunken and streaked with red, while a dirty gray stubble covered his jaw. The white shirt he wore was torn and stained with dried blood across his right shoulder, and a large bruise on his forehead had begun to turn deep purple.

"What happened to your shoulder?" she asked unsteadily.

"I got in the way of a bullet. Clumsy of me."

Carefully, she leaned over and kissed his scratchy cheek. "How bad is it? Can you move? Are you in pain?"

She was somewhat reassured by his faint smile. "Right now I feel like dancing a jig all around this damn room. What took you so long? Good Lord, woman, you look as if you've collected a bruise or two yourself."

From the doorway, Nat cleared his throat. "I'm afraid that was my fault, Mr. Forrester. Or is it Doctor?"

Alex lifted his head. "Doctor. And who the hell are you?"

"That's Nat Thorne," Valeri said hurriedly. "He helped me find you."

"How come I've never seen him before?"

"It's a long story," Nat said, coming into the room. "Right now we have more urgent business to take care of. How well can you trust your landlord?"

Alex blinked, laid his head back on the pillow and looked accusingly at Valeri. "Does he know?"

Valeri nodded. "Sorry, Alex, but I didn't have much choice. I needed his help. You weren't exactly easy to find."

Nat moved closer to the bed. "Look, I hate to intrude on your reunion, but I really need to know if we are safe here if the guy who owns this place should come back and find us."

Alex's face creased in a frown. "None of us are safe until this mess is cleared up. I don't think you have to worry about Harry, though. He seems harmless enough, though he does like to ask questions. I told him I needed a room for a few days. I think he accepted my story that I was on the road doing research for a book about small towns. I impressed upon him the need for privacy. Told him there were too many writers out there anxious to steal my idea."

"He didn't ask how you hurt your shoulder?" Valeri exclaimed, remembering how inquisitive the old man had been about her and Nat.

"He didn't see it." Alex waved a hand at the corner of the room where a jacket lay over the back of the armchair. "I was wearing my jacket."

"All the same," Nat said smoothly, "I think it might be better if we get out of here. How badly hurt are you? Can you move under your own steam?"

"Of course I can move."

To Valeri's relief, Alex struggled into a sitting position, wincing only slightly. "The reason I'm lying down is because I'm so damn bored."

He turned his scowl on Valeri. "What happened to you? I left you a message where to find me. I didn't think I was being that obtuse."

Valeri sighed. "We went to the gas station. All we found

was your message saying you'd gone into town for pop. You didn't say where.''

''Not that message. The one I left on your answering machine.''

Valeri exchanged glances with Nat. ''I didn't get it. What did you say on it? Nothing too specific, I hope?''

Alex narrowed his eyes. ''I was careful. All I said was that I had to get my car repaired. This is the only repair shop in Sylvan Springs. Since you were the only person who knew I was in Sylvan Springs—at least I thought you were—'' He shot another accusing look at Nat. ''I figured that message was fairly safe.''

''We're not the only people, Alex. Someone else has been in town asking about you.''

Alex looked alarmed. ''Sabhad?''

''His men, we think.''

''Dangerous man, that. He's already had poor old Simpson killed. Damn near killed me, too.''

Valeri gasped in shock. ''Paul Simpson? Your assistant?''

''I'm afraid so.''

''Why?''

Alex shot a glance at Nat. ''I'll tell you later.''

''It could have been the police asking for you, too,'' Nat said, apparently unaffected by Alex's obvious mistrust. ''They were all over Valeri's apartment when we went back there.''

''Went back there? I don't understand—''

Nat shifted restlessly on his feet. ''Look, Dr. Forrester, we can discuss all this later—''

''Alex. So where do you come into this?''

''Nat's right. We can talk about that later,'' Valeri said, standing up. ''We have to find somewhere safer to take you. Can you walk?''

''If you point the way. Can't see a damned thing without my glasses.'' He waved a hand toward his bedside table where a pair of reading glasses lay. "Those things aren't worth a damn. I found this place by sheer luck." He swung his legs off the bed and came shakily to his feet.

"Have you eaten?" Valeri asked, anxiously taking hold of his arm.

Alex nodded. "Junk food. I got a few supplies when I first got here. Harry sold me some soda. I didn't want to be too visible in town."

"That was good thinking." Nat looked at Valeri. "I'll help you get him downstairs, then I'll go get the truck. You wait in the garage with him until I get back."

"What if Harry comes back before you do?"

"Tell him Alex asked you for a ride. Before the old guy's got around to asking you too many questions, I'll be back with the truck. Just do the best you can."

Valeri couldn't help worrying as she helped Nat support Alex down the narrow wooden steps. He seemed so weak, not at all like his usual robust self. The past few days had taken their toll on him, she could tell.

Once Alex was safely on level ground again, Nat left to get the truck. He had barely gone through the door before Alex said slyly, "Nice-looking guy. What's he do for a living?"

"You don't want to know," Valeri said dryly. "Let's just say he works for himself and leave it at that."

"Ah. I thought as much." Alex tilted his head to one side. "You got anything going there?"

She could feel her cheeks growing warm. "No," she said firmly. "You know how I feel about that."

"You can't let one bad apple sour you on the rest. You have to start taking chances again sometime."

"Oh, is that right? Just like you did?"

"It's different for men. Some of us are better off on our own."

"Yes, I know," Valeri said, with just a trace of bitterness in her voice. "That's the problem."

Alex didn't respond to that, but Valeri had the feeling he understood a lot. She was relieved to hear the truck roaring back into the yard. A few minutes later Alex was safely settled in the front seat between them.

"Now where?" Valeri asked as Nat pulled out onto the road.

"Alex should have that shoulder looked at," Nat said. "Bullet wounds can be dangerous."

"It's only a graze," Alex assured him. "The bullet just nicked me. It didn't go in. Besides, I'd rather not answer any awkward questions right now. I assume the police are still looking for me?"

"As far as we know." Valeri decided she'd waited long enough to ask the questions. "What happened? All you said on the phone was that you were hurt and couldn't drive."

Alex sighed. "It's a long story. Can it wait until I've had a shower and a cold beer? I must smell like a polecat."

"We'll book into the Sunset Inn," Nat said. "It's just down the road."

"Is that safe?" Valeri asked, sending Nat a worried glance.

"We'll book in as Mr. and Mrs. Landers. They're all outside rooms. No one will have to know Alex is there."

"Who are Mr. and Mrs. Landers?" Alex asked, looking confused.

"My foster parents," Nat said, his foot on the brake as they approached the entrance to the motel. "It's a name I use now and again. It comes in handy to have an alias sometimes."

Alex gave Nat a shrewd look. Valeri could guess what he was thinking. Sooner or later, she would have to tell Alex about Nathan Thorne. Right now, though, she was more interested in what had happened to her father since she'd last seen him.

The transfer to the motel room went smoothly. It was still early enough in the afternoon for the parking lot to be fairly empty. Nat booked in, presumably charming the desk clerk in the process, Valeri thought darkly.

He soon emerged from the foyer, holding the keys to a room located at the far side of the building. The parking was in the back, out of sight of the road.

Within minutes they were all inside the motel room. Nat brought in the bags of clothing and tossed them on the bed. Alex insisted on taking a shower, and Valeri had to contain her impatience for a while longer.

"How does he seem?" Nat asked her when the rush of water safely drowned out their conversation.

"Weak, a little irritable—but I guess that's to be expected."

"He needs medical attention."

"I know," Valeri said unhappily. "But the second he walks into a doctor's office with a bullet wound in him the police will be on him."

"How are you holding up?"

She looked up and saw his eyes on her, full of concern. "Better now that I'm enjoying the luxury of a soft couch. After the last two days, I've acquired an intense dislike for anything that remotely resembles camping. I'm with Alex. From now on I take my vacations in a hotel."

He grinned. "You've never looked healthier. The rugged outdoors is good for you."

"I guess, if I want to develop knotted muscles in my calves and a leather complexion. Even my father looked horrified when he saw me."

"I'm sure after what he's been through, your father thought you were the most beautiful sight he's ever seen."

That look was back in his eyes again. She tried to look away, but couldn't. He was like a giant magnet, drawing her irresistibly toward him, in spite of all her misgivings. Right then she would have given anything in the world to feel his arms around her again, crushing her against his warm, powerful body with his mouth hard on hers.

She shivered, and his eyes narrowed. "Cold?"

"Tired. It's been a tough few days."

He smiled, and the tug of tenderness in her heart was almost painful. "You've held up incredibly well. You're a tough lady, whether you want to admit it or not."

She wasn't sure she cared for that comment. It sounded unfeminine. She was quite sure that Nathan Thorne's women were all ultrafeminine—the slinky, sensual types drenched in perfume, wearing painted faces and erotic, frilly black underwear.

The thought of him with other women hurt, and she looked down at her hands. Her nails were torn and she had grazes on the backs of both hands. She could just imagine what her face looked like. Not to mention her hair.

"Valeri..."

He'd spoken so softly that she wondered if she'd imagined it. She looked up to find his gaze on her mouth. Her heart skipped. She had to stop feeling this way about him. She had to remember what he was, and what he could never be. Men like Nathan Thorne were free spirits, beholden to no one.

"You're one hell of a woman, Valeri Richmond."

For some silly reason she felt like crying. "Thanks. You're not so bad yourself."

He grinned. "I consider that a real compliment after all the other things you've said about me."

She looked at him steadily. "That was before I got to know the real you."

His smile faded. "I was kind of hoping that you'd get to know me even better by the time this was over."

She couldn't seem to help herself. That little-boy hurt look was just too endearing to ignore. Deep down, she knew that he was an expert at arousing a woman's sympathy. She knew full well that every time she gave him the slightest margin, she was playing with fire. There was not the smallest doubt in her mind that he would take whatever she had to offer, and walk away without even looking back.

She knew that even if she let things get that far, she wouldn't be able to give him what he wanted. Not emotionally, anyway. And something told her that Nat would not be satisfied with anything less than the real thing. He'd know if she faked it. Just as Dan had known.

In any case, she wouldn't want him that way. If she couldn't be honest with him, then she'd rather not go through with it.

Even so, the part of her that needed him—the part that longed to be able to enjoy making love with him—propelled her to her feet.

"I wish things could have been different, too," she said softly.

His eyes burned, and the excitement winged through her veins. This time she could forget her fears. There was no time to make love. Only to hold him for a little while, and to feel his mouth hard on hers. This time she was safe.

She went to him and laid her hands on his chest. She could see the confusion in his face, and felt bad that she had put it there. She could be making things worse for both of them in the long run, but this might be her last chance of ever being this close to him again.

She wanted his kiss to remember, to hold in her heart in the lonely nights ahead. For as much as she tried to deny it, she knew Nathan Thorne would leave an emptiness that would never be filled.

"I'm sorry," she whispered. "I just want you to know that it's nothing personal."

"I'm glad to hear it. Does this mean that you've decided to trust me?"

She smiled. "Isn't it a little late to ask that?"

His eyes raked her face, full of expectations she would never be able to fulfill. He didn't have to know that now.

All he had to do was kiss her. Just one more time. One last time.

"Valeri," he muttered thickly, "don't look at me like that. Not unless you want me to—"

"I want you to," she said quickly.

His breath hissed out through his teeth. His hand gripped her upper arms as he pulled her roughly into him. The world spun around her, as it always did when he touched her.

There was nothing gentle about his kiss. It was all fire and heat and an urgency that made the blood race to her head. His arousal was swift, hot and hard against her belly, and she felt the familiar panic stirring deep inside her.

She fought it, concentrating on the sweet, rough pressure of his mouth on hers. When his fingers brushed her breast she made herself relax, and felt the first tingling heat of desire.

She tried desperately to hang on to it, reminding herself that she loved this man. *She loved this man.* Even as the startling thought embedded itself in her mind, the rattle of the bathroom door handle shattered the moment.

Nat let her go and moved over to the window, where he pretended to look out. She sank into the couch, knowing that he would need a minute or two to get things back under control.

She had trouble meeting her father's eyes when he walked out of the bathroom, looking altogether different in his change of clothes. "I feel halfway human, now that I've got rid of my caveman beard," he said, his knowing look full on Valeri's face.

She wondered how much he'd heard, or guessed. "Actually I think the caveman look suits you," she said lightly, hoping he wouldn't read too much into the tension that still crackled in the room. "Though I have to admit, you look better in a clean shirt."

"I bought it for when you turned up." Alex glanced at

Nat, whose back was still turned toward him. "I wanted to be presentable at least."

"I'm honored. How's the shoulder?"

"Feels better now that I've soaked it in hot water." He walked over to the bed and sank onto the edge of it. "Now I feel more like talking."

"I was hoping you'd say that." Nat looked composed again as he walked over to the couch and sat down next to Valeri. "I have to admit, I'm itching to know what all this is really about."

Alex gave him a long, searching look. "I'm a little curious as to how you became involved in all this, Mr. Thorne."

"We'll talk about that later," Valeri put in hurriedly. "Why don't you go first, Alex. What are these disks you say were stolen? How does Sabhad figure in all this?"

Alex's gaze switched to Valeri's face. "How do we know we can trust him?"

"I guess you'll just have to take my word for it," Valeri said levelly.

"Believe me," Nat said, "I'm on your side. I have a personal stake in this, too."

Alex wasn't going to be satisfied until he knew more, Valeri realized. "Sabhad tried to have me kidnapped," she said. "I would have been a prisoner in his house right now if Nat hadn't rescued me."

Alex looked grim. "I had a feeling that might happen. I waited all night for you, then when you weren't there by the morning I was afraid Sabhad had waylaid you. I called your apartment several times, then finally I called Sabhad himself."

Valeri gasped. "You did? When?"

"Right before I left the gas station. He told me he had you at the house, and that you would be returned home safely just as soon as I gave him back the disks. When he wouldn't bring you to the phone to talk to me, I guessed it was all a bluff. At least I hoped it was. I decided to lie low for a few days. I figured if you didn't turn up by the end of the week, I'd give myself up to the police. I thought they might have prevented you from coming for me."

He buried his face in his hands for a moment. "To be honest, I didn't know what to think. I was worried sick...." His voice faltered.

Valeri leapt up and rushed to his side. "Oh, Alex, I'm so sorry. I got in a car wreck and lost my memory for a couple of days, then Sabhad's men chased us and we wrecked Nat's car and had to cross the mountain on foot...."

She trailed off when Alex stared at her in horror. "No wonder you've got bruises. Are you all right?"

She gave him a reassuring smile. "I am now."

Alex glanced at Nat. "I guess I owe you a deep debt of gratitude for rescuing my daughter. How did you happen to come along?"

"Alex," Valeri said gently. "Nat was the man Sabhad hired to kidnap me."

Alex's jaw dropped. "But how—? I don't understand."

"I'll explain it all later in more detail. I can promise you though that Nat can be trusted. He hates Sabhad just as much as we do. I'd trust him with my life." She got up and went back to the couch. "Now tell us about the disks."

Alex hesitated for a moment longer, then sighed. "All right. I guess if you trust him, I'll have to trust your judgment. I have developed a revolutionary new process that could eventually replace oil as our major source of fuel. I first met Sabhad several weeks ago, when news of the project leaked out."

"It was deliberately leaked?" Nat asked, leaning forward.

Valeri could see the intense interest on his face, and felt cold. This is what this man lived for—international intrigue, the thrill of danger, the excitement of the chase. He would always live on the edge, and once he was gone she would never know if he was alive or dead.

This was all she would have of him now—the brief wonderful memories of their shared adventure. Soon he would be out of her life, leaving her more alone than she'd ever felt before.

The aftermath of her divorce was nothing compared to what she felt now. It had been more a matter of her pride being hurt when Dan had left. After a while, she'd even admitted to herself that it was a relief to be rid of him.

The thought of losing Nat was something else. No matter what she did in the future, she would live in the shadow of what might have been. If only things had been different.

Chapter 11

"As far as we can tell," Alex said, sliding up the bed to prop himself on the pillows, "the leak was an accident. Not that it was all that secret, but the media got hold of it a little sooner than we wanted. Anyway, as head of the project, I received a call from Sabhad's secretary in Riyadh. He informed me that Sabhad was on his way to the States and would like a personal conference with me. I told him that we weren't interested in making any deal with Saudi Arabia, but he wouldn't take no for an answer. Finally I agreed."

"So you met Sabhad before all this," Valeri said, painfully conscious—in spite of her interest in what her father was saying—of Nat sitting close to her.

"Yes. He invited me to dinner at the mansion. I felt quite honored to be invited there. That's quite a place."

"I know," Nat muttered. "I've seen it."

Alex sent him a shrewd glance. "As I expected, he offered me a very lucrative sum if I would sell him the fuel project. He suggested that it might be in the world's interest if his country developed the technique, since Saudi Arabia was a major supplier of the world's fuel."

"That was pretty arrogant, even for someone like Sabhad," Nat said, apparently fascinated by Alex's story.

"That's what I thought at the time." Alex leaned his head back and closed his eyes briefly. "Obviously they wouldn't want the project developed. I barely kept from laughing at him. Since he was willing to serve me a very nice dinner, however, I kept a still tongue and patiently explained that I could not do something that amounted to treason. I am, after all, a government employee."

"I bet he didn't like that," Valeri said, remembering the harsh voice she'd heard over the speakers at the mansion.

Alex shook his head. "On the contrary, he was very understanding about it. He accepted my decision, he said, and asked my forgiveness for his audacity. He said he was ordered to make the offer by his government, and he would take my answer back to them. We had a pleasant chat, and he was very cordial when I left."

"And you figured that was the end of it," Nat prompted when Alex paused.

"As a matter of fact, I did." Alex yawned. "Excuse me, I haven't slept well lately. Anyway, I didn't think too much about it until the night I was getting things ready to go to Washington. I was checking over the project one more time when I noticed that one of the specs was way off. I started to correct it, and the damn thing blew up on me. Virus. Wiped out everything on my hard drive within seconds."

"The whole project?" Valeri exclaimed. "How did that happen?"

"That's what I wanted to know." Alex's face looked forbidding. "I wasn't unduly worried right then, because I knew I had backup disks in the safe. I ran them, and that's when I knew we were in trouble. The entire program had been altered—completely sabotaged. Any layman could tell from those specs that the project wouldn't get off the ground. It would take months of work to reprogram even if I could remember all the steps, which is doubtful.''

"Oh, Alex,'' Valeri murmured. "You must have been devastated.''

"What about hard copy?'' Nat asked. "You must have notes, tables, graphs...stuff like that?''

Alex nodded. "Half of them are missing. Destroyed, I'd guess.''

Valeri felt sick. "Sabhad?''

"He was behind it.'' Alex shifted higher up the bed. "I figured he'd talked to my assistants and one of them had sold us out. The safe has a time lock on it. Short of blowing it up, you can't open it without the combination. Only three people had that combination—myself, Barrett and Simpson.''

"And now Paul Simpson is dead.'' Valeri leaned back against the couch. "How awful for his family. He had two kids, didn't he? Why did Sabhad kill him? Why do the police think you did it?''

"I'm coming to that.'' Alex looked around the room. "Is there any beer around, do you think?''

Nat got up immediately. "I'll go down to the tavern and pick some up. I'll bring back some sandwiches as well. We can't risk eating in a restaurant. Not that there's much to choose from anyway.''

Alex didn't give him any argument and he left, leaving Valeri to deal with her father's inevitable questions.

"Tough-looking devil, isn't he?'' Alex commented, the second the door closed behind Nat.

Valeri grinned. "You got that right.''

"All right, young lady, what's all this about the guy kidnapping you?''

Valeri briefly explained the events of the past few days, leaving out a few unnecessary details. She didn't think her father would appreciate Nat tying her to the bed, and she didn't want to talk about the kisses they had shared.

She avoided her father's eyes when she mentioned that she had spent two nights alone with Nat, and was thankful when Alex failed to comment.

"I don't understand how Sabhad could have pictures of you," Alex muttered when she told him that part.

"Nat thinks they might have been morphed on a computer."

"Of course. That's why Sabhad was so interested in my family. He asked for pictures, I showed them to him. He must have kept one of them for future use, in case it became necessary. I didn't think to examine them when I got back. I imagine he investigated all three of our families—" he frowned "—I wonder what he held over Simpson to make him sell out his country."

"It must have been something drastic."

"No doubt." He stared moodily at the floor for a moment, then lifted his head. "Anyway, how did you know where to find me?"

After she explained about the rental agreement, he let out his breath on a long sigh. "That was sheer luck," he said, shaking his head. "You could have searched this entire town and not found me."

"Nat suggested that I call the apartment to see if you'd left a message," Valeri admitted. "If I'd done that in the first place, I might have figured it out sooner. We just didn't think you'd take the chance to leave a message where someone else could hear it."

Alex smiled. "You don't give me much credit for being subtle, is that it?"

Valeri got up and went over to hug him. "I didn't know what kind of shape you were in. I wasn't sure you were thinking all that clearly. When did you get shot, anyway?"

"I'll tell you when your fellow gets back," Alex said wickedly.

"He's not my fellow." Valeri went back to the couch and sat down.

"But you'd like him to be."

It was a statement rather than a question, and she didn't bother to deny it. "It would never work out, Alex. Nat isn't the kind of man who could settle down in one place. He's not exactly a one-woman man, and I wouldn't settle for anything less. You know that."

Alex narrowed his eyes. "Not all men are like Dan. Don't make the mistake of cutting yourself off from happiness because of what one man did to you."

She sent him a gentle smile. "So what's your excuse?"

"I just haven't met a woman I want to settle down with. That doesn't mean I've stopped looking."

"I haven't noticed you bringing anyone home lately."

Alex leaned forward. "We're not talking about me, Val, we're talking about you. You have your whole life ahead of you. I just want you to be happy."

She felt tears prick her eyes, and blinked them back. "I know. I am happy. I have my work, and my friends. I have a good life."

"And you're lonely."

"Sometimes. Everyone is at times. Even married women. I know that better than anyone."

"But you don't have to be. Find a good man and settle down. Have kids. Make me a grandfather."

She laughed. "I knew you had an ulterior motive for this lecture. Anyway, I'm going to have a shower before Nat comes back. I can't wait to get back into my clothes and get the mountain out of my hair." She picked up the bag of clothes and headed for the bathroom, relieved for the excuse to end the painful conversation.

She was drying her hair with a towel when Nat returned. The bittersweet sight of him striding across the room, his arms full of grocery sacks and his dark hair ruffled by the wind, created an ache she knew would take a long time to ease.

He'd brought soda and beer, sub sandwiches and a tub of potato salad. He laid them out on the bed, and the three of them enjoyed a picnic, avoiding for a while the subject of Sabhad and the disks.

Nat kept Valeri and her father entertained with stories of some of his escapades, making Valeri cringe in horror at the risks he'd taken with his life.

She watched him as he talked, memorizing every expression, every gesture he made, knowing that this was all she'd have after he'd gone. She would remember this day for the rest of her life, she thought as she listened to Nat describing a remote village in the Thai jungle. She would remember sitting next to him on the bed, close enough to touch him, listening to his deep voice without him ever knowing that her heart was breaking.

When everyone was finished, she cleared up the remains while Nat showered. He emerged from the bathroom wearing the denim shirt and jeans he'd worn the first time she had seen him, his dark hair slicked down and curling the way it always did when it was wet.

Before she could look away, he caught her gaze and winked at her. The intimate gesture made her curl up inside, and she glanced at Alex. He was watching them both with a smug expression on his face.

Ignoring him, she settled herself on the couch again, feeling a rush of pleasure when Nat sat down beside her.

"Now where was I?" Alex murmured, looking up at the ceiling.

"You were telling us how you discovered that the material on the floppies was useless," Nat reminded him.

"Oh, yes." Alex reached for his beer and took a gulp. "Well, as you can imagine, I was in a state of panic. Here I was, due to leave for Washington the next morning to plead for a grant that would put the fuel project into production—and I had nothing to show them. I was shot down before I'd even started."

"So what did you do?" Valeri asked impatiently, as Alex paused for another gulp of beer.

"I called my assistants." Alex wiped his mouth with the back of his hand and put down the can. "I had a strong feeling that Sabhad must have questioned them about the disks, and of course, they both denied it. I told them that I would give them until midnight to tell me the truth. If I didn't hear from either of them, I was going to call the FBI and the CIA to report the theft of government material."

"I bet that got them nervous," Nat said, nodding his head in agreement. "No one likes playing with the big boys."

Alex smiled. "That's what I figured. Anyway, about an hour later Simpson called me. He said he had information about the disks, but wanted to see me in person. He said he didn't trust phones. He wanted to meet me in the lab at midnight. I asked him to make it earlier, since I had a plane to catch the next morning. He insisted that he couldn't be there before twelve. I should have smelled a rat right there."

"It was a trap," Valeri said, beginning to feel a little queazy.

"It was." Alex paused, his gaze on the floor. "I got there around eleven fifty-five. I let myself into the lab with my key card, but decided not to switch on the main lights, just in case. I was crossing the lab to switch on my table lamp when I tripped over something."

Valeri caught her breath.

"Simpson," Nat said, his voice hard.

Alex nodded. "He'd been shot. When I switched on the lamp, I thought at first he was dead. There was blood all over the place and his eyes were wide open and staring. But then he blinked."

Valeri curled her fingers into her palm.

"Did he say anything?" Nat asked, his gaze intent on Alex's face.

"I knelt down by his side, and I could see he was trying to say something. I leaned closer, but he was too weak to make any sense. I said one word to him—'Sabhad?' He nodded...and then he was gone."

"Poor Paul," Valeri muttered. "That butcher Sabhad deserves to die."

"I went over to my desk," Alex said as if he hadn't heard her, "and that's when I saw the gun. It was just lying there, right in front of my chair. At the same moment I heard sirens, and I knew I'd been set up. I figured Simpson must have called Sabhad and told him I was going to the CIA. This was Sabhad's way of killing two birds with one stone."

"You're probably right," Nat murmured.

"Well, I panicked. I picked up the gun, headed for the window and went down the fire escape. There was a Dumpster in the alleyway. It was stupid, I know, but I threw the gun in there, ran for my car and raced out of the parking lot at the back just seconds before the police cars pulled up in front. They never saw me."

"But they found the gun," Nat said, looking grim.

"Yes. They also knew what time I'd arrived at the lab. The key cards record names and times when people enter the lab. Simpson must have let the killer into the lab. The bastard probably waited until he saw my car, then shot Simpson and left the same way I did."

"What did you do after you left the lab?" Valeri asked. "Why didn't you come to my place?"

"And get you involved?" Alex shook his head. "I knew I had to get out of town until I could figure out what to do. I drove around for a while, then realized that by the next morning, Sabhad could be on his way back to Riyadh with my project. I couldn't let that happen. This discovery could change the entire economy of our country. I couldn't let them have it."

''So you decided to steal back the disks.'' Valeri sighed. ''It didn't occur to you to go to the police with the truth?''

''You know how long it takes to get through all that red tape? There was a murder. With all this garbage about inadmissible evidence nowadays, the police have to be careful they don't mess up. By the time they questioned me and I convinced them to search Sabhad's mansion for the disks, he'd be long gone. In any case, the chances of the police believing me were pretty slim. Sabhad is an influential VIP, and they only had my word that Simpson implicated him.''

''How did you get into the mansion?'' Nat crossed his ankles and leaned back as if he were thoroughly enjoying the story.

Alex grinned. ''I must admit, that was a little tricky. But by the time I reached the house in the early hours of the morning, I'd heard on the radio that the police were looking for me for Simpson's murder. I figured that my only chance was to keep Sabhad in the country long enough to prove my innocence. I didn't think he'd leave without those disks. Now I had no choice. I had to get them back. Or die in the attempt.''

''Oh, Alex,'' Valeri moaned.

''You've got guts, Alex, I'll say that.'' Nat glanced at Valeri. ''Just like your daughter.''

Alex grinned. ''She is a chip off the old block, isn't she?''

Valeri made a face at him and his grin widened.

''Anyway, I knew the wall was electrified. Sabhad had told me that. But the gates weren't. Besides, they were easier to climb. I left the car way down the road and hiked up the hill to the house. When I got there, the guard was sleeping. I bopped him on the head just to keep him that way.''

Valeri sat up. This was a side of Alex she would never have suspected.

"Don't look at me like that, Val," Alex said defensively. "I didn't do seven years in the army without learning a few things."

Nat looked from father to daughter, his face creased in amusement. "I get the feeling there's some family secrets coming out today."

"Obviously," Valeri said dryly.

"Anyway, I got over the fence and found the kitchen window over the sink unlocked. It was a tight squeeze, but I got in all right. I had no idea where to start looking for the disks. I have to admit, if I'd stopped to think things through, I would probably never have attempted such a foolhardy stunt."

Nat's concentration was once more centered fully on the man on the bed. "Where did you find them?"

"I got lucky. The very first door I came to opened into an office. There was a computer on the desk, and right there in front of it sat my disks. Unfortunately, while I was checking out the labels to make sure, I dropped my flash-light. I don't suppose it made that much noise, but it sounded to me like a bomb going off. I shot back into the kitchen and went out the way I got in. Not too quietly, I'm afraid. I'd just made it to the gates when all hell broke loose."

"The guard shot at you?" Valeri went cold, thinking of how close her father had come to being killed.

"Right. There were bells going off and lights flashing all over the place. The noise must have revived the guard. Luckily he was still a bit groggy, and his shots went wild. I caught one in the shoulder just as I dropped to the ground. My glasses fell off, but I couldn't stop to find them. I took off down the road and scrambled up the rocks to hide. I knew I'd never get down the mountain in my car without my glasses."

Valeri shuddered. "I'm surprised they didn't find you."

"Oh, they looked. But by the time they discovered my

car and realized I was still up there somewhere, I'd found a good place to hide between two rocks. That's a lot of area to search. They went right by me and never saw me. I worked my way down the mountain, found the gas station, and you know the rest."

"Well, I'm happy that it wasn't any worse," Valeri said feelingly. "You could have been killed."

Alex nodded. "I was lucky, I guess."

"You're not out of the woods, yet," Nat reminded him. "Sabhad's not going to give up that easily. He's already had men searching this town. It's only a matter of time before he catches up with you. We have to get out of here, preferably tonight after dark, and head back to Sacramento."

"I won't be any safer there," Alex said mournfully. "If the police don't pick me up, Sabhad's men will."

"We have to go to the police and tell them the whole story," Valeri said. "Now that we have the disks back, we don't have to worry about Sabhad getting his hands on them."

"There's still Simpson's murder—" Alex shook his head "—it will be my word against Sabhad. I was there, apparently alone with Simpson, my prints are on the gun, and I had a motive. Simpson had stolen my project and I could have been trying to get it back. The fact that I have the disks only makes matters worse. Sabhad could simply deny that I was ever at his house that night."

"But surely—"

"He's right," Nat interrupted. "Imagine what would happen if our police officers accuse a foreign dignitary of murdering a government employee and stealing government property, and then can't prove it? They're not going to take a chance like that."

"Right," Alex said, sliding his legs off the bed. "I've heard too much about innocent men going to jail for something they didn't do. I'm not prepared to take that chance. Somehow I have to prove that Sabhad is involved."

"It seems to me there's only one way," Nat said slowly. "We have to get Sabhad to admit he's involved."

Alex got off the bed and crossed the room to the bathroom. "It would probably be easier if I moved to Brazil." He disappeared inside, and Nat looked at Valeri.

"I think I might be able to pull it off. I'll wire myself with a recorder and pay Sabhad a little visit. I'll convince him somehow that I'm on his side, and with luck I could trick him into saying something that would incriminate him."

She shook her head. "It wouldn't work. You know that Sabhad is far too intelligent to be taken in like that. How are you going to explain why you took off with me right under his nose, and played hide-and-seek with his men for two days?"

Nat shrugged. "I'll think of something."

"No, it's too dangerous. I couldn't let you do that. Alex wouldn't let you do that."

The bathroom door opened on her last words. "Alex wouldn't let you do what?" her father asked, padding back to the bed.

Valeri repeated Nat's suggestion.

As she expected, Alex emphatically turned it down. "I can't let you take that kind of risk for me. Valeri's right—Sabhad would never go for it. He'd figure it out in an instant, and you wouldn't stand a chance."

"Unless..." Valeri murmured, her skin tingling with excitement as the idea took shape in her mind.

Nat gave her a sharp look. "Unless what?"

"Unless I go back with you." She was prepared for an argument, and wasn't disappointed.

Both men spoke at once.

"No way!"

"Are you out of your mind?"

"It will work." She leaned forward, her hand on Nat's knee to emphasize her point. "Think about it. Suppose we tell Sabhad that you've decided to take me back to him, now that you've had time to think things over? You could say that you were suspicious at first because I kept insisting I wasn't married to Sabhad. That part is true, anyway."

"Valeri—"

"Listen to me, Nat. Tell him the guard acted as if he didn't know me, and that's why you figured something was wrong. But after questioning me, you weren't convinced, so you're taking me back to get your money."

"Fine," Nat said grimly. "Then what happens? Sabhad admits he's responsible for the murder, then he just lets us go, right?"

"Nat's right, Val," Alex said, sounding worried. "Even if Sabhad were crazy enough to admit it, he's not going to let you go after that."

"Of course he's not. But what if we set up a checkpoint somewhere, where the police can hear what's going on? The minute they hear Sabhad implicate himself, they can move in and arrest him."

"And how do you get him to admit to murder?"

"You wire me instead of Nat," Valeri said evenly. "If Sabhad wants those disks badly enough to kill, he'll have to make some kind of deal. If he won't do it in front of Nat, he'll have to deal with me."

"Valeri, there's no way I'm going to let you put yourself in that kind of danger," Nat said firmly.

"It can work, Nat, I know it."

"I might not be able to help you if you get into trouble."

"Sabhad's not going to do anything to me until he has his hands on those disks. The police will be there long before that."

"We can't be sure of that."

"Nat's right, Val." Alex shook his finger at her. "Forget it. I won't let you risk your life for me. If anything happened to you, I'd never be able to live with it. No, you're not going. I'd rather take my chances with the police."

"You can't stop me." Valeri lifted her chin. "If Nat won't go with me, I'll go back alone."

"That's ridiculous." Nat surged to his feet and began pacing around the room. "There has to be another way."

"There is no other way." She watched him, willing him to agree with her. "You know it, Nat. It could work. This is my father's only chance."

After a minute or two, Nat halted, and looked at the other man. "I hate to admit it, Alex, but she's right. I guess it could work."

"No!" Alex looked pale as he got to his feet. "What if something goes wrong?"

"I'll take care of her, I swear it," Nat said quietly. "You'll just have to trust me."

Alex looked from one to the other. "I don't like it. I don't like it one bit. Sabhad is evil...he has a lot of men—"

"So do the police." Valeri shoved herself off the couch. "We're wasting time talking about it. Let's do it now." She looked at Nat. "What do you need to wire me?"

"A mike and a transmitter. CB radio. The old guy at the garage probably has what we need."

"Right." Valeri looked at her father, her excitement growing. "We'll take you back to the gas station. It's close enough to Sabhad's mansion to pick up a strong signal. At a given time, you call the police from the call box and tell them you're ready to give yourself up. When they arrive, you tell them to listen to the broadcast. With any luck, they won't have to wait too long to hear Sabhad incriminate himself."

Alex shook his head, his face creased in worry. "What if they won't listen?"

"You'll just have to persuade them—the way you persuade senators to give you a grant." She turned to Nat. "Tell him it will work, Nat. Tell him it's his only chance."

Nat's look of grudging respect warmed her through and through. "Let me know if you ever need a job," he murmured.

Alex still didn't seem convinced. "Mr. Thorne?"

Nat sighed. "The name's Nat, remember? I think we have to go along with it, Alex. I haven't known your daughter long, but I do know that once she's made up her mind, nothing I can say or do will change it."

Valeri sent him a swift glance. He was looking at Alex with a perfectly innocent expression. She had to wonder if he was referring to her rejection of him the night before. But this wasn't the time to worry about it now.

"How long will it take us to get set up?" she asked Nat.

"I'll go down to the garage and get what I need."

Alex glanced at his watch. "You'd better make it fast. Harry locks the place up tight at five."

Nat wasted no time in leaving. The door closed behind him, and seconds later the pickup roared out of the parking lot.

"I suppose you're determined to go through with this," Alex said unhappily.

"Wouldn't you do the same for me?" She had to admit, now that the decision had been made, she was getting butterflies in her stomach just thinking about it.

"Of course I would. But I'm a man. Men are supposed to take care of these things."

She looked up sharply. "Come off it, Alex. You've known me long enough to know that argument will get you nowhere."

"I've known you long enough to care very much what happens to you."

Her face softened at once. "I know. Please try not to worry. I'll be in good hands."

"You must think a very great deal of Mr. Thorne to put your life in his hands."

"I've seen him in action. He's pretty awesome. If anyone

can get one past Sabhad, it's Nat. And I wish you'd stop calling him Mr. Thorne.''

Alex grinned. ''Sorry. It's just that I find him somewhat intimidating.''

She smiled back. ''That's good. Maybe Sabhad will, too.''

She watched her father climb back onto the bed. He tried to conceal the wince when he laid back on the pillows, but she could tell his shoulder was hurting him.

''Let me look at that,'' she said, pulling aside his shirt collar to take a look. She caught her breath when she saw the ugly gash. It had started to heal, but she didn't like the look of the reddened skin around it.

''This settles it—'' she let his collar fall back ''—we go tonight. That shoulder needs attention and the sooner the better.''

''All right, I won't argue anymore. But I want to go down on record as saying that I'm not in the least happy about it.''

She grinned. ''I'll make a note of it.''

Restless now, she was anxious to get the whole thing over with. It seemed like years since she had been living a normal life, going to work every day in her plush new office, coming home to relax in front of the TV.

She wondered if she would ever be able to go back to that complacent life-style. She had a feeling that things would never be the same again, and it wasn't entirely due to her feelings for Nat.

Looking back on the last few days, she realized that she'd actually enjoyed the adventure, even though she'd been scared to death at times. She felt more alive now than she ever remembered, and it was going to be very hard to come down to earth when this was over.

As if echoing her thoughts, Alex said abruptly, ''You've changed.''

She had to smile. ''I'm not surprised. My face is probably black and blue, I've been in the sun for hours without my sunscreen, and my nails will never be the same again."

Alex shook his head. "I don't mean that. I mean *you've* changed. You seem more aggressive, more determined."

"More stubborn?"

"You've always been stubborn."

"Thanks."

"No..." He waved his hand in the air as if trying to think of the words. "I guess what I'm trying to say is that you seem to have acquired a self-reliance in the last few days that I've never seen before. You've lost that vulnerable look you used to have, as if you were afraid everyone was out to get you."

"Everyone is, now."

"That's what I mean. The old you would have crumbled in the face of everything you've gone through. Yet here you are, talking about marching into the lion's den with nothing but a cookie in your hand."

"I don't think Nat would care to be referred to as a cookie."

Alex shook his head in impatience. "You know what I mean."

She relented. "Yes, I do. I feel different. I feel as if nothing can stop me now. Whatever comes along, I can handle it. I guess I have Nat to thank for that. He gave me confidence in myself."

"He must be one hell of a guy."

Valeri colored. "He is. Just don't tell him that. He's got a big enough opinion of himself as it is."

"I think he'd like to hear it from you."

Her stab of pain was swift and excruciating. "Ever the romantic. Forget it, Alex. It's just not in the cards."

"Too bad," Alex murmured. "You two would have been an interesting combination."

"I doubt if interesting would begin to describe it." She tensed as the roar of an engine outside warned her that Nat was back. "Alex," she said urgently, "forget about Nat and me. Please. There just isn't any chance, and I'm okay with that." The door opened just then, cutting off Alex's reply. But Valeri knew by the way he looked at her that he wasn't convinced. Sooner or later he would be, when Nat took off on his next adventure. Now all she had to do was convince herself that she could live without him. That would probably be the hardest thing she'd ever done in her life.

Chapter 12

"I'll have to wire you," Nat said, as he unpacked the small box he'd carried in. "It's awkward to try it yourself."

Valeri's heart quickened. "All right. Where do you want me?"

Nat glanced at Alex. "In the bathroom, I guess. You'll have to take off your shirt."

"Oh, right." She headed for the bathroom, trying not to notice the sudden tension in the room.

"We won't be a minute," Nat muttered to Alex.

"That's okay, take your time." Alex's voice sounded casual, but Valeri could tell he was aware of her discomfort.

She waited for Nat to come into the bathroom with her, then half closed the door. Her pulse jumped when Nat shut it all the way. He must have caught her wary expression, because he said quietly, "I didn't want your father to hear what I have to say."

She pulled a face. "If you're going to stress how dangerous this is, I already know it. I'm not going to change my mind, Nat. No matter what you have to say. So you might just as well save your breath.''

The concern on his face when he looked at her warmed her heart. ''I don't want anything to happen to you. I don't know how well I'll be able to guard you if something goes wrong, or if I have to leave without you. I only agreed to go along with this crazy idea because I was afraid you'd try it on your own. But now I've had time to think about it—''

She went up on her toes and gave him a swift kiss on the lips. ''I'm going, Nat. Now get this stuff on me.''

He shook his head. ''You are one stubborn woman.''

She smiled. ''Yep.''

''And a gutsy one.''

''I don't know about that.''

''Well, I do. Take off your shirt.''

He made a big deal of sorting through the components on the counter while she unbuttoned her shirt. She slipped out of it and laid it on the counter, feeling self-conscious as she met his gaze in the mirror.

''I'll tape the transmitter under your arm,'' he said, showing her the small, flat box. ''I think the microphone will have to go inside your bra so it won't be seen in the neck of your shirt.''

Her heart thumped so hard she was certain he heard it as she lifted her arm for him to tape the box to her side. His fingers brushed her skin and she jumped.

''You okay?''

''Sure. Just antsy, I guess.''

''That's understandable. Just don't freeze on me when the time comes. If you think you can't do it, for God's sake tell me before we go in.''

''I'll do it.'' She could barely speak. His mouth was inches from her shoulder. She could feel his warm breath on her bare flesh, his fingers against her skin. The urge to tell him she loved him was almost irresistible.

Knowing what a mistake that would be, she bit back the words. Nat wasn't looking for love. And she couldn't give him what he was looking for.

"Okay, turn around."

She turned to face him, and his gaze moved down to her breasts. "I guess we can tuck this in here," he muttered, "but I'll tape it to make sure."

She held her breath while he tore off the tape with his teeth, then placed the microphone against the curve of her breast. The back of his knuckles pressed into the tender flesh as he attempted to tape the tiny microphone in place.

She couldn't breathe at all now. Her throat hurt with the effort of preventing any sound from escaping. Nat seemed to be having as much trouble as she was. The microphone slipped and he swore.

"Here," he said, handing it to her, "see if you can do it. I'm used to wiring men, not women. I'm too worried about hurting you."

She let out her breath in a rush and took the tiny instrument from him. After a moment or two she had the microphone secured, hidden just below the line of her bra. "That should do it," she said with relief.

"Good. Now put your shirt back on and let me take a look. That fabric might be too soft to hide the lines. You might have to wear the other one."

"I hope not," Valeri said, wrinkling her nose. "It's not clean."

"This isn't the time to get picky on me." He studied her figure with a detachment that might at any other time have been insulting.

His professionalism reassured her. If she had to do something really dangerous like this, she couldn't think of a better person to have by her side.

"Move around a bit, swing your arms, touch your hair, whatever," Nat murmured, watching her as she did as he asked. "It looks okay. I think you'll pass. Now let's get

Alex and get on the road.'' He opened the door for her and she walked past him into the room.

''All set?'' Alex asked, glancing at Nat.

''She'll do just fine.'' Nat looked at his watch. ''Are we ready?''

''I guess so.'' Alex looked at Valeri. ''You're sure?''

''I've never been more sure,'' she said, giving him a smile.

Although he didn't look convinced, he didn't say any more, and she led the way out the door, praying that she wouldn't freak out and let Nat down.

It was getting dark by the time Nat parked the truck in the forecourt of the gas station. After thoroughly checking around to make sure that there were no surprises waiting for them, Valeri got Alex settled in a corner of the ramshackle building with the cushions and bedclothes she'd borrowed from the motel.

As always, the heat of the summer afternoon had cooled considerably, and she shivered when the damp chill in the air penetrated her shirt.

''Are you okay?'' Nat asked as she straightened from her task. ''You don't have to go through with this, you know. We can always go back to plan A.''

Surprised that he'd noticed her shudder, she gave him a quick smile. ''Just cold, that's all. I'll be fine when we're back in the truck.'' She refused to admit, even to herself, that her insides felt like jelly. The slightest indication that she was losing her nerve and Nat would call it off. She had no doubts about that.

Nat gave her a searching look, then, apparently satisfied, turned back to Alex. ''Okay, we have our watches synchronized. Wait twenty minutes, then call the police. If they leave Carson City right away, they'll be here in about ten to fifteen minutes. That gives us thirty minutes or so to get to the mansion. It should be enough.''

Alex nodded, his face looking pinched in the half light.

"You will take care of my little girl, won't you? She's all I've got, you know."

"I'll guard her with my life," Nat said, reaching down to shake Alex's hand. "I've seen Valeri think on her feet. She's more resourceful than you think."

"Don't worry, Alex." Valeri dropped on her knees beside him. "Sabhad is not going to shoot us on sight. He wants the disks, and he'll need us alive until he knows where they are. By that time the police will be there."

"I hope you're right. I hope they listen to me. I—"

She shut him up with a finger on his lips. "I love you, Pop. Just look after yourself until we get back, okay?"

"I love you, too, honey."

She kissed him on his cheek, then got hurriedly to her feet. "Okay," she said brightly, "let's go do this."

She followed Nat out the door, and climbed back into the truck. Without Alex wedged between them, there seemed to be a lot of space between her and Nat. She would have liked to draw closer, but was afraid he'd interpret that as nervousness.

He looked at her once as he fired the engine, then concentrated on the road while he pulled onto the highway and headed once more for the mountains.

They passed little traffic on the way up, and in record time turned into the narrow road that led up to Sabhad's mansion. Nat said little, and Valeri was content to watch the stars popping out in the night sky. She refused to let herself think about anything.

Now that they were actually on the way, her nerves seemed to have vanished. High on adrenaline, she could feel her heartbeat racing, but apart from that she felt a strange feeling of calm inside, as if she were removed from her body and watching herself from a distance.

It didn't seem all that strange that she was taking part in a dangerous mission. She had lived with danger practically from the moment she had woken up in the hospital with her memory impaired; from the moment she had set eyes on the tough, rugged-looking stranger who had come to mean so much to her.

She glanced at his profile out of the corner of her eye. He sat staring straight ahead, his strong, capable hands on the wheel, his face expressionless. Pretty much as she'd first seen him the day he'd kidnapped her.

It all seemed so long ago now. A million years ago. She had been a different person then, and no matter how much she may hurt after he'd gone, she would always be grateful to him for revealing to her the real person trapped inside her. Her life would be different because of him—because of who she'd become in the last few days.

"You okay?"

His deep voice, coming out of the darkness at her, made her jump. "I'm fine," she murmured. "I'm looking forward to the acting job of my life. I have to pretend I hate you if we're going to convince Sabhad you're bringing me back against my will."

"I know. I intended to go over that with you before we went in. You should have no problem in pulling it off. After all, you've had enough practice."

She glanced at him. "I never did hate you, exactly. I was afraid of you, at first."

"And mad as a hornet, if I remember."

She smiled. "You were pretty high-handed, dragging me off in your car, insisting that I go back to my husband."

"To your daughters," he corrected. "I didn't give a damn about your so-called husband."

"I wonder whose daughters they are. Do you think they're Sabhad's? He must have a wife—from what the guard said when we got there."

"I can't imagine a man like him being the father of those two beautiful little girls."

There was a wistful note in his voice that tugged at Valeri's heart. No matter how much he tried to deny it, Nathan

Thorne wasn't as indifferent as he liked to appear. She wondered again what it was that had soured him on marriage and family life. She would probably never know.

Nat glanced at his watch as they approached the final curve in the road. "We're a little ahead of time," he muttered. "I don't want to go in too soon, in case the police get held up for some reason. Once we get closer they'll hear us coming from a mile off. This damn engine sets up enough echoes to wake the devil."

He pulled off onto a wide shoulder that passed behind a large outcrop of rock. They were practically invisible from the road, unless someone was right on top of them. He cut the engine and the roar shuddered into silence.

As keyed up as she was, Valeri was keenly aware of everything about him. The faint smell of the soap he'd used in the shower...the sound of his breathing...the slight creak of the seat when he shifted position.

The cooling engine cracked, making her jump.

"Getting nervous?" Nat asked softly.

She could see him clearly in the moonlight. He sat watching her, his expression guarded.

"A little."

"Good. I'd worry if you didn't feel at least apprehensive."

"I just don't think Sabhad would kill us in cold blood."

"He didn't seem to have any qualms about getting rid of your father's assistant."

She felt a spasm of fear. "I wonder why he killed Simpson?"

"Probably because he found out Simpson was going to spill the beans to your father."

"Then why did Simpson let him into the lab?"

"I doubt that it was Sabhad who actually did the killing. He doesn't strike me as a person willing to do his own dirty work. Simpson probably didn't know the man sent to get rid of him."

Valeri shuddered. "It must have been a dreadful shock for Alex, to find him like that."

Nat studied her in silence for a moment. "Valeri, you don't have to go through with this. There's still time to change your mind. I can just leave you here and come back for you later."

"I do have to go through with it, Nat. My father's entire future is at stake. I won't see him go to prison for something he didn't do."

"You do understand how dangerous it is? We'll be in Sabhad's house, surrounded by his men. There are no guarantees we'll come out of this alive."

She met his gaze. "I know. But I believe you can handle things until the police get there."

"There are a lot of things that could go wrong. The broadcast might not get through. The police might not want to wait and listen. They might think it's a put-up job to get Alex off the hook."

"And I could get killed the next time I drive around the block," Valeri said stubbornly. "You don't understand, Nat. I love my father. I'd do anything for him. I couldn't bear the thought of him wasting away in a prison cell for something he didn't do. I have to try, don't you see?"

He looked away from her, his fingers drumming on the wheel. When he spoke again, his voice was hushed. "I hope he knows how much you love him."

"I think he does. I like to think it's returned." How she longed to tell Nat that she loved him, too. In a different way, of course, but just as much. No, more. So much more.

The pain had started again, like a cold, hard knot in her stomach. Fate had given her one more adventure with Nat. If they came out of it alive—and somehow she couldn't believe that they wouldn't—then she would have to go on without him anyway. Nat would be gone from her life. This was the very last time she would be alone with him.

She squeezed back a tear, and took in her fill of him,

committing every tiny detail to memory. The way his fingers curled over the wheel. The slant of his wide shoulders in the denim shirt. The way his hair curled slightly on his neck. The rugged lines of his profile, as jagged and harsh as the rocks all around them. The sensuous curve of his mouth, that could be so demanding, yet so very gentle.

He turned his head suddenly, surprising her. It was too late to look away. Too late to alter her expression. His eyes widened, and he stopped breathing.

For a long moment they stared at each other—neither moving, neither breathing. Then, with an abrupt movement, he grabbed her arms and pulled her close, his mouth finding hers in a deep, demanding kiss that drowned out everything except the fiery touch of his tongue flicking hers and the pounding of her heart.

Without lifting his head, he tugged open the buttons of her shirt and slipped his hand inside. She tensed, and tried to draw away from his mouth, but he held her there with his other hand, refusing to let her go.

She felt a thrill of excitement, and made herself relax. This would be the last time. She would not spoil it by resisting him now. She loved this man. She wanted him. She needed him the way she needed air to breathe.

His fingers brushed the curve of her breast, then stilled. She remembered the microphone. He lifted his head and looked deep into her eyes.

"I don't know what it is about you that makes me forget what I'm supposed to be doing," he muttered, his voice husky with emotion. "We don't have time for this now, but one thing I can promise you. When this is over, I'm going to finish what we started here tonight. Count on it. Now let's get this thing switched on."

He kissed her once more, a hard, swift pressure on her lips, then he let her go.

Her fingers shook as she rebuttoned her blouse and combed her hair. So it wasn't over yet. She might have known that a day of reckoning would have to come. They'd been through too much together, started too many fires to walk away without some kind of resolution.

Her body ached for what he promised. But she knew she would only disappoint him. And herself. If the time came...when the time came...she would have to tell him the truth. She owed him that much. She would have to tell him that no matter how much she loved him, she could not respond to him physically. She would have to admit that she was frigid.

It was probably just as well, she told herself as the truck roared along the last few yards of road to Sabhad's mansion. Because even if lovemaking could be good between them, it wouldn't make any difference. This was Nat's life—he lived for the thrill of danger. He couldn't be happy doing anything else.

Either way, she was going to lose him. And it hurt like hell.

The truck was still a few yards away from the mansion when the searchlights sprang on at the gates. The beams swept back and forth across the road, picking them up in a blinding light as they approached the gate. Two guards appeared wearing army fatigues and carrying shotguns.

"Don't forget," Nat muttered, "you hate me. No matter what they do to me. You forget that and we're dead."

Now she was sick with fear. All her newfound bravado had vanished at the sight of those murderous-looking guns. Remembering her father's account of how he'd climbed over the gate with the guard shooting at him, she felt faint.

She sat as if carved from stone while Nat stuck his head out the window. "Nathan Thorne," he said harshly. "I'm bringing back Sabhad's wife."

The guards hesitated, looked at each other, and then one of them went back inside the guardhouse, apparently to call the main house. Seconds later the gates swung open and one of the guards beckoned them inside.

"Here we go," Nat muttered. "Just keep your head and we'll be fine."

Right then, all she could think about was running away. She couldn't do this. She couldn't act as if she hated Nat, not when she loved him....

The passenger door opened abruptly, and a rough hand grabbed her arm. She didn't have to fake her terror. She looked into the cruel face of the guard who stood there, his teeth bared in an evil grin.

"Allow me to assist you," he said unpleasantly.

Her flash of anger chased away the fear. "I can manage myself, thank you." She snatched her arm away from him, and his eyes darkened.

"Why you—"

"I'll take care of Mrs. Sabhad," Nat said, appearing at the guard's side. He shoved the man out of the way and grabbed hold of Valeri's arm. "Come on, lady, you're home."

Valeri flashed him a look of gratitude, and was rewarded by a fierce frown. "Give me any more trouble," he said in a low harsh voice, "and I'll give you a few more bruises."

The guard stepped back, scowling heavily.

Taking her cue from Nat, Valeri lifted her chin. "You touch me again, you disgusting barbarian, and you'll be singing tenor."

"Yeah, yeah, I've heard it all before."

He dragged her out of the truck, and she stumbled. His hand came out to steady her and she slapped it away. "Keep your filthy hands to yourself."

The guard began to smile again, obviously enjoying the byplay.

"Look, lady," Nat said with just the right amount of threat in his voice, "either you walk on your own two feet or I sling you over my shoulder. Take your choice."

"I'll walk." He was so realistic that he was making her nervous. She stalked off in front of him, but he caught up with her and kept her pressed to his side as they went through the door with the guards following close behind.

Valeri gaped at the sumptuous interior of the mansion. The marble entranceway was lit by an enormous crystal chandelier, and thick red carpet covered the wide curving stairway with its gold-tinted banisters. Obviously priceless paintings hung on the walls, and silk brocades and thick velvet drapes covered the windows in the sunken living room where Nat guided her toward a long, low cream couch decorated with gold tassels.

She had barely recovered from her amazement over the opulence of her surroundings when someone loudly clapped his hands. The guards stood at attention as a man entered the room, followed by a smaller man with bowed shoulders and a bald head.

Valeri's attention was riveted by the man who'd entered first. He looked magnificent in white robes caught at the waist by a wide, gold sash. He wore a white turban, and beneath it his eyes flashed dark and malevolent.

His swarthy face was dominated by a hooked nose, and his thick, cruel lips stretched in a smile over even white teeth. He fitted perfectly the western woman's idea of a *sheik*, and would have been devastating in a desert movie. Right now, though, standing in front of him in his own living room, Valeri felt nothing but loathing for the man who had killed, and would kill again no doubt, simply for greed.

"I wish I could say it's a pleasure to see you again, Mr. Thorne," he said in a thick guttural accent, "but after the trouble you have cost me, I would not be telling the truth."

All the time he spoke, his eyes never left Valeri's face. The queazy feeling in her stomach intensified as his gaze dropped to her feet, then slowly moved up her body with an insolence that made her cringe.

Remembering Nat's reaction when the man in the restaurant did the same thing, Valeri hoped he wouldn't make the wrong move. She didn't dare look at him, but kept her gaze on Sabhad.

She needn't have worried. Nat's voice sounded almost bored when he spoke. "I've brought your wife back, Sabhad. I believe you owe me some money."

Sabhad's gaze remained fixed on Valeri's face. "Really. May I ask what changed your mind? The last time my men saw you, you were racing in the opposite direction across the mountains with my wife."

"I am not your wife!" Valeri snapped. "I demand that you let me go at once."

"In my country," Sabhad said, a little too softly, "women do not speak unless commanded to do so."

"Well, you're not in your country now, Buster, you're in mine. And I speak when I damn well decide to."

She was unnerved to see a flash of amusement in his black eyes. "She is spirited, this one. She must have given you a great deal of trouble, I imagine, Mr. Thorne."

"You don't know the half of it," Nat said feelingly.

Valeri glared at him. "You can shut up, too, you ugly bastard."

Sabhad clapped his hands. "Enough! I would like to know why you left so abruptly, Mr. Thorne, and why you decided to come back, after all."

"I was getting to that." Nat's look of contempt was so real that Valeri had a moment of uneasiness. "She kept insisting she wasn't your wife, and at first she was so damn convincing. Then the guard didn't recognize her when I brought her to the gate…I guess I just panicked. After all, I could have been sent down for life if I'd grabbed the wrong person."

"But then she convinced you she was my wife, is that it?"

Valeri's heart thumped even harder. He wasn't buying it. She could see it in his eyes.

"She couldn't convince me she wasn't. I don't know why she's so damn determined not to come back here, but I figure it's none of my business. She's your wife—you fight it out with her. All I want is my money."

Sabhad nodded slowly. Valeri squirmed under that intense gaze. He reminded her of a hawk watching its prey for the right moment to swoop and strike. Any minute now he was going to deny everything. She had to get him to mention the disks. Anything that would incriminate him and bring the police in.

"You know very well why I don't want to be here," she said bitterly. "I'm not your wife. You tried to kill my father to get your hands on the fuel project. You've already killed one man for it. That's why you want me, isn't it? You think my father will trade the disks for me. Why don't you just admit it, you blackhearted murderer?"

Nat sent her a quick glance. "I don't know what she keeps jabbering about. I don't want to know. All I want is what you owe me, and I'll get out of here."

"I owe you nothing!" Sabhad roared, finally turning to look at Nat. "You think I'm stupid? You think I don't know when you're trying to double-cross me? You'll take the money *and* the woman, is that it? Well, you might be clever, Mr. Thorne, but you're not that clever. You try to take her out of here now and you'll both die."

"Now wait a minute—"

Sabhad stepped forward and swiped Nat across the face with the back of his hand. The vicious blow caught him by surprise and he staggered back before regaining his balance. The look on his face gave Valeri chills.

"You do that again," he snarled, "and you're dead."

At his words, both guards brought their shotguns up and aimed the barrels at his head.

"No!" She screamed the word before the thought was

fully formed in her mind. The instant it was out, she realized what she'd done. She could see it in Nat's eyes. Desperately she tried to recover. "I won't see any man killed in front of me," she said quickly. "Not even a bastard like him."

"Save your breath, Ms. Richmond," Sabhad said slyly. "Or may I call you Valeri? Believe me, this *desperado* isn't worth your pity. He'd sell his mother's soul to the devil if the price was right. I have met his type before."

Valeri bit back the hot retort. She stared stone-faced at Sabhad, and prayed for a miracle.

Nat wiped his mouth with the back of his hand. It came away with a bright red streak across it, and he gave Sabhad a murderous look. "Keep your goddamn money. And the woman. I'm sick of her anyway."

He turned on his heel as if to go, but Sabhad raised his hand. "Not so fast, Mr. Thorne."

The two guards crossed their guns in front of Nat, preventing him from leaving.

"Search him," Sabhad ordered.

Valeri closed her eyes as one of the guards patted Nat down thoroughly. Thank heaven she was the one wearing the wire. When she opened her eyes again, the guard was handing a gun over to Sabhad.

"I didn't think you'd come in here unarmed," Sabhad said, tucking the gun in his robe.

So he'd kept the gun with him all the time, Valeri thought, wondering where he'd hidden it. She felt sick, wondering what Sabhad might do to him. All this was her fault. If he hurt Nat, she'd kill the bastard somehow.

"Mr. Thorne, I think it's safe to say that you know about the disks that Dr. Forrester stole from my office. I would hazard a guess that you also know where they are. I suggest that you go back to Dr. Forrester and tell him that I have his daughter in my custody, and that she will come to no harm as long as he is cooperative. He is to give the disks to you, and you will bring them back to me. Once I have them, Ms. Richmond will be free to leave."

Nat scowled. "And what if I can't find Dr. Forrester?"

Sabhad smiled his evil smile. "Oh, I think you'll find him, Mr. Thorne. You see, if you're not back here with the disks within twenty-four hours, then Ms. Richmond will meet with an unfortunate accident. I trust I make myself clear?"

"Very clear," Nat said grimly.

"Oh, and I suggest you don't contact the police. After all, there's that little matter of Paul Simpson's murder. I'm sure the police would be happy to know of Dr. Forrester's whereabouts."

"My father didn't kill anyone," Valeri said hotly.

"Maybe," Sabhad said smugly, "but the police are convinced your father shot Mr. Simpson. It might take him a while to explain how he came to be in possession of the gun. Very stupid of him to throw it in a trash bin. But very convenient for me, of course."

"How did you know—" Valeri began, but Nat silenced her with a warning look.

"I'll get the disks for you, and I'll bring them back," he said harshly to Sabhad. "Not for the woman, but for the money. You pay me double when I deliver or I hand them over to the police."

Sabhad stared at him a long time, but Nat refused to look away. Finally Sabhad said softly, "You drive a hard bargain, Mr. Thorne. You shall have your money." His gaze returned to Valeri. "Meanwhile, I'll keep Valeri entertained until you return." Once more he raked her up and down with his hot gaze. He didn't exactly lick his lips, but the greedy expression on his face left no doubt what was on his mind.

Valeri swallowed. She glanced at Nat, but his expression was hard as he stared at Sabhad. "I'll be back," he said, the threat in his voice evident to everyone in the room.

"I'm sure you will," Sabhad said smoothly. "But just to make sure, I'll send an escort along with you." He clapped his hands three times and a door opened across the room to reveal two husky, dark-skinned men in business suits. They marched across the room and stood one on either side of Nat.

"I wouldn't try anything stupid, Mr. Thorne." Sabhad smiled. "My men are heavily armed and very quick on their feet. One wrong move, and I promise you, they will hurt you."

Valeri's heart filled with terror. Her mind buzzed with anxious questions. Had the police heard the broadcast? How long would it take them to get there if they did? What would happen to Nat once the men found out they'd been tricked? And what was going to happen to her without Nat to protect her?

The fear rose up to choke her. She looked desperately across the room at Nat. He sent her one hard look, as if to reassure her, then strode across the room to the entranceway with Sabhad's henchmen hot on his heels.

The heavy door closed behind them with a thud, and the sound of it echoed in Valeri's heart like a death knell. She looked back at Sabhad, and cold hands of fear clawed at her heart when she saw the lust in his eyes.

"Now, my dear," he said softly, "I have you all to myself."

Chapter 13

The door closed behind Nat with a loud thud, and his blood ran cold. He'd been shut off from Valeri, unable to lift a finger to help her. And he knew what Sabhad had in mind. He couldn't mistake that look in his eyes, those soft innuendos.

The thought of what the man might do to her drove Nat crazy. She wouldn't stand a chance against him. He knew what men like Sabhad were capable of, and it didn't bear thinking about.

Not only that, but if the bastard tried to rip her clothes off, he'd find the wire. Nat didn't like to think how Sabhad would react to that. Valeri's life could be in danger.

He strode across to his truck and opened the door. He couldn't afford to waste much time. He certainly couldn't take the chance of waiting for the cops to turn up. If they turned up at all. He had to do something, and fast. But not here.

He'd wait until they were outside the gates, out of sight of the ever-vigilant cameras. He didn't need Sabhad's entire entourage down on his head. As it was, he was in for a tough time.

Nat settled down behind the wheel and waited for the two henchmen to squeeze in beside him. Their breath smelled of garlic, and their clothes stank of nicotine and a spicy odor he couldn't identify. The man closest to him shoved his elbow viciously into his side, and Nat's skin crawled. It was going to be a pleasure taking care of these two.

He drove out through the gates, and watched in the rear-view mirror to see them close behind him. His mind worked feverishly. How best to do this? Overturning the truck seemed like a good start. They were armed, and Sabhad had his weapon. It seemed as if they had all the advantage, but Nat had learned a long time ago never to leave anything to chance. He still had a few surprises up his sleeve, and he was well aware that he would need every one of them if he was going to survive.

He waited until the first sharp turn in the road. The men were staring ahead, suspecting nothing. He could almost feel the adrenaline pumping into his veins, increasing his heartbeat, his blood pressure, his metabolism. These were the moments he lived for: the seconds before he put his life on the line.

He felt as if he were soaring like an eagle, power flooding his body and his mind. This was life; this was living it to the hilt. He was invincible. He was unbeatable. He was Nathan Thorne.

With those thoughts pounding in his brain, he gave the wheel a vicious twist. The tires shrieked in protest and the truck bucked, fighting the momentum that kept it going one way while the wheels took it another.

The two men let out a startled oath and a gun appeared in Nat's face. He ducked, jerked the wheel again, then curled his body in a ball as the truck became airborne, then crashed back to earth and slowly toppled over the edge of the steep incline.

Valeri looked around the room to which she'd been escorted by a silent woman with a black veil hiding her face. It was a bedroom even more luxuriant than the lavish reception room she'd just left.

The bed was a four-poster, draped in blue-and-gold chiffon, and covered with a gleaming silver-blue spread and white satin pillows. Low armchairs in blue and gold rested beside tall, floor-to-ceiling windows draped in the same silver-blue as the spread.

Swirls of pale turquoise and salmon pink decorated the plush gold carpet. An ottoman sat at the foot of the bed, and Valeri perched gingerly on the edge of it.

She'd been surprised when Sabhad had dismissed her. Surprised and immensely relieved. She'd imagined all kinds of horrible situations, but it seemed as if he wasn't interested in her the way she'd feared.

She crossed her ankles and stared down at her scuffed and worn shoes. They looked out of place resting on that luxurious carpet. She wondered what Nat was doing, and how long he'd keep the men driving around before he admitted he wasn't going to take them to her father.

She didn't want to think what would happen then. She had to trust that Nat could take care of himself. He'd been through some pretty hair-raising experiences and had survived so far. She had to believe that he would survive this.

As for Alex, she could only hope that the police listened to him long enough to hear what was said earlier. If they didn't—if it had been for nothing—then they were all in a bad situation: her father in the hands of the police, Nat in the hands of Sabhad's hit men, and her in the hands of Sabhad himself.

They had to listen, she told herself fiercely. She wouldn't let herself think otherwise. Any minute now they'd come bursting through that door and tell her it was all over—that Nat and her father were safe and that she was free to go.

As if in answer to her thoughts, the door opened abruptly. For a single second Valeri thought her wishes had been granted, but then her heart sank. It wasn't the police who stood there, but Sabhad. And he was no longer wearing his robes and turban.

He wore instead what looked like a long nightshirt, and the smile on his face told her she was in serious trouble.

"Ah," he said, coming into the room and closing the door behind him. "Alone at last."

Valeri was in no mood for jokes. She watched him take a key from the folds of his shirt and lock the door. Looking wildly around the room for a possible weapon, she realized that the tops of the tables and the dressers were bare. Obviously this was a guest room.

She fought the panic that urged her to beg for mercy. She had to stay in control—to play along with Sabhad long enough for the police to come and rescue her. And they would come, she promised herself. She had to hang on to that.

She got slowly to her feet and moved across the room to the windows. She could see nothing in the darkness outside, but it made her feel a little better to know that the outside world was just a pane of glass away from this... harem.

She didn't know what had brought the word into her mind. She only knew the thought of it made her feel sick. Forcing her voice to sound casual, she said, "You have a beautiful house."

"Thank you, my dear." Sabhad crossed the room and sat on the edge of the bed. "But it's not mine. I only lease it when I come to your beautiful country on business."

She flicked a glance at him. He was watching her the way a cat watches a mouse, giving her just enough room to move, knowing he could reach out at any time and trap her.

She searched desperately in her mind for something to say that would keep him talking. "I imagine the U.S. is a lot different from Saudi Arabia."

"It is, indeed. This is a beautiful country filled with beautiful women."

"You have beautiful women in your country, too."

"Ah, but they do not excite me the way western women excite me. There is something about your smooth, alabaster skin that sets my soul on fire."

Deciding that she was approaching dangerous ground, Valeri changed the subject. "How did you get those pictures of me?"

Sabhad laughed, obviously very pleased with his cleverness. "I'm an expert with a computer, as you might have guessed. I have all the latest software from your country as well as from Japan—sophisticated software that can do many things, like transplanting one face for another."

Valeri nodded. "I thought so. But where did you get the picture of me in the first place?"

Sabhad raised his chin and stared at the ceiling. After a moment he lowered his gaze, and looked broodingly at Valeri. "I invited your father here for dinner. We talked, he showed me pictures, I kept one."

"So you had all this planned all along," Valeri said bitterly. "You intended to frame my father for murder."

"Not at first—" Sabhad sighed "—I had hoped to persuade him to sell me the project. When he refused, I approached his assistants with the same offer. I had pictures of all their families, in case I should need them for leverage. Luckily, Simpson accepted my offer after giving it some thought. Apparently he was deep in debt and in danger of losing his home. He saw this as a way out."

"But why did you kill him?"

Sabhad shrugged. "He got cold feet. He called me and

told me your father was going to the CIA. He wanted out of the deal. Of course, I couldn't let that happen. I told him that I would change your father's mind—that he was to call Dr. Forrester and arrange to meet him at the laboratory at midnight. I would be there to persuade Dr. Forrester to see things my way."

"And Simpson believed you?" She couldn't believe the scientist could be so gullible.

"Simpson was desperate. He was grasping at straws."

Valeri thought about Simpson's fatherless children. "What about the two little girls in the picture," she said, suddenly remembering them. "Who are they? Are they your children?"

Sabhad's expression changed. He got up abruptly, smoothing down the folds of his shirt. "Enough questions. They are boring me. We have better things to talk about, you and I, Valeri."

With her tongue, she moistened lips that had suddenly gone dry. "Like what?"

"Such as how we are going to pass the time until Mr. Thorne gets back here with the disks."

He took a step forward, and Valeri moved back. A small padded bench in front of the window caught her behind the knees and she sat down heavily.

"Come, my dear," Sabhad said, moving closer. "Don't be shy. I'm sure you've had men make love to you before. You have never had a man like me, however. I can guarantee it."

"You're right about that," Valeri muttered. She tried to remember all the moves she'd learned in a self-defense class years earlier. She wished now she'd paid more attention. All that came to mind was a swift knee in the groin. She'd have to resort to that if things got serious.

Sabhad stood in front of her now, one hand outstretched to touch her cheek. She jerked her head away, out of his reach.

He smiled, making her squirm. ‘‘Don’t resist me, Valeri. You know you will submit to me in the end. Why not make it pleasant for both of us? There is so much I could teach you.’’

Her stomach churned so badly she thought she might throw up. ‘‘I’m not interested in anything you might have in mind,’’ she said curtly.

‘‘Ah, but I could make you interested, if you give me half a chance.’’ His hand snaked out so suddenly that she had no time to react. Sabhad’s cruel fingers grasped the back of her neck and forced her forward while his lips fastened on hers, wet and disgusting.

She lifted her hands and shoved hard against his chest, but he was stronger than he looked. He trapped her hand easily, and twisted her arm behind her back.

She gasped when the vicious pain bit into her shoulder. Twisting her head, she tore her mouth from his. ‘‘Let me go, you bastard, or I’ll make you sorry you ever set eyes on me.’’

Sabhad chuckled, a triumphant sound that chilled her blood. ‘‘Such feeble threats, my dear. But I like my women spirited. Fight all you like. I shall win in the end.’’

He pulled her closer, putting pressure on her bent arm. The other hand closed savagely over her breast, squeezing so hard she cried out in pain.

Sabhad grinned. ‘‘See, my dear? You like it.’’

He pressed his body closer, until she could feel his arousal. Filled with a loathing she couldn’t describe, she put all her strength into the upward swing of her knee.

Sabhad sidestepped, and she caught him on the thigh. He grunted and shoved her toward the bed so hard that she lost her balance. She stumbled and ended up sprawled across the beautiful spread. Before she could move, Sabhad was on her, trapping her legs with his, bending her hands back above her head.

Terrified now, she struggled, but he only grinned, his

garlic breath nauseating her. ‘‘Relax, Valeri,’’ he whispered. ‘‘This will be a pleasure, believe me. Be nice to me, and I might even decide not to kill you when your lover comes back.’’

‘‘He’s…not my lover….’’

‘‘Your lips lie, Valeri, but your eyes cannot….’’

She struggled with all her strength, but she knew she was fighting a losing battle. Tears spurted from her eyes, and the room swam in a salty haze.

His hand ripped the buttons from her shirt, and she screamed—a loud, shrill yell of desperation. Sabhad swore and clapped his hand hard over her mouth. ‘‘Do that one more time and I’ll slap you into silence,’’ he muttered.

He dragged her shirt open, and his hand stilled.

Too late, she remembered the microphone. Sabhad uttered something in his guttural language. ‘‘So, you betray me. You will die for that….’’

The room exploded into bursting sparks of light and pain as his hand cracked across her face. She screamed again, bracing herself for the next blow…and heard instead the shattering, splintering sound of broken glass.

Sabhad lifted his head, then suddenly he was gone… hauled off her bodily by two strong, tanned hands.

‘‘All right, you sniveling bastard,’’ Nat snarled. ‘‘You’re gonna pay for this.’’

Struggling to sit up, Valeri watched in terror as the two men fought. Sabhad was strong and quick on his feet, but Nat was taller, and what he lacked in speed he made up for in sheer bulk. After an exchange of blows, he landed one that lifted Sabhad off his feet and sent him crashing against the wall. The stunned *sheik* slumped to the floor, his chin resting on his chest, his eyes closed.

‘‘Nat!’’ Valeri slid off the bed and flung herself into his arms. ‘‘Thank God. He was going to…going to…’’

‘‘I know.’’ He silenced her with his kiss, soothing her

ragged senses, smoothing away her fears with his hands. "It's all right now. We—"

A loud thumping on the door interrupted him, harsh voices calling out in the language she couldn't understand. She looked up at Nat, and saw for the first time the gash across his forehead. "Nat, you're hurt!"

He rubbed at his head, then looked at his blood-smeared fingers. "Lucky I've got a hard head. I had to make a quick entrance." He nodded at the shattered window.

She went cold when she thought of how badly he could have hurt himself. For her. He'd risked his life for her... again. How could she not love him?

"We have to get out of here," Nat said urgently as the pounding on the door became a heavy thudding. The wood creaked as if to emphasize his words.

But Valeri had heard something else. She held up her hand. On the night air came the reassuring wail of sirens, approaching fast. "Enter the cavalry," she said, smiling in relief.

"I'm so relieved that everything turned out all right," Alex said, looking up at Valeri from his hospital bed. "But you took a terrible chance. Had I not been so weak and irrational, I would never have agreed to let you go."

"You didn't have much choice," Valeri reminded him. She bent down to kiss his cheek. "I'm just happy to see you looking so much better."

"Of course I'm better. How about you?"

"Much better after a good night's sleep. They kept both Nat and me in overnight for observation. I haven't seen him this morning yet."

"I'm told I can go home soon."

She smiled. "I know. I checked with the front desk. They have your release papers all ready to sign."

"Then I can go home now?"

"As soon as Nat gets here. He's with the police, filling in all the details for their report."

"So Sabhad is behind bars?"

"For the time being."

"What happens to him now?"

"I guess it will depend on what arrangements our side makes with Saudi Arabia. The important thing is that you're completely cleared of suspicion in the murder. The police heard enough to satisfy them on that score."

Alex nodded. "Thanks to you and Nat. Now I'm ready to go home, I can tell you. I've already called the opticians, and they're rushing my order for new glasses. Meanwhile, I have a pair of old ones that will get me by until the new ones are ready."

Valeri patted his shoulder. "I'm glad to hear it. I'd hate to think of you groping around like that for days."

"How is Nat? Thank heaven he turned up in time. It was a miracle he got away from Sabhad's men."

At the mention of his name, her smile faded. "Apart from a nasty gash on his forehead, and a few cuts and bruises he collected when he rolled the truck, he seems okay."

Alex narrowed his eyes. "He's leaving."

She nodded, trying to swallow past the hard lump in her throat. "He's driving us both home, and then he's going back to San Francisco. He called his agency. They have a job for him in the Philippines."

"What sort of job?"

Valeri shrugged. "He didn't say. I didn't ask."

"You love him?"

She blushed. "I care for him a great deal."

Alex nodded. "He seems like a great guy. What is it—his job that you can't accept?"

She looked down and followed the line of weave on the white bedspread with her finger. "That's part of it."

"You don't approve, is that it?"

She smiled, though her heart was breaking. "It doesn't exactly make for good husband material."

"You could work things out. After all, he doesn't work all the time. If you loved him enough, you could be satisfied with the in-between times, couldn't you?"

"Maybe. But then if he loved me enough he could give it up, and do something else. And I just can't see him doing that for anyone."

Alex winked. "Stranger things have happened."

She shook her head. He didn't understand, and she couldn't tell him. How could she explain to her father that it could never work between her and Nat because she couldn't give him what he needed? She'd already failed in one marriage because of her problem. It would break her heart to have Nat for a while, only to lose him later.

She looked up as the door opened and the man so prominent in her thoughts walked in. Seeing him again like that, with a small thin bandage covering the gash in his head, her heart turned over. He looked so audacious, and just a little dangerous. She fell in love with him a little bit more every time she saw him.

"I'm ready to play chauffeur if you two are ready," he announced, grinning at Valeri. "That's if you feel you can trust my driving."

"Well, I'm not so sure about that." She turned to Alex. "For an ex-race driver, he's not too sharp on the bends."

Nat pretended to look hurt. "Just because I managed to wreck a couple of vehicles?"

"Make that three if you count mine."

Nat sighed heavily. "That's the thanks I get. Just no pleasing a woman, that's what I always say."

"Typical male response."

"Quit arguing, you two, and get out of here so I can get dressed," Alex said plaintively. "I've already been here longer than I want to be."

Nat put his hand on Valeri's shoulder and guided her to

the door. ''Don't worry, Alex, I'll deal with her. She'll be purring like a kitten by the time I've finished with her.''

Valeri shuddered. ''Now you sound like Sabhad.''

Nat followed her out into the hallway. ''He sweet-talked you?''

''If you can call it that, yes.''

''The man's got more style than I gave him credit for.''

Valeri frowned. ''How can you say that? How can you—''

''Relax.'' Nat grasped her shoulders and pulled her into his chest. ''I was just teasing. Sorry. I guess it's a sore subject.''

''Very,'' Valeri said grimly. ''Did the police say what was going to happen to him?''

Nat shook his head. ''They were being pretty close-mouthed about it. My guess is that they'll deport him to stand trial back there. One thing's for sure, he'll never set foot in this country again.''

''That makes me feel a little better. You never did tell me how you got away from Sabhad's men after you rolled the truck.''

Nat dropped his hands, the cold, closed expression she knew so well spreading over his face. ''They missed the knife in my boot when they searched me.''

He didn't have to say any more. She didn't want to hear any more.

They both looked at the door as it opened to reveal Alex, fully dressed and, much to Valeri's relief, looking more like his old self.

He talked incessantly for the three hours or more it took for Nat to drive the rented car to his townhouse in Sacramento. He invited Nat and Valeri inside, but Valeri was anxious to get home and into some clean clothes. She waited until she was sure he could manage for himself, then she left him alone with a promise to call that evening to check on him.

"Does he mind living alone?" Nat asked as he drove into the city.

"No more than I do." Valeri looked out at the buildings flashing by without really seeing them. "He's very self-sufficient, and he's been alone a long time. To the point where he prefers it now, I think."

"He's a nice guy."

"Thank you. Actually, he said the same about you."

"He did?" Nat looked pleased by that. "I hope his daughter shares his views."

"I was the one who vouched for you in the first place, remember?"

"Ah, yes. So what about you? Do you prefer living alone?"

She thought about it before answering. "There are some things I like about it. Being able to eat when I want, what I want. Being able to read in bed at night without someone complaining about the light being on."

"But?"

She shrugged. "It's lonely. Sometimes I wish I had someone to share the evenings with."

"But not enough to do something about it, right?"

She looked at him, startled by the comment. "What made you say that?"

"Just a hunch."

He swung the wheel over and she realized they had arrived at her apartment complex. Now she felt nervous again, her heart thumping the way it always did when she was alone with him somewhere. She couldn't stand the thought of saying goodbye to him, yet she didn't know if she wanted to be alone with him in her apartment.

"Aren't you going to ask me in?"

She looked up at him, her insides melting at the expression in his eyes. Unable to deny him anything when he looked at her like that, she said lightly, "Of course. Would you like to come in?"

He grinned. "I thought you'd never ask." He swung out of the car and came around to open the door for her. "As you can see, I got you home safely."

"So you did." She climbed out and walked past him to the entrance. "I never had a moment's doubt."

"Is that why you white-knuckled the dash all the way home?"

She pulled a face at him, while something twisted painfully inside. How she would miss these moments...the lighthearted banter between them, the serious discussions, the excitement of never knowing when he was going to kiss her....

She pulled up short at her door. "I don't have a key. It was in my purse that I lost in the fire." Only now did she realize that there were no cops in the parking lot. They must have been called off last night.

Nat gently shouldered her aside. "Allow me." He looked at the lock. "Hmmm...dead bolt. Hold on a minute." He fished out of his pocket what looked like a small packet of miniature tools. A moment of fiddling with one of them and he had the door open.

Valeri looked up at him. "Is that legal?"

Nat lifted his eyebrows. "Would I do anything illegal?"

She smiled sweetly at him. "Would a cat eat fish?"

With a pained expression, he held a hand over his heart. "Oh, how this woman wounds me."

She laughed. "It would take a lot more than that to wound you, I'd say. Come on in, I'll fix you a drink."

"Sounds good to me." He followed her into her spacious, neatly furnished apartment, his eyes drawn immediately to the vibrant wall hanging draped above the fireplace. "Nice," he commented. "Where'd you get it?"

"My mother made it." Valeri looked wistfully at the tapestry depicting a child in a white dress enjoying a summer picnic in a shady wood. "She copied a picture she'd taken of me when I was eight."

"Your mother was very talented."

"Yes, she was." Valeri cleared her throat. She would never understand why her mother went to such great lengths to keep her from her father, and she found that hard to forgive. But she couldn't deny the fact that she missed her mother, at times quite painfully.

"I'm sorry." Nat's arms came around her from behind. "I seem to have a knack for saying the wrong thing lately."

She leaned back against his chest, enjoying the quiet strength she always felt emanating from him at times like this. "It's all right. I'm feeling a little overly emotional right now, I guess."

"Well, here, maybe this will help." He turned her in his arms, and as she had known he would...hoped he would...covered her mouth with his.

The fire in her veins flared up instantly. She clung to him, threading her fingers through his hair as the world slowly faded out of sight. His hands roamed her back...her sides...his thumbs caressing the curve of her breasts.

He lifted his head, his mouth inches from hers. "I made you a promise last night," he murmured. "I'm here to keep it."

Oh, how she longed just to accept what was happening and enjoy it. But she couldn't. She couldn't let things go all the way, only to freeze up at the last minute.

She pulled back, resisting the pressure of his arms. "I'm sorry, Nat."

She saw bewilderment and pain in his eyes, and felt like crying. "What is it with you?" he demanded harshly. "Why do you blow hot and cold like this? One minute you're all soft and warm, promising me all kinds of wonderful things with your eyes, and the next you're freezing up like a...a...damn virgin."

She pulled out of his arms and turned away, determined not to cry. "I'm sorry, Nat. It's not that I don't want to—it's that I can't."

"What the hell does that mean?" He flung himself into her armchair and crossed his ankles, looking ferociously up at her.

She pulled in a long breath and knelt in front of him. "It means that I am physically unable to respond to a man. Any man. My mother had a horror of sex, which was why Alex left. She considered the whole thing evil and dirty. She did it with my father because it was her duty, but after I was born she moved out of his bed and never went back."

Nat looked even more bewildered. "But you know better than that, don't you?"

She nodded. "Yes, I do. I talked to a therapist and I read all the books. But all those years of growing up and being told that it was evil to let a man touch me has had a profound effect on my mind. My body wants to enjoy it, my mind won't allow it. My first marriage failed because of my hang-up."

Nat tilted his head back and let out a sigh. "Why didn't you tell me before? You must think I'm a jerk...."

"No." She laid her fingers against his cheek. "It isn't your fault. You didn't know. Nat, that's why I've never met anyone else since my divorce. It was why I could be so sure that I wasn't married to Sabhad. Any man that I become involved with would have to accept me for who I am. He would have to love me for my mind and my personality, and not my body. Because I don't know if I'd ever be able to enjoy the physical side of a relationship. There are not many men willing to accept a woman on those terms."

Nat gave her one of his helpless, little-boy looks that could tear her heart apart. "Valeri, I don't know what to say. I have to admit, any relationship I've ever had has always been based for the most part on the physical aspects. I don't know how to love a woman any other way. All this just blows my mind."

"I know." Valeri could hardly stand the ache that spread

throughout her body when she got to her feet. "That's why I had to tell you. I just couldn't let you think I was normal, when I knew I would end up disappointing you."

He stood up, too, his fingers grasping her chin. "Don't you ever say that," he said fiercely. "Don't you ever say you're not normal." He kissed her hard, then let her go. "You are the most normal woman I know. You're just different."

"I'm sorry, Nat."

He shrugged, and the expression on his face broke her heart. "I'm sorry, too. The problem is, Valeri, you need a man who can fulfill your special needs. I'm just not that man. I never will be. I'd only end up hurting you."

She nodded, gritting her teeth so that she wouldn't cry. "I'm sorry, too, Nat. But I can't regret meeting you. It was an...interesting experience."

He gave her a crooked smile. "Yeah. It was. Well...I guess I'd better leave."

Her throat hurt with the effort to hold back the tears. "You take care of yourself, okay?"

"You, too, sweetheart." He bent his head and gently touched her lips with his. It was a kiss of regret...a kiss of goodbye. "I'll never forget you, Valeri. Think of me now and again?"

She managed a weak smile. "How could I ever forget the devil who kidnapped me?"

His gaze moved over her face as if committing it to memory. "You know what they say," he said softly. "Better the devil you know..."

"Than the devil you don't," she finished for him. "I'll remember that." *Always,* her heart echoed. For there would never be a man alive who could make her forget Nathan Thorne.

Chapter 14

Time had no meaning for Valeri in the weeks that followed. She went back to the office saying as little as possible about her adventures, which made interesting news in the papers for a day or two. She refused to be interviewed by the reporters, and after a while they gave up to chase after more topical subjects.

Alex improved quickly, and rescheduled his meeting in Washington. He was waiting to hear any day the outcome of his petition. He asked her once or twice if she had heard from Nat, but after getting her negative answers for a while, refrained from asking her again.

She was relieved about that. Any mention of Nat's name brought fresh pain, reopening wounds that hadn't had time to heal. She lost the enthusiasm for her work and left more and more to her assistants, until one day, her chief advisor and good friend Corie Anderson sat her down in the office and proceeded to lecture her.

Corie was happily married and the mother of two small children. Valeri had often admired the way she managed her family life without letting it interfere with her job. Right now, however, she looked more like a mother than she did an employee.

"This business was built on your name, your record," she said, while Valeri sat slumped in her chair. "Without your input our customers are not happy."

Valeri looked up, shaken out of her lethargy. "I haven't had any complaints."

"Oh, they're satisfied, they're just not ecstatic about the results—the way they should be if we are to have their repeat business. There are a lot of PR companies out there—some a good deal cheaper than us—who can satisfy them just as well. It's your special touch, your talent, your ideas that keep the customers coming back to us."

Valeri sighed. She couldn't seem to fight her way out of the cloak of depression that sometimes threatened to smother her. "I just can't seem to come up with anything anymore. I lay awake at night trying to come up with ideas, and everything is blank. Maybe the blows I took to my head have destroyed my creativity. Maybe I've lost it all."

Corie perched herself on the edge of the desk. "Nonsense. You can't lose your creativity that way. If you want my opinion, Val, I think you need a break. All that excitement you had was bound to end with a letdown. You're just burned out, that's all."

The feeling of desolation that had robbed Valeri of so much sleep lately almost overwhelmed her. "I don't want a break. I'd go crazy sitting around doing nothing."

"I hate to be the bearer of bad tidings," Corie said gently, "but that's exactly what you've been doing for the past three weeks. What you need is something to stir up your creative juices again."

Valeri fought her irritation, knowing that her friend was only trying to help. "So what do you suggest? I go shopping in New York?"

Corie grinned. "Sounds like a good start. Actually, I was

thinking more along the lines of an African safari, a trip to Hawaii, or a cruise, maybe. Start a new hobby. Go somewhere or do something you've never done before."

Valeri gave her friend a hopeless look. Nothing appealed to her. Nothing could compare to the excitement of watching Nathan Thorne smile at her, or feeling the strength of his arms about her. "I'll think about it," she promised.

"Do more than think about it." Corie slipped off the desk. "Do it. If you don't, you won't be able to do it later on, you'll be too busy fighting to save your business."

Valeri waited until Corie had left the office, then wandered over to the window. The sun-drenched street below hummed with the light traffic that would become a roar in another hour or two when the rush hour started.

She watched the cars hustling for space, threading in and out among the slower trucks and buses. Nat was probably in some jungle somewhere, surrounded by the fragrance of tropical flowers and the calls of exotic birds, instead of the strident horns and stinking exhausts trapped by the static heat of the city.

As always, the thought of him again tore open the barely healed wounds. No matter what she did, she couldn't get the memories out of her mind. She heard his voice a thousand times a day, whispering her name. She'd wake up in the night, her body aching with an inexplicable need, tormented by the memory of his arms holding her close, his mouth hot on hers.

She had to stop torturing herself like this, she told herself, as the now familiar ache spread rapidly through her body. Corie was right. She had to snap out of this gloom and doom. A cruise sounded like a good idea.

Before she could change her mind again, she crossed the room and picked up the phone. Within minutes she had herself booked in a single cabin on a cruise ship heading for the Caribbean.

* * *

The bar stank of body odor and strong tobacco. The heat was suffocating, the kind of steamy heat that can drain the energy and fog the mind. Smoke curled around the dim lanterns on the walls and the noisy jukebox in the corner, while bamboo curtains hung limply in the doorway, barely moving without a breeze to stir them.

Nat stared down at the dark stains on the table and wished he were anywhere other than Manila. The job had created frustration right from the start. Nothing had gone right. His contact hadn't turned up, and he'd wasted days trying to find out what happened to him.

By the time he'd been offered a replacement, the timing was off and he'd had to replan the entire operation. Now he was stuck in this goddamn hole until the timing was right. Whenever that might be.

The American he'd been sent to rescue from a Manila jail must have given up hope by now. He was due to be executed in a few days. All diplomatic attempts at gaining his release had failed. Now his only hope rested entirely on Nat's shoulders, and Nat couldn't do a damn thing to help the poor bastard because his hands were tied by the useless idiots who'd been sent to help him.

He twisted his glass viciously in his hands, and stared down at the swirling whiskey. He was losing his edge. The job was going sour on him and he didn't know why.

He'd even begun to think lately that he was too old for this life of constant threat and danger. He was going to be forty in a few months. He'd been lucky so far, but how long would his luck hold out?

He was getting tired, slowing down. And that wasn't good. Not only his life, but the lives of many others, depended on him staying on his toes. Maybe he should get a checkup. Maybe the physical beatings he'd taken over the years were finally having an effect on him.

He lifted the glass and drained it in one gulp. Slamming it down on the table, he beckoned to the waitress, who was lolling against the counter watching him out of the corner of her eye.

He knew she'd been watching him for the past half hour. He was aware of every woman in that bar, accompanied or alone. He knew which ones might be interested, and which ones to avoid. He watched the waitress now as she sidled up to his table, one hand resting provocatively on her fleshy hip.

"More whiskey?" Her voice purred from her full lips, more a caress than a question.

He looked her over. Her white blouse hung from one shoulder, dipping low enough for him to see the curve of her succulent breasts. Her rounded hips swayed slightly, drifting the long black skirt about her bare ankles.

When he looked up she was smiling, her eyes hot and inviting. Dark brown eyes, full of promise...and they did nothing for him. Absolutely nothing. It was as if he were dead inside, drained of all sexual response. He just wasn't interested. And for Nathan Thorne, that was a significant first.

"More whiskey," he said curtly, and watched the invitation die in her eyes. She flounced away, her hips bouncing from side to side in her anger, and he knew he would have to wait for his whiskey. He looked around the bar, sizing up the rest of the women. More than one of them met his gaze, sending him body signals with a slight movement of their heads, or a touch of fingers to the lips.

He knew all the signs. He could read them clear across a jam-packed room. At one time he would have taken his pick and played the game. Not now. There wasn't one woman there who could raise the slightest response in his weary body. There hadn't been since he'd left the States.

He stared across the room, oblivious now of the hot glances coming his way. *Not since he'd left the States.* He thought about that, long and hard. Gradually he was forced to face the truth—the facts that he'd refused to accept until now. He hadn't been interested in a woman since the day he'd walked away from Valeri, and left more than just a memory behind.

He wasn't interested in women anymore because they weren't Valeri.

He could have all the sex he wanted with little more than a flick of his fingers. But the truth was, he felt more excitement just by holding Valeri in his arms than anything he remembered with other women.

Just thinking about her...the way her dark hair blew across her forehead, the way her eyes lit up when she looked at him, the funny little smile she gave him when he teased her, the feel of her, warm and exciting, in his arms...just thinking about all that woke up his body again.

He sat there for a long time, stunned by what had happened to him. He was unaware of the sulky waitress slamming down his drink. The sultry heat no longer bothered him—he couldn't see the come-hither smiles of the women, or the warning scowls from their suspicious men.

He saw only a nude body, bathed in moonlight and framed in the doorway of a ramshackle hut on a cold night in the Sierra mountains. And in that moment he knew that his life would never be the same again.

Ignoring the whiskey on the table, he got to his feet and threw some bills down in the puddle spreading beneath his glass. He had a lot of thinking to do, and some tough decisions to make. He still had a job to take care of, but when it was done, he would be free to chart a new course. Now he had to decide where that course would take him. And how much he was willing to risk.

Valeri tapped on the door of Corie's office and stuck her head inside. "I'm going down to pick up my tickets for the cruise," she said when Corie looked up with a smile.

"Good girl. Why don't you take the afternoon off and

shop for some new clothes for the trip, while you're about it.''

Valeri pretended to frown. ''Are you trying to get rid of me?''

''If it will bring back the vibrant, energetic, enthusiastic Valeri that we all know and love, then yes, I'm anxious to get rid of you. Go have fun. We'll manage here.''

That was the problem, Valeri thought as she closed the door again. They could all manage very well without her. She just seemed to have lost all ambition. The work no longer interested her.

Maybe she should think about doing something else, she thought as she pushed through the revolving door that led to the street. Corie would be only too happy to take over the reins. In spite of her flattering comments, Corie was every bit as proficient and talented as she claimed her boss to be. The customers were more than happy with Corie's ideas. Valeri had checked with them and heard nothing but glowing praise.

Deep in thought, she didn't notice the tall figure standing directly in front of her until she'd bumped into him. ''Oh, excuse me—'' Her breath slammed into her throat. It couldn't be. And yet it was.

''Hi, there, sweetheart,'' Nat said, flashing his crooked grin. ''You need a ride?''

She could only stare up at him, speechless and suddenly afraid. Why had he come back? Why now, just when she was beginning to pick up the pieces of her life again?

He tilted his head to one side. ''You're looking a little worried. Afraid I'll wreck the car again, I guess. Well, I can't say I blame you. I guess I do make a habit of it.''

She couldn't believe he was standing in front of her—tall, tanned and looking as incorrigible as ever. He wore jeans and a khaki work shirt, and looked thinner than she remembered. She gazed at him hungrily, filling her mind and her soul with the sight of him, in case he should suddenly vanish again, leaving her empty and in pain.

His grin faded a little as she continued to stare at him wordlessly. "You are happy to see me, I hope?" he asked, sounding more uncertain than she'd ever heard him before. "I mean, if you're not...just say the word, and I'll walk out of your life and you'll never see me again. Only, you'll have to tell me to go, because I'm not budging until I hear you say the words."

She cleared her throat as the ridiculous happiness bubbled up inside her. What did it matter why he'd come back or how long he would stay? He was here now, and she was damn well going to enjoy him.

He was looking worried now, and there was something lurking in his eyes that made her pulse race. She could be mistaken, but he almost looked afraid. That wasn't an emotion she normally attributed to Nathan Thorne.

"Valeri...I'm sorry, maybe this isn't a good time..."

She finally found her voice. "Will you please stop babbling, you itinerant bum, and kiss me," she ordered unsteadily.

His grin came back, and she felt wonderful. "Be my pleasure, ma'am," he said, "but not here. I've got a few things I want to say to you, and I want to do it in private."

Her heart seemed to leap into her throat. Stamping out the hope before it could take flight, she suggested tentatively, "My apartment?"

"Perfect. Your car or mine?"

"I'll drive. I want to get there in one piece."

He shook his head. "Man! And they say an elephant never forgets."

He accompanied her to the car, his hand possessively on her arm. How she loved his take-charge attitude. He made her feel special...protected. It had been a long time since she'd had anyone protect her. Alex, bless his heart, was not the protective type, much as he worried about her.

Nat took the keys from her and opened the door, waiting until she was settled behind the wheel before closing it. She watched him stride around the car, still unable to believe he was actually here—tangible and so undeniably appealing.

He slid in beside her, invoking all the memories she'd fought so hard to suppress. She wanted to touch him, to hold him, to kiss him until she had no more breath. She felt ridiculously shy, wondering if she looked the same to him, or different.

She wished she'd worn something other than the rather plain blue suit. Something softer and more glamorous. She should have had her hair cut weeks ago.

"Relax, I'm not going to attack you, I promise."

The words, spoken in his deep voice, unsettled her. "I'm not worrying about that," she said, a little stiffly. "I was just wondering if I'd left my apartment tidy enough for visitors."

"Don't worry, I won't even notice. After where I've been the last few weeks, your apartment is going to look better than a luxury suite in a five-star hotel."

Determined to steer the conversation into safer channels, she asked brightly, "So what have you been up to lately?"

She began to relax as he launched into a vivid description of Manila, and some of the problems he'd run into. Although he sounded the same, she sensed something different about him, though she couldn't put her finger on it.

The minute she closed the door of her apartment behind them, she felt the tension creeping over her once more. Nat actually seemed nervous, and she couldn't imagine what it was that he had to tell her. She slipped off her suit jacket and laid it on the back of the armchair. "Can I get you a drink?"

"Later." He looked at her, his eyes warm on her face. "Sit down, Valeri. There's something I have to tell you."

She sat on the edge of her couch, with the familiar thumping of her heart pounding in her ears. He stood for a moment looking down at her, then he moved over to the fireplace and looked up at the tapestry.

"I know what it is to grow up without a father," he said softly. "I never knew mine."

"I'm sorry." Her whisper barely left her lips. She sensed now that what he had to tell her was painful to him. And likely to be painful for her. He was going to explain why he wasn't the man for her. She braced herself, hoping it might be easier to accept if she knew why.

Nat drew out a long sigh, then began speaking in a low voice that was sometimes difficult to hear. "My mother never married my father. I don't know if she ever knew who he was. She was a drunk, and took out her frustrations on my hide. One night when I was three years old, she took off somewhere while I was asleep, and left me all alone to wake up in an empty apartment. I never saw her again."

Valeri pressed her lips together to stop the sound of distress from escaping.

"The county put me in three different foster homes. My first foster mother screamed abuse at me every chance she got. My second stood by without saying a word while her husband nearly killed me with his belt. The third tried to rape me when I was fourteen. That's when I got smart and left town. I've been on my own ever since."

As hard as she tried, she could not stop the tears from spilling over. He still stood with his back to her, and she couldn't see his face. His head was down, though, and she could hear the pain in his voice.

"I never knew what it was to have a woman love me. I could never trust any woman, so I kept all my emotions locked up in a neat little box, where no one could get at them. I figured that as long as I didn't give a damn, no one would ever hurt me again."

He paused, and the silence went on for so long that Valeri knew she had to say something. Moving her lips with difficulty, she said quietly, "Nat, it's all right. I understand."

He turned to look at her then, and she almost cried out at his ravaged face. "Valeri, when I watched you put your life on the line for your father, I finally understood what real love could be. It took me a while to realize it, but I want to love someone like that. I want to be loved like that."

She was crying in earnest now. She tried to speak, but he stopped her with a raised hand.

"Let me finish. Any woman who would risk her life for someone she loves is a woman I'd trust with my life. I need you, Valeri. I want you—with or without the sex—and I swear I'll spend the rest of my life trying to earn the kind of love you're capable of giving."

She struggled valiantly to stop the flow of tears. "Nat, you deserve so much more than I can give you. I love you with all my heart, but it just wouldn't work. I would give everything I have to be able to respond to you physically. But I can't. I don't know how. Sooner or later, it wouldn't be enough. You'd want more than I could give."

He knelt before her, his face so full of tenderness that she ached with love for him. "Sweetheart, you have to learn to trust me, just as I learned to trust you."

"I do trust you, Nat. I trusted you with my life when you promised to get me out of Sabhad's house alive. I couldn't have gone in there if I hadn't trusted you to keep that promise."

He reached for her hands and pressed them against his chest. She could feel the steady beat of his heart, warming her, reassuring her. "Then trust me now, Valeri. Trust me with your body, as you do your mind. Let me show you how beautiful making love can be. You taught me how to love emotionally. Now let me teach you how to love a man physically."

The panic stirred and the tension gripped her body again. "Nat, I don't want to disappoint you."

He smiled. "You won't. We'll take it one step at a time, and I promise I won't force you to do anything you don't want to do."

Still she hesitated, part of her longing to go to him, the other part afraid.

"Trust me," Nat whispered, and leaned forward to touch her lips lightly with his own.

She returned the pressure, then, as he drew back, she allowed him to pull her to her feet.

"Where's the bedroom?" he asked, brushing her fingers with his lips.

She shivered. "Just down the hall."

"Do you have a full-length mirror anywhere?

"Yes, in the hallway."

"Good." He took her hand and led her into the hallway. He paused in front of the mirror and made her face it, standing behind her to look over her head. "I want you to watch," he said softly. "Watch how your body responds to me, and mine to you."

He reached from behind her and began unbuttoning her shirt. His wrists rested against her breasts, making them tingle as he moved down. She found it hard to breathe, impossible to speak.

She looked at her face in the mirror. Her jaw was set, her mouth pinched, her eyes wide and scared. She made a deliberate effort to relax the muscles in her face.

He pulled her shirt out of her skirt and undid the last button. Very slowly he slipped the shirt off her shoulders and free of her arms. "You look so good," he murmured in her ear. "You have no idea how many times I've imagined you just like this."

She could see the rapid rise and fall of her breasts, trapped in her bra. Her throat ached with the effort of keeping her breathing even. She met his gaze in the mirror, and he smiled. "You're doing fine," he whispered, then lowered his lips to her shoulder, where he trailed a kiss all the way to her neck. His mouth felt warm and moist against her sensitive skin.

Her knees began to sag. Something began to coil tightly low in her belly. She felt his fingers on her back as he unsnapped her bra. Carefully, he slipped the straps from her shoulders, and let the bra drop to the floor.

Her bared breasts felt as if they were swelling, the nipples standing out like hard pebbles. She felt an urge to thrust them forward into his hands as his fingers gently cupped them.

"Look how beautiful you are, Valeri," he murmured huskily. "See how your body responds to my hands when I do this." His thumbs brushed her nipples, and she whimpered.

Now she could feel the tension slipping away from her shoulders and her back. A new kind of pressure took over, a deep, pulsing sensation, a sweet ache of longing.

She watched his strong fingers unzip her skirt and ease it over her hips. Her half slip fell to the floor, and she stepped out of the puddle of clothes, closer to the mirror.

He slowly crouched, drawing her pantyhose down her thighs to her ankles, where he lifted each foot out of its shoe and drew the stockings off her feet.

She waited—her lungs aching with the effort of breathing—for him to remove her panties, but he straightened instead, and trailed another kiss along her shoulder.

With his lips still buried in her neck, he unbuttoned his shirt and tugged it off. She watched, mesmerized, as his hands went to his belt and unbuckled it. Her throat constricted as he eased his zipper down, then moved away from her so that he could push his jeans down his long legs.

When he was free of his shoes and socks he straightened again, and looked at her in the mirror. "Just so you know," he said softly, "I love you, Valeri. I think I have ever since

I put you to bed in that motel room. I wanted you then. But that was nothing compared to the way I want you now."

The last of her reservations vanished when she watched him ease his briefs over his hips. He was beautiful. A proud, arrogant male in full arousal. Now all she could think about was relieving the torment that gripped her body.

He took off her panties while she watched in the mirror. He ran his warm, roughened hands over her entire body until she was trembling with the hot need that would not let her go. He kissed her, starting with her mouth and working his way down until she could no longer stand. Then he caught her up in his strong, tanned arms and carried her to bed.

Never in her life had she felt like this. Flying without wings, floating through clouds, soaring through space. His gentle fingers tormented her, thrilled her, excited her until she felt she could stand no more. Just when she was on the point of begging him to stop, he rolled onto his back and pulled her down on top of him.

"Kiss me," he muttered, his voice thick with emotion. "Everywhere. All over."

She did as he asked, his excitement feeding hers as her lips glided over his body, down his belly, along his thighs.... The sound of his harsh breathing, the sharp little groans, were a symphony of excitement and passion to her ears. She couldn't give enough, take enough.

Finally, with a groan, he flipped her on her back again, and once more the magic of his fingers claimed her soul. This was what it was like to love a man, she thought, exultant in her own pleasure. The sensations she'd heard so much about and had never really believed real were finally hers to indulge in.

Her body writhed and arced of its own accord, responding to the insistent fiery touch of the man who knew exactly how to inflame her with an ever-intensifying need.

She cried out, again and again, marveling at the sound, at the urgent response of her body. She wanted him inside her. She craved the release he kept so tantalizingly out of reach.

At long last, he raised himself above her. This was the moment she had waited for, and in that instant a flash of doubt cooled the heat ravaging her body.

His eyes burned with his passion as he looked down at her. "Relax, sweetheart," he muttered hoarsely. "Trust me. Trust yourself. Let go, don't fight it. Give in to it, let it take you where you want to go...come to me, baby...I need you so much."

"I need you, too." She gripped his shoulders as he eased himself into her, and then her body arced again.

His slow, steady rhythm built the pressure up inside her, higher and higher, until she lost all track of time and space. There was no panic, no feeling of dread or frustration. No guilt, no stigma, no humiliation. There was only him and her and the primitive beat of their bodies as they rocked together, faster and faster, striving for the exquisite pinnacle of release.

They reached it together, in a final, shuddering, turbulent upheaval that shook the bed.

She lay for a long time in his arms, spent and unbelievably content. She could have stayed there forever, half dozing, half dreaming, alone with him in a safe, warm haven of pleasure.

Soon he moved, however, disturbing her peace. He propped himself up on his elbow and looked at her. "I don't suppose you'd consider feeding a hungry man?"

She smiled. "If you don't mind taking a chance on my cooking."

"I'd take a chance on anything you did."

She stared into his eyes, marveling at what he'd accomplished...what she herself had accomplished. He'd made a whole woman out of her. She would love him forever for that.

"Thank you," she said softly.

He raised his eyebrows. "For what?"

"For loving me."

He leaned down and kissed her soundly on the lips. "You'd better get used to it. There's a lot more where that came from."

She was afraid to ask the question, but she had to know how long he would be hers before she had to say goodbye to him again. "How long can you stay?"

He tilted his head in the gesture she found so endearing. "You trying to get rid of me already?"

She shook her head. "Never."

"Good, because that's exactly when I'm going to leave. Never."

She stared at him, afraid to hope, terrified he didn't mean what she thought he meant. "But your job?"

He shook his head. "It wasn't a job. It was a way of life. I'm out of it for good. I settled that before I came here. Even if you weren't prepared to take me on, I knew I was finished in that line of work."

She had thought she couldn't be any happier. She'd been wrong. She felt bursting with it. "What will you do now?"

He shrugged. "That kind of depends on you. I was hoping we could do something together. I know you have a pretty successful business going, and I'd understand if you wanted to keep it, but I have to tell you, I don't know the first thing about public relations, and I'm not sure I'd be any good to you there, so I was wondering if you'd consider doing something else for a change. I'm not pressuring you in any way, of course. I'd understand if you—"

She shut him up with her fingers on his lips. "You're babbling."

"You seem to have a habit of making me do that."

She stretched out her body in sheer delight. "Well, as a

matter of fact, I was getting a little tired of PR work. I'd like to do something a little more exciting. What do you suggest?''

His eyes crinkled at the corners as he smiled at her. ''Oh, I don't know. I have some money saved up...we could charter boats in the Caribbean, run a skydiving school, hunt sharks...whatever appeals to you.''

She grinned up at him. ''All of the above.''

''Whatever it is, you can be sure we'll make a go of it. How can we miss with two adventurous souls like us working together?''

Her eagerness caught her up in a whirl of excitement. ''We'll come up with something fitting for a devil.''

He kissed her again. ''How would you like to be married to a devil?''

She caught her breath. ''You're proposing?''

''Isn't that what people do when they want to get married?''

She smiled through her tears. ''Well, it's not too romantic but I guess it's the best a devil can manage.''

He lifted a tear from her cheek with his finger. ''So what's the answer?''

She pretended to think about it. ''I guess it would be an adventure.''

''Is that a yes?''

''That's definitely a yes.''

''Then that's settled. Now let's go eat. We have a lot to discuss and we think better on a full stomach, remember?''

She remembered. She would always remember their first days together with a special kind of bittersweet nostalgia. No matter what happened in the future, or how long they were together, that's how she would always see him—the fierce, arrogant mercenary intent on taking her back to the daughters he thought she'd abandoned.

The devil she knew.

Only now she knew him better. She could understand

now what had driven him those first few hours she'd known him. His own mother had abandoned him, and he wasn't going to let that happen to two innocent little girls.

He had opened up his heart to her, and he'd led her into a world she had only dreamed about. He was her man, and she would be his woman until the day she took her last breath.

* * * * *